BEDFOL

9 38769240 X6

25 JUN 2011	2 2 NOV 2010
1 8 AUG 2007	1 8 DEC 2010
30 Aug 2007	2 3 FEB 2011
1 3 SEP 2007	
1 0 JUL 2008	
1 0 MAR 2009	
3 0 MAR 2009	
1 2 AUG 2009	
0 2 SEP 2009	

BOOKS SHOULD BE RETURNED
BY LAST DATE STAMPED ABOVE

Moreland
and Other Stories

by

Frederick A Read

First Published in 2007 by
Guaranteed Books

an imprint of Pendragon Press
Po Box 12, Maesteg, Mid Glamorgan
South Wales, CF34 0XG

All stories copyright © 2007 by Frederick A Read
Original cover image Copyright Scottish Tourist Board
This Collection copyright © 2007 by Pendragon Press

Cover design & typesetting by Christopher Teague

ISBN-13: 978 0 9554452 1 7

Printed by Biddles Ltd, King's Lynn, Norfolk

www.guaranteedbooks.com

Dedication

I wish to dedicate this book and my thanks to three people, although not necessarily mentioned in the right order.

To the librarian who I have met or spoken to that have offered their support in ordering advanced copies of this book and who have also avowed their support when my ten novel 'Adventure' series which is also due for publishing.

To the local retailer who has done the same to help me in providing a small retail outlet in their little part of the world.

To the stalwart reader who have taken the decision to buy this book from your local retailer, and I hope that you enjoy its contents. If so, then you should enjoy the rest of my books. As what the lovable Irish comedian would say, "Come 'ere, there's more!"

Your support means that I can now go forward and have my "Adventures of John Grey" published, which has been written in the style of C S Forester's 'Hornblower' series.

I hope you enjoy these four stories, especially if you enjoy letting your imagination wander and discover the settings to where my characters have found themselves.

Acknowledgement

To my dear wife ANNE, who has spent many a lonely evening for several years, in front of the goggle box being engrossed in her own little world of the soaps; whilst I am engaged slaving over a steam driven computer word processor trying to produce a worthy tale for you readers.

To a newly found diamond and my favourite proof reader, Ann. Farquhar from Hereford. Without her beady eye (albeit a myopic one), my descriptive and flowing prose would not be possible. Long may she be able to put the Queens English for punctuation marks etc. into my manuscripts to make my rambling stories more acceptable to you the discerning reader.

Table of Contents

1
Going to By Bys

107
Lucky Creek

137
The Crow's Nest

179
Moreland

Going to By Bys

Peter swung his legs over the side of his bed, making his warm feet feel the instant contact with the cold flagstone floor.

He winced at the sudden natural recoil action of his body to this temporary unpleasantness as he swiftly crossed his room to wash, before cladding his tall muscular body in warm clothing, in readiness for the start of another day of hard work.

"Morning, Mother. Its eight o'clock and I should have been out long before now.

"Morning Peter. Your father said not to waken you too early, and for you to get yourself rubbed down all over, with that bottle of lotion he has left for you." Helen replied as she nodded to a large blue bottle on the table.

Peter looked at the dreaded bottle and recognised it as his father's panacea for any aches and pains.

"Must I, Mother?"

"Yes. Ask your sister to rub it over you when she comes back."

"But Mother!" Peter protested in vain, as he knew not to argue.

"Patricia has been up all night in the nursery stable. When you've had your breakfast, meet her in the wash house so she can put it on you."

Peter tucked into his large breakfast with gusto, even at six feet tall and over fifteen stones, his mother still called him a 'growing lad'.

Having finished his meal, Peter stood up and went over to collect his lunch box that his mother had ready for him.

"What's in it today? Maybe one of your giant oggies[*] with lashings of onions?" Peter asked as he licked his lips at the thought of yet another home made feast that would await him for his dinner.

"Think of it as a surprise. After that meal you've polished off which was enough to feed an army, you want more? Just as well I've bred children with healthy appetites, isn't it." Helen rebuked mildly, as she reached up and tussled his blonde curly hair.

Peter just grinned, pecked Helen on her cheek, picked up his lunch box and ambled down through the long building, and through the door that led to the wash house.

This is where everybody changed from their 'house clothes' into their 'work clothes'.

When coming in from work, the family hygiene regime dictated that everybody would have to strip off, put all their dirty clothes into the large vat of hot water for washing, and take a shower before changing into the clean house clothes. Even all footwear was to be treated by special chemical agents to reduce chances of diseases and unwanted bacterial infections.

Peter stripped off his house clothes and went over to the clean pile of work clothes that was laid out for each member of the family.

"How are you this morning Peter? I'll bet you're feeling a bit sore and stiff from your exerts yesterday."

---

[*] 'Oggies' were first created in Devon during the 15th century, as a pastry filled with meat and vegetables for the lunch boxes of the tin miners. Also a favourite meal by the Cornwall sailors since King George III, now referred to as 'pasties'.

"Morning big sister. Yes, feeling a bit stiff. Father has left his bottle of stuff for you to rub into me. But if you've just been up all night, then I'll wait until later." Peter replied, as he saw his twin sister emerge from the cloud of steam the hot shower created.

Peter and Patricia were nineteen year-old twins. Although they grew up side by side, Peter now did his work outside, whereas Patricia was rapidly establishing herself as a vet. She, tall, slender and curvaceous; he, standing full head and shoulders above her, very muscular and tanned by the seasons.

"Oh no you don't. I've just spent all night helping two mares to foal. You're just a mere man, Peter. When I've finished with you, you'll feel like a frisky stallion if I know you. So just stand there until I dry myself off." Patricia ordered as she dried her hair, before wrapping the large towel around her body.

Peter lay down onto the steam heated flagstones as Patricia knelt down beside him and massaged his body all over with the creamy lotion.

He felt the lotion sending spears of warmth, and a tingling feeling all over him, as he watched his sisters gentle but firm and probing fingers that seemed to play an unwritten tune all over his body.

"Right then. That's you done. I was careful around your dangly bits, so you'll be okay. I'm going for breakfast and bed now." she announced, as she re-corked the liniment bottle, then kissed his forehead as he rose up.

Peter thanked her, and stood up in front of her to put his heavy work clothes on, oblivious to his state of arousal.

"Now then big boy. Put that away or Angus will get angry in case he thinks you're going to do him out of a job." she teased, as she saw the effect the ointment had on him.

"Yes Peter Plumstead, don't you know it's rude to point that thing at us! Besides, there's bigger ones than that on the farm."

came two harmonious voices from out of the clouds of steam.

"Ha ha! Then it serves you two right for looking too close." Peter replied as he started to put his clean work clothes on, and saw that his other two sixteen year-old twin sisters were emerging from the hot showers, giggling and laughing to themselves.

"Whatever you're feeding it on, it's not working." Jilly teased.

"Never mind Peter, it'll make some lucky girl very happy as long as she feeds it right." Jenny quipped as the three girls started to tease him further.

"Now then girls. Leave your poor brother alone. He's still a growing lad and is doing his best." Helen said, as she entered the wash-room, and smiled at the sight of her children as naked as the day they were born. This was not a problem, nor an issue in the family for them to be prudish; as the facts of life were happening all around for them to see.

"When you girls are dressing I'll have your breakfast ready. Peter, your father has gone over to your Uncle Cyril's place with Angus, but says to see your brother Clive before you start."

"Clive over in the milking parlour? Only I've another heavy day ahead of me again."

"He should be back by now for his breakfast." Helen started but was interrupted by a deep booming voice from behind them.

"What's the problem little brother?" it was his smaller, second eldest brother, Clive who had stripped off and was entering the shower area.

"I was just telling him what your father said, but you can tell him now. I'll have your breakfast ready; just let me get the girls off to school."

"I'm off to bed mother, so I'll just have a glass of cream instead." Patricia said quietly and kissed Helen on her cheek before leaving and brushing her long hair as she went.

"But father has taken the tractor and trailer, Mother. How are we getting to school now?" the twins asked in unison.

"It's all right Mother. I'll be quick and take them down in the Land Rover." Clive volunteered.

Helen piled the dirty clothes into the large copper vat full of hot water, then turned to the twins and told them to get some fresh butter and milk from the larder as they passed to go into the kitchen.

"The twins have worked well this morning Mother. The stables and the piggery have been mucked out and clean again. They didn't have time for the rest, so I'll see to our feathered friends when I come back." Clive said proudly.

"Yes, they're learning farmyard skills well." Helen agreed with a smile.

"What am I doing then Clive?"

"Ah yes. I need the blacks with me today. The whites and greys are to stay resting. You are to take two of the chestnuts and two of the blacks, then hitch them to the flat wagon. From the grain silos, make and stack about forty sacks of assorted grain onto it, then take it over to Charles's place. The new millstone you put into place yesterday has been ground down and Charles is ready for milling. Bring the team and trailer back via Cousin Frank's saw mill and Father will meet you there just after dinner time."

"What's Angus over there for?"

"Uncle Cyril's got a new herd of heifers for Angus to tup. So Angus will be staying overnight and be brought back later tomorrow."

"That's good Clive. I've still got that fencing over at the water meadow to complete, and the By landing stage to make, before the barges can come in again."

"I'll expect Charles will give you a hand once he has finished milling. The barges are not due for another few days, and anyway, I've two clamps of root vegetables to shift over there."

The two brothers talked as they dressed, taking time to reflect their workload for the day, then left to go their own separate ways.

Peter worked methodically at his task of sacking and stacking the grain. He made it look easy as he threw the heavy sacks onto the flatbed wagon as if they were bags of cotton wool. When he was finished, he walked over to a water barrel and drank from a mug that was tied up and immersed in it. He then got a large bucket and filled it up and gave each horse a drink whilst he prepared himself for his trip.

He clicked his tongue and spoke softly to his horses as he walked between them when they pulled the heavy wagon. The shire horses dwarfed Peter's six foot frame, as he led them gently but firmly, over the soft grasslands.

Their soft rhythmic plodding soon gave way to the clip-clopping sound as they left the fields and made their way along the narrow farm track that was the remnants of a Roman road. It was a typical farm track that was flanked with shrubbery and grassy banks; with the occasional break in them that had a gate or stile as access into the fields.

After a little while, with Peter deep in thought on his instructions for the day, he passed the familiar old wooden direction sign that was leaning over as if to point up the hill towards High Knowle Woods[*]. With another side pointing downwards to his place, Low Knowle Farm & Shire Horses, with the third one faintly showing the direction to where he was going, Notte Waterfall & Mill.

He knew all the lanes, roads, and short cuts that criss-crossed the valley and the entire surrounding countryside. This lane would take him a couple of miles along the floor of the shallow valley, crossing a river ford and round the base of the High Knowle to the other side behind the forest, to where his eldest brother Charles and his new bride were living.

---

[*] The word 'Knowle' is an ancient, probably Anglo Saxon word for an 'elongated hill', which rises up to form a curved slope leading to a higher flat part of the land. The modern version is probably 'knoll'.

"Hello Peter! Didn't expect you today. How are you?" Came a melodious voice from behind a washing line, draped full of linen and other clothing.

"Is that you Claire? Good morning who ever it is." Peter laughed, as all he could see was a pair of shapely legs walking along the bottom of the washing line until Claire finally appeared.

"Patricia gave me the Knowle Farm special this morning, and I haven't stopped since. That stuff don't half make you try to work it off!"

"I'll bet that was a sight for sore eyes. Painful too if it gets in the wrong places." Claire chuckled and wrinkled her freckled nose.

"I've brought about eight tons of mixed grain. Charles in the mill?" Peter asked quickly to change the subject. The Knowle Farm liniment was the stuff of ancient folklore, local legends, and the local answer to all ailments for man and boy alike, with most women and girls not excused either. But nobody daring to 'lose' the recipe or skimp on the ingredients in the making of it because in everybody's eyes, it was that powerful.

"Yes. He asks if you'd take it over and empty the sacks into his holding hopper. He'll drain it from there. Best see to your horses first, then come in for a cuppa." Claire suggested breezily.

Peter led the horses through the yard and positioned the wagon next to the mill hopper. He tethered the horses to the rail next to a watering trough, then got a bale of hay for them to eat, before he finally re crossed the yard and entered the converted barn that was home for Claire and Charles.

Peter saw a vase full with a big bunch of bluebells and cowslips on the all-purpose, wooden table, which was showered by the sunbeams streaming through the now very clean and curtained windows.

He sat down on a three- legged stool next to the table and was given a large mug of tea and a roll spread with home made butter and honey.

They chatted a while until Charles came ambling through the wide wooden doorway.

"Hello Peter. Keeping the missus' company?"

"How's the millstone Charles?" Peter asked in reply.

"Okay. I've managed to get it ground down and eased. Now suddenly I'm back in business, and its' all thanks to you dear brother, because I certainly couldn't shift it, not even in a month of Sundays." Charles replied as he nodded his head to Peter, as Claire handed him his tea and roll.

"Father has taken Angus over to Uncle Cyril's for tupping the new heifer herd. Maybe we'll have a few more prize animals in the herd when the time comes."

"Aye. That's for sure, isn't it wench?" Charles replied as he stood up behind Claire, putting his arms gently around her, cuddling her and kissing her neck and bare shoulders.

"Mmm! Delicious woman flesh!"

"Oh! Why sire! Please unhand me! My man will be after you with the dreaded Knowle liniment." Claire giggled, fluttered her eyelashes at him as she nestled deeper into his arms.

"On no! Not *the* dreaded liniment! He wouldn't dare!" Charles said in mock horror, and kissed her shoulders even more.

"Oh yes he would. And he'd use the biggest bottle he could find." Claire replied, keeping the little charade going.

"What's all this then?" Peter asked, as he witnessed the impromptu bonding between his brother and his new bride.

"Let me! I'll tell him." Claire said with a chuckle and pushed Charles gently back down onto his stool.

"I'm with child, and its due around late harvest time. Isn't that great?" Claire announced proudly as she blushed, her cheeks turning a deep pink.

"Congratulations Claire, Charles." Peter whooped.

"We'll have a big celebration. Time to pick the beast for fattening, get the apples pressed and."

"Whoa, not so fast young man! As the mother don't I get a

look in?"

"You men are all the same." Claire interrupted in mock admonishment.

"Yes. She's right Peter. Time to consider all that when we get the official nod from the Doc sometime this afternoon." Charles said in response.

"But Patricia has been up all night with two foaling two mares, and another is due soon to drop hers. Peter said innocently and with concern.

Claire laughed and shook her head at the two brothers.

"Tut tut! For shame on you men! It's not the same. I'm a woman, not a horse or a cow in the field, so show some decorum if you please. Patricia is a fine, up and coming vet, but we females of the human kind are different and need proper doctors and the like."

"I suppose you're right." Peter conceded, scratching his head wondering what the possible differences were, that Claire had spoken about.

Charles laughed at Peter's apparent puzzlement and naivety.

"Well there you go. Anyway, that's enough excitement for today Peter. Let's get your wagon unloaded. I understand you've got to meet father over at the saw-mills. Only, I've got some seasoned lumber for you to use on the By's landing stage. You are to leave half your team with me for a couple of days so that I can gather in the grain for milling."

"Glad you mentioned that Charles, I only need two shires for the return trip. But I'll need to give it to Frank to cut it to the sizes I need."

Both men stood up, and in turn, pecked Claire dutifully on her cheeks.

"Be good boys now won't you." Claire said laughingly in response, and gently ushered the men out of the house, as they strode purposefully out to complete their morning's work.

Peter led his horses to a large pile of cut timber next to the mandatory watering trough, then climbed up onto his trailer for a while, listening to the noises of the saw mill.

"Afternoon Peter. Come to pick up your fencing?"

Peter turned around in his seat and watched his oldest cousin Frank, walk slowly towards him. He owned the sawmill and had his younger brothers and other men to help him work it.

The large, barrel-chested man with his ginger beard flecked with wood chippings and sawdust coming towards him, seemed an awful spectre to anybody else but Peter.

"Aye! I need about sixty stakes and about a hundred cross staves. Did you get the galvanised staples and the reels of round wire?"

"No. Ken said he'd bring them over when he comes back from Pa's farm. But you can have as much as you want, because I'm clearing the place for the heavy lumber that's due up to the Notteham's landing stage any day now. Is that the hardwood from Charles's on the back of your wagon?"

"Yes. He's got a lot more there to be shifted. But I've got the wrong type of wagon, so I've only brought enough for now. I still have some fencing to complete by the water meadow. So maybe you'll have it cut ready for me, say the day after tomorrow?"

"Okay Peter, that'll hold. Must get back. I'll get the lads to unload your wagon, but if you need anything else just holler." Frank stated and walked back into the large cavernous timber framed building that housed all the steam powered machinery which operated the massive array of saws.

Peter watched his cousin go as he started to open his lunch box.

"Ah! Mothers 'surprise' lunch. Two cheese and onion wedges as thick as doorsteps, and five apples."

When he had finished his wedges he ate one apple and gave his two remaining horses the rest.

"There you are my beauties. Just a little treat for your hard work today." Peter said softly and patted each horse gently on their necks. He was taught from a very early age to treat his animals well and always remembered his father's words:

'The shires are the gentle giants that will always do your bidding if you treat them right. If you don't, then watch out Peter, not even Angus would go near them.'

Peter waited until the saw mill workers unloaded his wagon before he moved the pile of fencing onto it.

He was tying the load down, when he saw his father riding Peter's black hunting horse towards him. The four horse team and the black exchanged horsey greetings as all three started to drink from the trough.

"Hello father. I'm all loaded up except for the wire and staples. I understand that you'll be bringing them over from Uncle Cyril's?"

"They're on the back of the tractor back at the farmstead." Ken informed him.

"Had your lunch yet? I'm starving. So I'll go over and have a bite with Frank. If you want to move off, I'll catch up with you by the top end of the dyke."

"See you later then." Peter replied as he watched his father dismount and walk across to the sawmill.

Once more Peter walked between his two giants as the bundle of fencing swayed on the back of the wagon. He made his way steadily along, crossed the ford and along the edge of the water meadow, then up the gentle gradient of a hill to a ridge that was in fact the remains of a dyke that was topped with a low hedge.

As it was half way up the gentle slope, it made a natural border and a marker for each field. In fact it was a man made feature that ran parallel for several hundred yards with the brow of Low Knowle.

The dyke was deemed to be made around the 12th and 14th century, as a classic strategic ploy used in those days and probably used in many of the famous battles that were fought throughout the centuries, in those very same fields.

The bundles of fencing were dumped into the dyke, which was dry at this time of the year, but filled up like a miniature reservoir during the winter. But just one of Peter's favourite places when hunting rabbits, wild fowl and even the odd trespasser.

'That should do it for today. Judging by the spoor, I'll bring my longbow and rifle tomorrow. About time we had rabbit stew again.' Peter mused as he climbed onto the now empty wagon for his ride back to the farmstead.

On the way back he heard his Father shouting at him and looked round to see that he was galloping fast to catch up.

"Peter. It looks as though some of your new fencing has been deliberately cut down." Ken said breathlessly as he walked his horse alongside the moving wagon.

"It's cut between the old landing stage and the start of the water meadow. It seems, we've had unexpected guests on the land who might just pay us another visit. They must have been here earlier and come by river. That sector was not worked today, so somebody must be in the know of our whereabouts, or just lucky to be able to get away with it."

"Do you think it could be the Cutlers up to their old tricks again?" Peter asked as he flicked the reins to keep the horses moving.

"Hmm! I don't think so, although when I shot the last one, Jed Cutler said he'd get even. But we haven't seen them since, and that was over three years ago before you took over, if I remember."

"Well whoever they are, they'll get the usual welcome. I don't suppose they'll be back again much before the moon is up, so I'll get some supper and prepare for an overnight guard. I'll use my night sights and the hide on the high knowle."

"Why over there Peter?"

"I have a perfect view of the entire valley from our farm right down to Frank's sawmill. The valley is oval shaped formed by the knowles, about two miles wide at the water meadow, and some four miles long from the eastern high bluffs to the western low bluffs at By By's. Mind you that's as far as the crow flies, but seems a lot less in my telescope, Father." Peter explained.

"Only as big as that? It seemed much bigger in my day, but it sounds good Peter. Best get home and we'll discuss it over supper. See you soon." Ken stated, as he turned and galloped away in front of him, leaving Peter to walk his horses along behind.

The Low Knowle shire horses were a very rare breed and world famous. With an average of twelve raised every year and kept on the farm to be sold. Each one of them worth thousands, making them very attractive targets for any would be horse thieves.

Peter's mind was full of ideas and thoughts on how best to deal with this latest problem.

Amongst his many duties on the farm, his principle duty was the 'Land Ranger', or the 'Rustler and Poacher catcher.'

He was given this very responsible job by the farming community and had taken it over from his father. Also because Peter was a crack shot with a rifle and an accomplished archer, and had won many a competition in hunting skills and was able to use either weapon to great effect.

When he arrived back into the courtyard of the farmhouse, he unhitched the wagon and pushed it into the wagon shed.

Then after seeing to his horses, he went through the family routine of the wash house and finally arrived into the kitchen with his clean house clothes on.

"Evening Peter. I suppose you're hungry again?" His mother greeted as she placed a large bowl of broth on the table in front of him.

"Hello mother, hello big sister, hello little sisters." Peter greeted everybody in turn as he dutifully pecked Helen's cheek.

"Ahhh! Mother's delicious soup! If there's enough left, can I take some with me tonight?" Peter asked, as he sat down to eat.

"Tonight Peter? Where do you suppose you'll be going?" Patricia asked lazily as she stretched and stifled a yawn then curled herself up in the large leather sofa again.

"Hasn't Father told you? It appears that we've had unexpected guests on the land and he suspects rustlers are using the river." Peter said after clearing his mouth from food.

"Hello Mother. Hello everybody." It was Clive's turn to greet the family and sit down to his equally large bowl of soup.

"Rustlers did you say Peter?" Clive asked as he slurped up a spoon of soup.

"Slurpy slurpy oink oink!" the twins chanted as they teased Clive's eating habits.

"Hush girls! Never mind Clive. Listen to what's been said." Helen said sharply, with a menacing look at the twins, which had its effect and silenced them.

"Yes Clive! I'm taking my rifle and night sights over to the high knowle. I might be out overnight. If you can, I'd appreciate it if you'd bring a large spotlight and make yourself a cover with the fencing timber I left in the dyke today. You only need to stay for about three hours of moonlight, from say nine o'clock onwards.

"Maybe Father could bring his twelve bore and the big spotlight, and position himself in the secret hollow of the tree opposite the landing stage."

"Hello Ken. Sit yourself down and have your supper." Helen greeted, as her husband emerged from the washroom corridor.

"Hello family!" he replied as he kissed his wife and heard the chorus of greetings from his off-springs.

"So you want me to use the hollow tree trick. Why not Clive?" Ken asked as he sat down to the table.

"I've put Clive in the dyke, because he can move out without being seen. He will only be on lookout for about 3 hours or until I arrive to take over. As the farm owner to confront these people, you need to be as near to the point of contact as possible. Besides, you're more familiar with the river to be able to cross over it." Peter explained.

Ken nodded his head in acknowledgement, and smiled at the cunning plan that his son was about to hatch.

When Ken and Clive were eating their soup, Peter then went on to discuss the details of his plans. Whilst the men were talking things over, the girls listened quietly, daring not to interrupt them, as Helen made up a lunch box for them to take.

Peter had his soup flask, but the others had sliced meat sandwiches, which the others teased him about as being the favourite.

"Now then boys! Peter is the General so he gets the soup." Helen teased and kissed each one as they left. She wagged a finger at them and said sternly "You men come back in one piece do you hear. I've enough work and worry around here without any of you adding to it."

"Yes Mother!" all three men replied in unison, then started to sing "Hi Ho, Hi Ho, Hi Ho Hum!" as they marched down the washroom tunnel in single file.

It was a distance of time between the going down of the sun that immersed the land in total darkness and the emergence of the moon that bathed the land again in a silvery sheen; that found Peter settled down in his concealed den. He scanned the terrain below him with the telescopic night sight, to help him see in such darkness.

The built-in automatic range-finder told him the straight distance between himself and the dyke, or to wherever he pointed it.

He knew every range and real distance by heart through years of hunting, so took no notice of it. Instead he watched his two men-folk arrive at their hideouts and then watched them prepare themselves for their vigil, before his own scanning took over. *'Phase one complete'* his mental check-list noted.

His concealed hide was his little arsenal where he kept his spare weapons, but he had his own little armoury at the farmstead, where he made his own ordnance such as bullets, snares and traps. He even made his own bows and arrows, using the same age-old methods as those made since the 12th century, and made from the very same local woods around him.

Even the different arrow heads he used seemed to be aplenty, and could be found in many of the surrounding fields, especially when they were being plowed for the next crop.

Many a hare or rabbit, let alone poachers and rustlers were bagged using his trusty longbow that he held in his hand. He favoured the silence of the bow for shooting intruders and game, whereas his long rifle was noisy and too powerful at short distance, so he used it for targets much further away.

His objective was to wound the rustlers not kill, and in truth, he was a one-man army, but they wouldn't know the difference in Peter's deadly skill with his weapons. That was why the local constabulary were perfectly happy to let Peter continue his humane way of dealing with this perennial problem, as it saved them several man hours and reams of paperwork, in doing it themselves.

The moon was up and full, and with the sounds of the nocturnal animals and wildlife around him, Peter saw a movement in some bushes down to the right of Clive. A large fox emerged from it and furtively looked around, before trotting its way up the slope, making its way towards the farmyard for a meal of chicken.

'Hah you scallywag! I'll pin your tail to the ground for you before long, just wait and see'. Peter mused, as he took aim with his rifle. 'Bang! Mr. Fox. Your tail's just been shot off. Lucky for you I have other guests to sort out first.' Then put his rifle back down to scan around again.

'Nearly time for Clive to leave, judging by the moon-time. I'd better slip down now to relieve him when there's no apparent movement along the river. Phase two now in force.' Peter thought to himself as he mimicked the fox, by taking a furtive look around before moving off.

"Clive! It's me!" Peter whispered as he startled Clive by tapping him gently on the shoulder.

"Bloody hell! You nearly gave me a heart attack, where have you just sprung from? How did you cross the river, as I never saw you?" Clive swore again as he turned to see Peter crouched behind him.

"Shhh! Sound travels further during the still of the night. I haven't seen anybody yet, but that doesn't mean there's nobody around."

"Well, I best be getting home now Peter while the coast is clear."

Peter put his finger to his lips, indicating to Clive to be quiet, then pointed down along the valley to where the old landing stage was. He raised four fingers, and mouthed the words, 'four men with two dogs.'

Clive looked down through the low hedgerow and saw the intruders using a pole to push a mumblebee[*] along.

Peter used his fox call to signal his Father that the intruders were here and for him to prepare according to phase three of his plan.

"Clive. I want them all to get off the boat before I start

---

[*] A flat bottomed boat that was used to transport livestock over water.

flying arrows at them. I need to get closer to them, but once I've killed the dogs and hit two of the men, you point to and switch the light onto them." Peter whispered into Clive's ear.

Clive nodded and whispered that he understood and got ready as Peter left him to get closer to the intruders.

The first dog died without a whimper, the second just yelped and died before the men realised something was up. One of them was hit on the thigh, which made him fall to the ground screaming with pain. A second one was hit on his arm that made him drop whatever he was carrying.

"We've been ambushed by the bleeding Indians. Look at the arrows flying at us." One screamed.

"We've been rumbled. Let's get out of here before we all get skewered." shouted another.

"Bastards! Just wait 'til I get my hands on those bastards firing these bleedin' arrows. I've been hit in the leg, and now there's some shit-faced bastard shining a dirty great searchlight in my face." Another swore vehemently.

The third and fourth men behind the first two to get hit, turned and ran towards their boat to make a getaway, but ran straight into the waiting gun of Ken.

"Okay pals! Step this way with your hands up." Ken shouted as he switched his search light on, and shone it straight into their faces.

"Okay then. Now let's see who you are. Drop your weapons and come over here now, before I shoot you down." Ken snarled his orders to them.

One of the men was about to raise his weapon to shoot, when an arrow thumped into his leg, making him over-balance and fall into the river.

"There must be a whole tribe of them up there just waiting to scalp us. Do as he says for gawd's sake." whined the one with the skewered arm.

Ken had them all sitting down in the boat with their hands tied behind their backs by the time Clive and Peter arrived. The ambush had worked perfectly

The four men looked at Clive and especially at Peter, with his longbow slung over his shoulder and the rifle in his hand.

"Well if it ain't the Lone Ranger and Tonto," sneered one.

"We'll git you for this you crazy bastards. We don't like people sneaking up on us like that." drawled another.

"It looks like we've just bagged a gang with a tidy sum on their heads. They've tried this stunt several times around here and Notteham, before now. Allow me to introduce you to the Langley Brothers, who steal to order and ship the animals abroad for a nice profit." Ken announced, then with a secret wink to his sons and in a loud voice said.

"Our livestock will be safe once we've strung them up. Have you brought the ropes?"

"String us up? Ropes?" the four men asked in fear.

"Yes. We've got the Royal approval to hang horse thieves and shoot other intruders. Now which do you want to be done for?" Peter asked with menace in his voice. Although he knew it was not strictly true, it served his purpose.

One of them, apparently the ringleader sneered.

"Hah! You can't strung us all up at once! Anyway we'll tell the law."

"When we've done just that, who'll know it was us? Anybody can still lynch horse thieves. But you'll be dead by then anyway." Clive baited with simple logic.

"Look Mister! We only came for one lousy animal. You've killed our dogs, which have a government licence. We have our rights and want compensation for our troubles." the ringleader persisted arrogantly.

"Look pal! The way I see it, you've come to rob us, and got caught. We can shoot you now as rustlers or string you up for horse thieves. Your choice, which is it?" Ken demanded sharply as he approached them with his rifle pointed at them.

"Before we do all that, we need their next of kin." Peter announced as he kept up the pretence.

All four men gave their details to Clive, who wrote it all down on a small scrap of paper, but made it look as if he was only a country bumpkin who couldn't read or spell properly, thus making the men exasperated even more by spelling everything to him.

"Right then you lot! Let's get you to the local nick. Sergeant Phillips will have a nice warm noose to slip around your necks when we get there. Mark my words on that." Ken baited once more.

The four men started to whine and whimper, promising the moon if only they were set free to go back home again.

Clive and Peter had maneuvered the craft into the middle of the river, and with its engine now switched on, they moved quickly down the river to the bridge that links the local village of By By's that straddled it.

The tradition is that whoever lives, or is on one side of the river is in By, and anybody living or is on the other side, was in By's. This worked both ways, so that those opposite to you, would always be in By By's.

Ken had announced to the four men and teased them again, that they were going to by by's, as you would tell a child they were going to bed. The men thought that they were going to be lynched anyway and started another bout of wailing and protests.

When they all arrived at the police station, Sergeant Phillips was sitting at his desk drinking from a mug and reading the local newspapers.

"Well hello Ken. Who have you got for us this time?" He asked with a frown on his face.

"Bill. We have apprehended the Langley brothers and we claim the reward money for them. They have been shot with arrows, so their wounds will be fleshy but clean. They brought along two rabid dogs, which have been put down humanely. You can put the proceeds of the rabid dogs into your most favourite charity, but the farm can do with the reward money." Ken said evenly.

"Thank you Ken! Peter has done well tonight. I'll get these villains put away safely." Phillips replied with a beam on his face.

"Right you lot. Down the corridor and pick a cell to your liking. They're all the same, so no squabbling." Phillips commanded to the Langley's, who shuffled past Ken with glowering looks, mouthing obscenities at him.

"I'll be over to get the usual statement from you later on tomorrow Ken. Its gone midnight, are you fixed for transport back?"

"Thanks for offering Bill. We've come down in the Langley's boat. You'll be able to retrieve it from the landing stage as and when. But wait until Peter has finished repairing the stage. Say in three days, Okay?"

"Right you are Ken. See you later."

Ken and his two sons left the station, climbed back in to the boat and in no time arrived back at the landing stage where it all started. After tying it up, they left for a well-earned rest before starting just another day on the farm.

The clear cold water of the water meadow flowed gently around Peter's legs, as he drove his fencing posts into the soft muddy ground with his heavy sledge hammer.

"This will still give the animals plenty of water to drink even when the river is low, and prevent them getting stuck in the mud of the river," Peter said quietly to himself as he stopped to look at his completed handy-work.

"Morning Peter!"

Peter looked round and saw his old school chum, floating slowly towards him on an open barge that had a motor bolted to it to propel it along.

"Hello Tom! Haven't seen you in ages. How's the family?"

"All right I guess. Our Susan's asking after you."

"As you can see, I'm up to my proverbials at the moment, but tell her I'll see her in By Bys on Saturday, about eleven."

"That's a fine looking fence you're putting up. What's your depth now?"

"Just over two feet; but it will be down to less than a foot later on in a couple of months when the river is low. I have the landing stage to re make, but this fencing will keep the animals out of the river and also let you know you'd go aground if you came near it. At least that's the idea."

"That's a good idea. This type of craft is a converted mumblebee, and can float in less than one foot of water when empty, but needs a good three when fully loaded."

"This stretch of the By from our farm going down to By By's, is the shallowest part and only about four feet at its deepest place including at the landing stage."

"Well there's a lot of deep mud that's built up around there Peter, so be careful you don't get stuck in it. If I were you, I'd wear a safety harness tied to a solid piece of fencing or that tree trunk over there, to haul yourself out of."

"Thanks for the tip, maybe I'll do just that." Peter said with a nod.

"See you Peter, must go now. I'll tell Susan to expect you. I'll be there with Wendy. Usual time and place?"

"Yes. See you." Peter shouted and waved as Tom floated further away from him.

It took Peter all day to complete fencing off the water meadow on his side of the river By, which is joined by the river Notte further up river.

He was caked in mud by the time he got back to the farm and was glad of the welcoming hot shower if only to try and warm himself up.

"Evening dear brother! Pass the soap will you." Patricia asked as she stepped under the cascading hot water and joined him.

"Hello big sister! I've been in cold water all day. But am real glad of this lovely hot stuff. What about you?" Peter asked as he shoved the wooden bucket full of soft soap towards her.

"I've been in the stable nursery all day. As one mare started, so another decided to join in and they dropped their foals simultaneously this afternoon, which makes four foals in two days, and I'm knackered."

"You're knackered? I don't suppose the mares are feeling all that great either, with you poking your arms inside them all the time."

"Ha ha! What do you men know anyway. Just squirt your thing and go." she teased and threw her flannel at his body.

"Careful or my Susan'll be after you." Peter laughed as he managed to dodge Patricia's well-aimed flannel.

"Speaking of which, Claire told me yesterday that she is due to drop a child around harvest time."

Patricia laughed again then rebuked him for his choice of words.

"It seems that Claire's been feeding her man well then. When is Susan going to feed you, Peter?"

"Feed me what?" Peter asked with a puzzled look.

"Oh Peter, you silly lovely boy. Never mind. But I'm going to miss you when you grow up!" She giggled and kissed him on both cheeks.

Both finally left the showers and got dressed into their house clothes, then walked side by side down the corridor to the kitchen where they greeted Helen with a peck on her cheeks.

"Hello Mother! Peter just told me that Claire's having a baby. Due around harvest time."

"Oh that will be nice. I'm a Grandma at last. I was beginning to think that my boys were dry." Helen said jovially.

"Just wait until your father hears of the news. Fancy Claire not telling us sooner."

It was a good evening by the fire for the customary family get-together, and for the Plumstead's to rejoice in the news of Claire's baby.

This was the time when the television got shut off, so that the family exchanged news, views, or talk about the days work, and what the following day's farmstead events had in store for them.

"Peter. You've done a good job down at the water meadow. I've just brought your timber over for the stage. Frank says that he'll send more if you need it." Ken said slowly as he drew deeply upon his large pipe, filling the room with the aroma and clouds of tobacco smoke.

"There's a storm brewing judging by the clouds building up way over beyond the bluffs towards Mutch Pitm." Clive stated absentmindedly.

"That'll suit Charles, but it means that my work on the stage will be held up again." Peter answered in the slow moving conversation, as he warmed his legs by the open log fire.

"We'd have the day off school too, and we could get on with our history project, couldn't we Mother." the twins said in harmony.

It was another early night to bed for the Plumstead's, as the morning would see them securing the farm and animals against the pending storms.

Peter met the twins coming into the showers as he was leaving to get dried off and dressed for the next period of his day's work.

"We've had a fox in the chicken run last night Peter, but it wasn't able to get through the new wire you put up. For you to know it, it's got a lot of fur missing."

"It must be the one I saw the other night. I would have shot him too. But thanks for the tip little sisters." he replied, and continued getting dressed in silence.

The heavy wooden door swung open with a cold gust of wind and banged itself loudly against the solid stone walls, as Clive entered the wash house, pushing hard to shut the door against the strong winds.

"Ah Peter! Father says that you've got to hitch up a double team to the heavy wagon, with the flatbed coupled onto that, and sack up all the remaining grain. I'll give you a hand for the stacking but I've got the herd and the other animals to look after before the bad weather breaks upon us. So you'll be on your own going over to Charles's place. Father will meet you there when he's brought Angus back."

Peter looked out of the high window and down over the valley below them to see the menacing storm clouds building up.

"We'd best not go down by the By as it will probably have risen somewhat. The poor people of Mutch Piddling[*] in the Marsh must have got a soaking last night judging by what's coming our way Clive."

"Yes! John told me that the Piddle had overflowed its banks this morning and has flooded Mutch again. The Notte should be next to empty into the By to make it flood too."

"John? John Walters was here?" Peter asked in puzzlement, guessing correctly the name as the only other Ranger for the whole valley.

"Yes. He was tracking down a rabid dog that somehow had crossed the By to our side. He says for you to look out for it, as it's already killed several sheep over towards Bymouth."

---

[*] A Piddle is attributed to an Anglo Saxon word for a stream, but also means urinating. In this case a person called 'Mutch' was always seen urinating in that particular stream that flowed through the local village, hence the name.

"I'll have to take my rifle with me then in case I spot him on the way back. It must be serious for John to track so far east as this, Bymouth is a good ten miles away from here."

The brothers walked swiftly out into the courtyard and made their way towards the stables, where they met Patricia attending the new foals.

"Morning big sister!" Peter greeted.

"Morning dear brothers. Big Sam the gander was attacked and killed last night. Judging by the teeth marks, it's not fox, but something else like a dog."

"John Walters was over earlier, he said there was a rabid dog roaming around. Peter will sort it out when he comes back. In the meantime Patricia, keep the doors securely locked at all times, we don't want a rabid dog loose in here." Clive said matter-of-factly.

"What, my John? Over here?" Patricia asked with concern.

"Oh! Yes he did ask me to tell you that he's been up at the Bymouth Manor estate for the last few days. Said he'd be coming back with my Susan, for the Saturday market, weather permitting. Also said to see you about elevenish by the clock." Clive explained as he remembered the message, which made her blush slightly.

"There you are then big sister. We're all going to By By's together now." Peter chuckled and smiled, as he thought of his own meeting.

The two men worked through the early morning and did not stop until all the grain was stacked and tied down on the big wagon and flatbed cart.

Helen came over to them bearing a flask of tea.

"Here you are boys. Get this down you." she said with a flourish as she poured the hot tea into two mugs.

"Peter. Your father rang to tell you that he's on his way home now, for you to wait and not to try and move the double team yourself." she said quickly.

"Good! I was a bit concerned about that, so I can get back

to the herd now. You'll be all right now little brother." Clive said with relief in his voice as he reached up and patted his taller brother on the shoulder."

"Thanks Mother! But I could have handled the team. But it means now that I too can relax and keep my eyes skinned for this rogue animal."

Peter drank the last remains of his tea and gave the mug back to his mother's waiting hand.

"That will keep me warm for another while, but Father had better hurry up or we'll get caught in this lot on the way back." Peter stated as he looked up at the sky again.

"Well, lets go then Peter." Ken's booming voice came from behind him.

The eight shire horses pulled steadily at their harness as the heavy wagon and its trailer gouged out deep tramline tracks across the soft grassy surfaces of the fields.

Ken was walking his animals and calling to them by name as they went along, whilst Peter sat precariously on top of the bulging sacks, keeping a look out with his binoculars.

The trip to the mill was slow but sure and uneventful as they arrived to be greeted by Charles.

"Morning Father, morning Peter. It seems that you're the first to arrive. Your wheat can go straight into the feeder hopper, as will Cousin Jimmy's when he arrives. All the other types of grain will have to be stored in their silos."

"We've brought you about ten tons of wheat, four of corn and two of maize, Charles. That's the lot from our silos now, except for a ton of oats and we need that for the horses." Ken said loudly as he pulled the team to a stop.

"That's just fine. You can leave the four whites and the flatbed wagon here as I'll be using them later on. Let's go for a cuppa as I'm sure you both need it." Charles invited.

"Morning Claire!" Ken and Peter said in unison as they met her standing in the doorway.

"Morning both! Come in and sit for a while."

Claire waited on the men before sitting down to her own refreshment.

"Charles will be working like a Trojan very soon, as the Notte is getting stronger enough for him to use his third stone." Claire opined.

"Yes. The story has it that Mutch Pitm has been deluged and we're next. The Notte and By will both be in full bore by tomorrow morning I expect, but lets hope it clears up for Saturday's market day." Ken replied.

"It looks as if I won't be able to get the stage done until the water has gone down. Let's hope my new fencing survives as I don't fancy another day standing up to my waist in freezing water." Peter said as he joined in.

The conversation ebbed and flowed for a little while longer before Ken stood up and started to get back to the tasks in hand.

"Thanks for the cuppa, Claire. No doubt you too will be busy with all these visitors Charles is expecting very soon." Peter said gratefully.

"Yes! Claire's café is now open to business. A girl has to make a living somehow." She replied with a grin on her face as she escorted the three men out of the house.

The water wheel was spinning much faster on its axle than when they arrived, which meant that the rest of the grain sacks to be drained down into the feeder hopper were sucked down quickly into the grinders, giving Ken and Peter a much needed shorter unloading time.

The horses were lined up again and headed out of the courtyard, moving much easier with just one empty wagon, as they lumbered down the track.

Peter rode 'shotgun', with his rifle in his lap and his favourite longbow between his knees as he sat next to Ken.

They didn't speak for all the time they rode back to the farmstead, just concentrated on the job each had to do. It was nearly mid afternoon when they arrived home, with the storm clouds getting darker and angrier looking by the minute.

"We'd better get the animals stabled and the complex secured double quick Peter. I'll see to the horses, you start locking up on the left side. Get Clive to double up and get his side of the buildings secured. By the look of things we've only got about an hour before this lot drops on us."

Peter never answered but grabbed his longbow and in one blurred motion, fired an arrow towards the door of furthest outbuilding.

There was a dull 'thwack' sound followed immediately with a loud howl and yelping that seemed to get fainter as Peter fired another arrow that produced another 'thwack' and an even louder howl.

The sudden piercing howls and yelping started to unsettle the team of horses Ken was leading back into the stables.

"What the hell was that? Whoa! Steady on boys! Steady on! Come on get in there." he said softly, calming down his animals before he forced them into the stables.

"That dear Father, was what John Walters and I had been on the look out for." Peter said quietly as he took aim with his high powered rifle and shot the mortally wounded, escaping animal dead in its tracks.

"That was the rabid dog that was attacking animals all along the valley. Let's hope it was a loner, a pack of them could do serious damage to the entire farming community."

Patricia came racing out of the nursery stable looking pale and trembling like a leaf.

"You've got him then Peter, it somehow got into the nursery. It attacked and killed one of the mares and her foal and has left dear old Pongo bitten nearly to death when he came in to protect me. I managed to chase it outside before it could reach me." She gasped and started to cry. Peter put his arm protectively around her and held her close until she stopped crying.

"I saw a movement coming from over there by the door of the milking parlour, but had to use the longbow in case I spooked all the animals. But I shot it dead anyway. Father has the horses under control now by the sound of things, so let's go and see to poor old Pongo. Unless he can be saved, I'll have to shoot him too."

"No Peter. I'll see to the dead foal and Pongo. You get that dead animal double wrapped in polythene bags and take it to the police. Mind you don't get any of its body fluids on you when you do, as it's highly contagious."

"Okay big sister. I'll do as you ask."

Ken came striding over to them asking if they were all right.

"Just as well you used your longbow first Peter. The sudden noise in this courtyard would have reverberated a great deal and really spooked the animals. It took me all this time to calm them down. We've got a storm brewing over us, which might set them off again. So we'd best get finished and cleaned up for the night. Have you seen Clive, Patricia?"

"No Father, but he should be in the milk parlour finishing off."

Peter ran over to the parlour with his rifle still in his hand, calling as he went.

"Over here Peter! Over here quick!" was the reply.

Peter ran to the back of the building and saw Clive sitting down on the floor, swearing profusely, and holding his legs.

"The bastard came out of nowhere and bit me several times before I managed to stick it with a pitchfork and chased it out of the barn. It attacked two of my best milkers before it came at me. One of the cows is now dead." Clive explained as he groaned and winced in pain.

"Patricia!" Peter shouted at the top of his voice.

"Patricia come quick! It's Clive."

She arrived slightly ahead of Ken and quickly assessed the situation. She grabbed the Emergency First Aid kit box off the wall and began to treat Clive with its contents.

"Dad! You get the Land rover out. Peter! Carry Clive over to it and help me take him to hospital. Clive! How long ago was it since you were bitten?" Patricia asked calmly but demanding a swift answer from Clive.

Ken sprinted away and came back with the vehicle and Peter lifted and put his brother gently into the back of it.

"Peter! Clive needs a special injection! Perhaps Dr Long might have something in his surgery. Phone him to see, otherwise we've got a dash on our hands to Bymouth hospital. Clive has only got about an hour left before the fever symptoms take over.

Father, you drive whilst I tend him." Patricia's coolness and veterinary skills had taken charge of the situation as she commanded her men-folk at will. This was her undisputed territory and expertise on the farm, and nobody in the family ever questioned her orders.

Peter came back with the news that the doctor had an antibiotic serum, and was on his way over.

"How far and how long will it take him to get here Peter? Only if we can have Clive bathed by the time the Doc gets here, it would be more beneficial than treating him in the back of a Land rover."

"Three miles on a good day, but because of the By is in flood, a slight detour, so about five miles in total. And say twenty minutes maximum" Peter explained to his anxious sister.

"Father! Ask Mother to get plenty of clean towels ready, and I'll need a large bowl of ice to keep Clive's temperature down.

"Peter! If you're correct, then we'll get Clive into the showers and have him washed down first in warm water, then with an antiseptic rinse. We'll have him all ready for the Doc there. There's nothing we can do for the dead animals, but I need to see to the other animals the dog came in contact with, in case they too develop the virulent disease."

Peter scooped Clive up in his arms again from the back of the vehicle and took him into the washroom, where he found the twins changing into their work clothes.

He briefly explained to them what had happened to Clive, what Patricia was planning, what he had to do, and started to strip Clive for bathing.

"You go Peter, leave him with us. We'll bathe him and wait with him until Mother arrives with the Doc." the twins urged, as they took over from him.

Peter just nodded and thanked them, then left to continue with his original chores, meeting his Father on his way around the buildings.

"Father, I'll lock up and secure everything, you go and help the girls seeing to Clive, he's heavy and they might not be able to lift him." Peter suggested.

"Your mother will be there to do that, and Patricia will soon be there to meet the Doc. I'm best settling the animals down, as its going to be a long day ahead of us tomorrow." Ken spoke gruffly then added.

"You finish off doing this then help me in the milking parlour. It will need decontaminating if I know what to expect next. The rabies virus is just as deadly as any on the farm, including anthrax or foot and mouth, Peter."

Peter went swiftly around the several outbuildings that formed the wide hexagonal courtyard. He checked the generator and boiler rooms before seeing that the livestock were okay and safe.

The storm heralded its start with the day turning swiftly into night, as the winds started howling in the trees and the rains just lashing down, drumming loudly onto the roof slates. All of this was lit up with flashes of lightning accompanied with ear battering thunder, which was constantly rumbling overhead.

"Dr Long. Glad you could make it, although your return trip will not be as pleasant." Patricia said as she nodded to the smallish but very rotund figure of the doctor coming through the front door.

She explained what had happened and what she had done in the way of emergency first aid, with Long nodding his head and selecting items from his black bag.

"You have done well, even for a vet, Patricia! Let's hope this will settle him down a bit." Long said as he injected Clive with the serum.

"I will give him a sedative as well and put a few sutures into his wounds. That injection I have given him isn't the correct one, but it will have to do for now. The effect of the drug will only last a couple of hours and I had only just the two hypodermics in my surgery.

"So I'd better let you have the other one in case, but he really needs a bigger dose with a different serum and immediate hospital treatment. He will drift off to sleep soon with this drug, but keep the ice packs on him to help stem the fever."

"We'll phone the hospital to tell them to expect us, and we'll get you a replacement injection on our way back, doctor." Patricia replied gratefully.

"I would come with you dear girl, but I've got another two house calls to do. Best you let him rest a little while to let the serum take over. Hopefully the storm will ease off in the meantime for me to get back.

Give him a cup of weak tea with plenty of sugar before he falls asleep, that will help his shock system recover."

"What a good idea Doctor. We can all have a cuppa, as there's nothing like one to calm the nerves." Helen suggested

The impromptu tea and biscuits were welcomed by all, and seemed to cheer everybody's spirits up.

"Thank you for your hospitality Helen, but I'm afraid I must be making a move to get back in time for the surgery now." Long stated.

"If you wait, we'll prepare Clive and take him to the hospital in the Land rover. Better travel in company down to the main road, just in case you get stuck somewhere in your little car, Doctor." Ken suggested.

"Yes, thank you Ken, that's a good idea. There is a fallen tree at the bottom of the lane, but by the sound of this wind there may be plenty more going back on the road to By Bys. When you get to the hospital Patricia, show them the serum needle I gave. It will tell them exactly what to give next."

Patricia nodded at the instructions and prepared herself for the trip.

"You'll have to go Peter as I have to stay here to see to the animals. Take the dead dog with you to the hospital in case they want to take samples from it. But drop it off at the police station on your way back." Ken ordered sharply.

Peter just nodded, lifted Clive up gently and carried him out to the waiting vehicle, whilst Helen draped an oilskin over the both of them.

Within minutes the two vehicles moved steadily down the narrow winding lanes towards the main road to By Bys.

"It's a long time since I've driven this thing Patricia and my licence only allows me to drive it 'off road'. How's Clive doing?" Peter asked loudly as the vehicle bounced along the uneven surfaces of the lanes, being buffeted by the storm.

"He's sleeping the drug off. But once we get onto the main road we'll be okay. Just as long as we all arrive in one piece." she replied stoically.

The drive to the hospital was a perilous one for the Plumstead's, tree after tree seemed to throw themselves at their Land rover as they were passing, causing Peter to swerve violently to avoid crashing or being hit by one.

"Talk about the funfair dodgems!" Patricia said excitedly as she watched Peter wrestle with the steering wheel.

"Sorry about this! But needs must Patricia. Nothing is going to stop me, not even that police patrol wagon that's been trying to chase after us for the last couple of miles. We've got about half a mile to go for the turn off to the hospital. So get ready for a swift exit left."

He turned the vehicle sharply into the hospital lane entrance, causing it to skid violently and tilt onto two wheels before it slammed safely back down again. But they arrived slowly and sedately at the entrance to the A&E door where they stopped, with the chasing police car coming to a skidding stop and facing them as if to block them off.

A patrolman got swiftly out and ran over to Peter who was about to get out of his vehicle.

"Now then sir! You have violated too many traffic and safety laws to mention. I am arresting you for dangerous driving."

Peter just ignored the policeman, brushed him aside and calmly walked to the back of the land-rover where he picked up his sleeping brother and gently carried him into the hospital where nurses were standing wondering what all the commotion was about.

Patricia arrived quickly by his side and announced to the inquisitive nursing staff that the patient was her brother, and that he was suffering from an attack by a rabid dog. The serum given and that he is in need of immediate serum treatment, and decontamination.

Her announcement seemed to galvanise the nurses into action who took Clive off Peter and rushed him into the depths of the hospital. Patricia carried on talking to the nurses as she went with them, leaving Peter to see to the irate policeman who was inspecting every detail of the Land Rover.

Having watched and heard what was said, the policeman seemed to have a change of attitude when Peter came over to him.

"Having a spot of trouble sir? Maybe you could fill me in with some details. Just for the record, you understand sir." he asked quietly.

Peter introduced himself then told the policeman what had happened and showed him the dead animal in the back.

"I brought it here in case the doctor wanted some samples. If not then I shall be taking it back to the sergeant at the By By's nick."

"Very well then sir. I'm satisfied with your story and I'll say no more about this. Only, next time you take a left-hand turn like that, make sure you have a good set of tyres, and that nobody is coming the other way. You get my drift?" the policeman said wearily as he tapped his lapel badge.

Peter just smiled and thanked the departing policeman then waited in the A&E foyer for his sister to come back.

Several hours passed, and although the storm was still raging, it was a much gentler ride back to the farmstead for the twins.

Peter put the vehicle away safely and went to join his sister in their obligatory shower and antiseptic rinse, before entering the family sanctum of the kitchen.

"Hello you two! You've been gone ages. I tried to phone the hospital but the line has gone dead. What's happening to Clive?" Helen asked anxiously.

Patricia explained their journey in every minute detail, which had the younger twins listening intently and enthralled with it.

"Talk about a good story. That's the best we've heard for a long time." they said quickly.

"Tell us more."

"Lucky the copper took your story in good faith, Peter. It sounds as if he's new around here and was trying to earn brownie points. Bill Phillips will put him right though." Ken observed, then asked, "How much was the reward on this one Peter?"

"Don't know Father. But whatever it is, the sergeant says by rights it's going to John Walters even though I killed it."

Peter answered quietly, as he knew that he and John would share it between them on Saturday.

"So who's a lucky girl this Saturday afternoon then?" the twins piped up as they threw their cushions at Patricia and commenced to tease her.

Patricia just blushed, and threw the cushions back at the twins again telling them to grow up.

"That's just what we're doing big sister." was the reply, as the cushions were sent flying back to her again.

"Now now then girls, its time for bed. The weather is here for at least another day, so you two can stay in bed until breakfast time." Helen stated, which was greeted with a cheer from the twins as they jumped up off the sofa and did Helen's bidding.

When Helen came back into the living room Ken started to discuss the re scheduling of the workload to cover Clive's temporary absence. That, and the enforced inactivity on the land due to the bad weather.

Patricia advised them that the nursery stable and the milk parlour had to be decontaminated before any more animals would be allowed back in again.

"All in all, a few bad days in store for everyone, especially for poor Clive stuck in the hospital." Helen concluded somberly just as the lights flickered and went out, leaving them all in the glow of the dying fire.

"Better get turned in now while the going is good don't you think Ken?" Helen asked lazily as she stretched herself and made for the bedrooms.

Ken moaned about wanting to do so but had to see to the lights.

"It's all right Father. I'll see to it, you can go with mother. You might as well get turned in too dear sister. It's probably something simple, so I'll use the access corridor to get there." Peter volunteered as he fumbled and reached for the hurricane lamp and lit it with a taper.

"Okay then Peter if you're sure! Any problem with the boiler, come back for me."

"But nobody has used that side corridor for ages Peter." protested Helen.

"Don't worry mother, I go down there several times a month. Two years ago I discovered another tunnel leading off and down some steps to a couple of stone clad rooms, and it's where I make my archery equipment and my bullets. In fact it's just the perfect place for it."

"That's where Peter keeps his souvenirs and battlefield artifacts that he keeps finding. Isn't that so Peter." Patricia informed everybody.

"But how do you know that?" Peter asked with surprise.

"That's easy dear brother. The twins told me that they saw you going there and they followed you down. They saw a lot of the artifacts you have found, and they catalogued them as part of their history project that they keep mentioning from time to time.

They took one to school to show their teacher, who said it was a very valuable item. And that really speaking, you should hand them all over to the Bymouth museum."

"Well I never!" breathed Helen as she turned to Ken.

"Fancy our Peter being a secret hoarder of national treasures."

"I don't care what he keeps down there as long as he doesn't blow us all up with his gunpowder. I kept all mine in the outhouse where the carts are now kept. I thought I knew this farm complex inch by inch. Where abouts is this tunnel Peter? It sounds like some sort of a dungeon or something. I wonder what else you've found." Ken replied.

Peter never answered his father, but walked swiftly down the washroom corridor holding up the lamp to see where he was going.

The washroom corridor linked up with the rest of the tunnel system, which was originally built as part of the underground workings of a very large 13th century castle. But the castle was repeatedly attacked and destroyed before being rebuilt again, over the millennia and eventually ended up as abandoned ruins.

However, it was the Plumstead's forefathers in the early 17th century, who took it over and used those ruins to construct the entire Lower Knowle farmstead building complex.

They had used the same material, foundations and shape of the original castle, but only as a single storied building. With the tunnel uncovered and converted for use as an access corridor, you could reach all the other parts of the building without stepping out into the open.

The morning was dark, drafty and damp as Peter rose from his bed to start his morning rounds of the farm. He had worked long into the early hours of the morning, repairing the boiler that produced the hot water for the steam turbines.

They turned the dynamo to generate the light and heating system for all the buildings in the complex.

When he stumbled into the brightly-lit kitchen for another check around the farm, he saw his mother up to her elbows in flour, kneading dough. He felt ashamed at his selfish thoughts of being the only one up this time in the morning.

"Morning Mother! Didn't expect to see you up so early. What time is it?" He greeted as he pecked her on her flour-smudged cheek.

"Morning Peter. Its six o'clock and I expect you're hungry. Sit down and I'll give you some breakfast." Helen offered cheerily.

"You'd gone a long time, when did you finally get to bed?"

"About four o'clock. I fixed the boiler but on the way back, I had to put a tarpaulin over the chickens shed, as all that part of the main roof got blown off. Fortunately the felting was okay to keep them dry, otherwise we'd have soggy chickens flying around everywhere."

"Patricia went to down to the nursery stable around that time, funny you didn't see her. I expect she's sleeping in her little caboose there and should be back any time now."

"Father still in bed then?"

"No. The cows need milking twice a day so he got up about an hour ago to decontaminate the milking parlour. He should be back soon for his breakfast."

"So I'm the last to get up again! Silly me to think I was the only one up this morning." he said with a touch of sarcasm.

Helen came over and ruffled his curly locks.

"Never mind son! After all, you were the one out in the storm when we were all tucked up in bed fast asleep." Helen replied with a smile as she appeased him.

"Such is life on a busy farm dear son." she added stoically.

"Amen to that!" Peter replied as he started to tuck into his breakfast on a plate that any dustbin lid would look puny against.

Ken arrived into the kitchen from the washroom corridor, and sat down at the head of the table where Helen had his place set out for him.

"Morning Peter. From what I've seen, you had a busy night last night. What time did you get back?" he asked.

"Morning Father." Peter replied in response.

"The back end of three, nearly four, I guess. I'm on my way out now, is there anything I need to know or get you?"

Ken rattled off what was needed immediately, paused then added.

"I've decontaminated the milk parlour, so if you would, take the pile of straw I've left under some logs, and burn the lot. Logs and all Peter, as I don't want a rabies virus epidemic starting from this farm."

"I'll be a while getting round to doing all that Father. I have a suspicion of another rogue dog or fox roaming around the place. Once I'm satisfied it's not in the home farm, I'll start."

"Can you at least get the parlour hay in before you start off. I have to start milking in about half an hour."

"Six bales did you say?"

"Yes, and just two now for me please Peter." Patricia asked as she too entered the kitchen, kissing him and Helen on the way past to sit down at her place at the table.

"Morning Father. I've decontaminated the nursery stable and checked the milk parlour you did. I'm satisfied they've been given a good scourge. I'll burn the contaminated hay Peter, as I've got to spray the around the boiler as well."

"There you are then. That's the day sorted Father." Peter said cheerfully, as he left to go down the washroom corridor to change.

"I meant to ask him to check the phone lines down the lane. It's still dead and I was hoping to phone the hospital to see if I could visit Clive." Helen said slightly crestfallen.

"I've got to go over to By By's to get some veterinary supplies; I'll look for you as I go along Mother." Patricia offered, which cheered Helen up visibly.

"Clive will need his toiletries and other things. Can't you take me to the hospital instead?" she asked eagerly.

"Yes and maybe you can get me some tobacco while you're at it?" requested Ken.

"All things are possible dear parents, but I must get some sleep first. I'll be going to By Bys about ten, so you'll all have to wait until then." Patricia said quietly as she rose to go to her bedroom.

Peter had completed his rounds and was loading a handcart with hay when he saw Patricia and Helen climbing into the Land Rover.

"Hold on a minute!" he shouted to them.

"I think it's got a damaged tyre from the debris on the roads last night. There's a spare one in the garage. I'll put it on if you'll just wait a moment." Peter advised them and left to get it.

It took him only a few minutes to change the wheel, much to the relief of his womenfolk.

"See what I mean Patricia?" he said as he held up the damaged wheel.

"That last tree we bounced over has left some of itself in the rubber. We have another spare one, so you don't have to buy one just yet."

"I what? I only started off with a simple pick up of much needed veterinary supplies. Now I'm going to the shop for tobacco, the garage for tyres and to the Bymouth hospital. God knows where I may end up or when I can get back!" Patricia stated with exasperation.

"Such is life on a busy farm dear sister." Peter replied softly, and placed a kiss on her forehead.

"Now where have I heard that one before?" Helen said softly as she smiled at them and climbed into the waiting vehicle.

Patricia drove off swiftly, leaving Peter alone to return to his chores.

Peter completed his extra chores and was on his way to prepare for dinner, when he met the twins who were also coming into the washroom.

"Morning Peter!" they said in unison.

"Good morning little sisters. The chicken coop had its roof blown off but I've fixed it now. It looks as if you'll have to change the bedding straw, so I've left you two bales just inside the door." Peter explained.

"Why thank you. We wondered what the extra straw was for." the twins replied, then talked about their chores for a while longer whilst taking their mandatory showers.

"I understand that you two have a history project on the go. What period are you doing?" Peter asked warily to test them.

"We've got a history exam soon about the dark ages between the Twelfth and Fourteenth century." they stated.

"Tell me more! I know something about that period as I did almost the same history period too." Peter said with a straight face, and feeling that he'd find out a lot more from them, if what Patricia has told him.

"You do? That's great! Then you can help us with some of it after we've done our afternoon chores." they said excitedly.

"Yes, this valley is steeped in battle history of that period, and I can show the various things dotted throughout the valley for you to look out for. There's a lot of things that went on all around this valley, from the eastern bluff, right down to the western bluff at By Bys, judging by all the bits I keep finding." Peter explained to try and exact some response from his sisters.

"Yes we've seen your." Jilly started, but was hushed quickly by Jenny.

"Ahah! I smell the blood of two little Indian girls." Peter said triumphantly.

"Two little borrowers who leave their marks all over the place."

"Peter! We didn't mean any harm, honestly." Jilly said with remorse.

"Your biggest mistake is that you both forgot that I can read tracks and follow an animal for ages. What I can't understand is why you leave the place in such a mess."

"All right Peter. We own up to following you down the tunnel two months ago. But we only drew what we saw and left everything as it was. We've only been down twice since and won't be going back." they said with a scared look on their faces.

Peter noticed that look and asked what was wrong to spook them.

"We think it's spooky down there and we kept hearing clanking noises. We're afraid it might be ghosts who have come back to haunt the place."

"I haven't seen or heard anything, and I go down there quite a lot. In fact I was coming back along the tunnel at four o'clock this morning, and I didn't see anything then. It's probably the water going through the pipes." Peter said, as he tried allay their fears and thoughts.

"Well if you say so Peter. But we still have to finish the study off, for our exams." Was their hesitant reply.

"I tell you what. If you want anything else to trace-draw, or find out about, tell me and I'll come down with you. How's that then girls?" He said to cheer the girls up again.

"Yes! That suits us fine Peter. Thank you!" they said gratefully, and happily skipped their way in front of him towards the kitchen for dinner in the knowledge that their big brother would protect them.

"Hello mother, big sister!" all three chanted as each entered the kitchen and shattered the silence of the room.

"Hello you three. Sit down and have your stew. Patricia, hand me over the teapot dear, I'll make a fresh pot for us." Helen said loudly over the noise of the chairs being dragged over the flagstone floors.

Peter looked at Helen's' face and saw she was looking worried and upset.

"What is the matter mother?" he asked with concern.

"Is it something to do with Clive?"

"Yes mother." the twins joined in.

"How is Clive?"

Helen looked over to Patricia, then went slowly towards and into the hallway corridor, leaving Peter and the twins with deep concern and puzzlement on their faces.

There was a moment's silence before Patricia cleared her throat, which made the three turn their heads towards her.

"Patricia. What is the matter? Tell us, we've got a right to know." Peter asked sharply, which prompted the twins to demand the same.

Patricia stood up slowly and faced them, and with almost a whisper she said.

"Clive had to have both legs amputated from the thigh down, last night. He suffered a heart attack but was resuscitated, then nearly died again from the massive anti rabies serum he was given. He's now in a seclusion ward of the Intensive Treatment Unit until he gets better.

He'll be in hospital for at least a month, with a further year or so, going in and out of the orthopedic ward and therapy unit."

Peter stood up and caught the twins in his arms as they rushed to him weeping. Patricia came over and joined the embrace as she too started to weep. He stood there hugging them, like a sentinel silently guarding his sisters, with the anguish of his brother's loss of limbs tearing at his heart, and tears slipping down his cheeks with relief that Clive was still alive.

After a little while when the weeping stopped, he thought of saying something flippant or cheerful just to lift his sisters up from their gloom.

"Well never mind dear sisters. Think of it this way, maybe they'll give him longer legs and he'll become taller than me. That way you'll have two big brothers to plague now, instead of just me. And he won't be able to duck under his cows anymore, instead he'll be able to just step over them."

The twins stopped their sniffles and started to giggle quietly at what he said. Patricia slapped his arm sharply at his remark.

"Trust you! You lovely great hunk. Wait until I tell your Susan about you." she said quickly as she reached up and kissed him.

"That's from us girls."

Helen had arrived back into the kitchen again, in time to see and hear this little intimate scene and came swiftly over to Peter. She stood up on her tip-toes and kissed him tenderly on his cheek and said.

"You're a chip off the old block Peter, only taller."

"Does father know yet, Mother? Only he's been in and out of the stables and the milking parlour all morning." he asked.

"Old blocks? I know what Helen?" Ken asked as he entered the kitchen.

The girls fell absolutely silent as Helen gripped Peter's hand.

"You'd better sit down dear. I'm afraid it's Clive." Helen started, but Peter hushed her and took over the duty of informing him.

Ken stood still and looked around the room with puzzlement.

"What be the matter son? Go on, I'm listening." Ken demanded.

Peter glanced around at the girls and his mother, then faced his father.

"It appears that Clive had both legs amputated during the night." he commenced, and related to him exactly what Patricia had said. When he finished, Ken sat down in his chair with a thump and a shocked expression on his face.

Ken stared at Helen then at Peter for a moment, then stood up slowly and went to look out of the kitchen window. Nobody spoke for several moments until Helen came up to him, put her arms around his waist and rested her head against his back.

Ken's face showed great trouble and anxiety as he turned round to her and kissed her, which made her and the girls weep again.

Peter stood holding his three sisters but looked directly into his father's eyes.

Not a word was spoken between them. But in that look they both knew that although Clive had had a very narrow escape and both were glad he survived, life without him around the farm would be extremely difficult for them to cope with.

When Charles got married and left the farm to run the mill, it was a huge blow to Ken. For Ken had been struggling ever since to catch up with the financial hole the farm was slipping further into, as each season passed.

The loss of Charles' input as the farm's land manager was one thing, but the loss of Clive's input as livestock and dairy manager as well, was a fatal blow.

Two key members of his family gone from the farm within six months meant that it was now impossible for Ken to meet that financial burden, even though he still had a powerhouse in Peter to rely upon in the family's struggle to keep the farm going. The family knew that Lord Bymouth had loaned them a substantial amount of money to develop the shire horse stud, and took the deeds to the farm until such times as it was it all paid off. Times were going to be harder for them all now.

"Well Father!" Peter said eventually, to break the ice and the despondency everybody seemed to have lapsed into.

"As I've said to the girls, it's not as bad as it seems. It's not as if he has gone permanently, he's only in hospital for a while getting his legs seen to. Maybe they'll give him some stilts to walk on and he'll come back taller than me."

"Just think Father, he'll be able to drive the cows to By Bys without stopping now. The poor cows won't know what hit them until they reached the market."

Ken glowered at Peter for a moment, then suddenly a flicker of recognition appeared on his face as he realised the practicality of what Peter said.

"Trust you Peter! Yes Helen, I think you're right. He is definitely a Plumstead." Ken declared as he went over to Peter and put an arm around his son and gave him a few gentle pats on the back.

"Peter! You and I will sit down this evening and work out a priority of everything, sort things out in general and even slow things down for a while until Clive is fit again." Ken said softly.

Peter just nodded his head slowly as if to draw a line under this incident.

Helen and Patricia both breathed a sigh of relief as they saw that their men-folk were already starting to 'raise the drawbridge and man the ramparts' to try and get things back to almost normal again.

"Can we please finish our dinner now Mother?" the twins asked in a loud whisper, which returned Helen swiftly back into her usual stoical self.

"Why yes, of course you can. Will everyone please sit down, so we can finish our dinners together." she announced softly, as everybody rushed to obey her command with noises of chairs being scraped across the floor and various requests of passing this or that from across the table.

The following morning saw that the storm had blown itself away and left much brighter and calmer weather ahead, as everyone went about their early morning tasks.

Saturday had arrived and as it was the monthly payday, everybody was eager to go into the village for a well-earned afternoon off.

The entire population of the Bye valley congregated in the village once a month, which coincided with payday and their market day. As everybody was related to each other in one way or another, it was the time that family ties were renewed again in one big extended family get together.

Peter and Patricia met their sweethearts and were in the Young Farmers' club at the back of the cattle market, enjoying a drink with all the others, talking about the latest news and about Clive's near death, when Sergeant Phillips approached them.

"Peter, can I have a word?" he asked civilly.

"Afternoon Sergeant!" Peter replied affably. "How can I help you?"

"One of the high knowle farmers has complained to me about your shooting target practice last week, and I was meaning to talk to you about it the other night. It seems that you have a few extra scarecrows dotted all over the valley that you use for range practice, both for your longbow and firearms."

"Yes Sergeant Phillips. Please continue." Peter encouraged as he guessed what to expect next.

"Well, one of the scarecrows that you shot at turned out to be this farmer who was standing behind it at the time, doing it up. Fortunate for him your arrow stuck into the centre pole instead of going straight through it. May I suggest that you use the ancient and traditional target range provided, and more often, as the law requires. Or at least do something to those scarecrows so that if you do shoot bullets or arrows at them, nobody standing behind would get hurt."

"Thank you for telling me sergeant. I will be more careful, and if you see this person, offer him my apologies and I'll make it up with a brace of pheasants or wildfowl. If I know him, he's rather partial to wildfowl pie. Mind you though sergeant, he's fortunate I was using an old longbow and lighter arrows at the time, and that I was not aiming at him otherwise he'd be dead, five hundred yards away or not."

"Well I'll tell him anyway Peter. That's my public duty done, now I've told you." he said to conclude that topic.

"How is Clive? The whole village has heard of his trouble."

"Lost both his legs. He's out of commission for a while, and we're trying to cover for him as I've said. He should be back almost to normal self once he's got his new legs fitted I dare say."

"Well Peter! We, the missus and I that is, wish him a speedy recovery."

"Thank you sergeant, I'll tell him."

The sergeant nodded his head and left Peter to return to his circle of friends.

"Peter! Tell your dad that the tannery is full again. It will take at least another six weeks for the process to complete, and my dad said that I can be spared to help out for that time." Tom volunteered.

"Why that's decent of you Tom. Best get your dad to tell mine though, just in case he's got somebody from the Farmers' Guild to come over."

"Yes. I have a couple of weeks off as well, so I can come over and see you more often too lover boy!" Susan whispered loudly into his ear as he sat down next to her.

"Ooh! Listen to that! So just who's a lucky man then?" Patricia teased as she overheard the whisper.

Peter blushed and drank from his glass without answering.

"Speaking of which, John! When are you going to make an honest woman out of me, I'm getting to be an old maid now." Patricia said as she turned her attention to her fiancé.

It was John's turn to blush.

"If it were me, it'll be the Mayday festival." he started to say.

"Well it certainly isn't anybody else my lover boy, so why wait? And by the look of you, you're in need of a good feeding." Patricia joked.

That girlie remark from her made all the other girls laugh, and even more so, at the puzzled looks their boyfriends gave them.

"You've got one ring on your finger, so the next one will probably be during the Harvest festival. Anyway I thought its' supposed to be the girl that sets the day?" John finished with a smile and planted a kiss on Patricia's lips, to prevent her speaking again.

The afternoon slipped into the evening, most of the people had left and all the stall holders packed up and gone, leaving the village almost deserted, save for the odd straggler.

Peter and Patricia kissed their lovers and waved them goodbye as they waited with the Land Rover for Helen and the twins to arrive back on the last rural bus from Bymouth. Ken had the tractor and was already back at the farm waiting for them all there.

MUTCH PITM via BY BYS, stated the abbreviated neon lit sign on the front of the single-decker bus, as it stopped noisily at the clock tower. The bus let off half of its passengers and took on a few more before it motored its way through the village and out of sight towards its own destination.

"Hello Patricia, Peter! Look what we've bought!" the twins greeted excitedly as they rushed up to him, each holding up a carrier bag.

"Hello you two, hello Mother!" Peter said softly as he opened the door of the Land Rover and helped Helen into it.

Everybody climbed into the vehicle which Peter drove whilst Patricia talked to the twins, otherwise it would have been a silent trip back to the farm.

The family had their supper and discussed the day in their customary way, winding down by the fireside, enjoying each other's company.

"So Clive will be able to come home for Easter then, that's good." Peter remarked, as topics were discussed one by one in the slow, unhurried conversation.

"Tom will be staying to help out for a few weeks Helen. He can use a spare room in the other wing, instead of the hired hands place over the boiler room." Ken informed her.

"Time for bed now girls!" Helen said after a while, as the Plumstead's prepared themselves for the usual By Valley Parish, Sunday routine.

All early morning chores done first then the outing to By By's church service and Sunday school for the children under sixteen.

The villages' single church provided services for the Catholics between nine and ten o'clock, and the Protestants between ten-thirty and eleven-thirty, with the two pubs and all the shops shut for the day. Only essential work got done on that day, nothing else, as observing the Sabbath day was still a part of the valley's customs.

But for Peter and John, apart from their personal radio link between themselves and Sergeant Phillips, it was their full day alone out on the 'range' as anything or anybody else found roaming around out there, would be deemed as intruders.

Peter routinely saddled up his hunting horse and loaded it with his weaponry and any other equipment needed, before he led it out through the gate of the courtyard. With a single leap up into the saddle, he trotted his horse across the fields to begin his day.

The stillness of the morning was shattered and full of noises echoing across the valley, as the farmers' vehicles took the Sunday worshippers to and from the village. The main road from By By to Mutch Pitm ran straight and true along the bottom of the valley on the high knowle side, with the meandering river on the low knowle side. So both Rangers knew that any trouble or unwanted strangers would probably wait until the afternoon when nobody was about for them to come and try anything.

This was the usual time when Peter would be sitting in his little hideout looking around with his powerful binoculars, with his rifle at the ready, as would his opposite number John, in some other place further away.

To while away his lonely vigil, sometimes he would focus his range finder on different scarecrows and pretend to shoot them.

It was during such a time when the sergeant's words filtered into his thoughts 'standing behind the scarecrow' and 'making it more safe for his target practice.'

'But of course. We could have intruders hiding behind scarecrows and I wouldn't see them. Worse still they might be dressed up as one and I wouldn't know it unless they moved.'
He whispered to himself as he scrutinised each one in turn, through his high powered binoculars.

His search was fruitless, so he spent the rest of the day criss-crossing the valley checking each one until dusk. The only things he shot and bagged during the day, were several hares and rabbits, and the furless fox that managed to cross his line of fire. At the end of the day, for Peter, it was a good one for hunting and a peaceful one for the valley community once more.

It was Monday morning, and Peter was working on the landing stage, up to his waist in cold water again. The storm had washed away parts of the bank on the other side of the river, with some of the soil deposited around his work area, thus creating a quagmire of thick mud.

'It's deeper than I thought. Just as well I'd decided to use a safety harness as Tom suggested otherwise I might get stuck so fast, I'd not be able to climb out again.' He muttered to himself as he stumbled on yet another unseen obstacle under his feet.

He was about to put a wooden support strut for driving down into position, when he saw something coming slowly up to the surface of the mud that started to glint as the water washed the mud off it. It looked very heavy and made of metal, so he took hold of it and dragged it out of the water then threw it gently onto the bank on his side of the river. Suddenly Peter was surrounded with several other pieces of the same glinting bits of metal, which were sent the same way as the first one.

'What's all this? Where's it all coming from.' He wondered as he looked around for any more items. He looked over to the other side of the river bank to where the hollow tree was, and saw several other strange looking objects sticking out of the bank. He recognised some of the items and went across to retrieve them from their resting places.

"The water must have disturbed some sort of ancient burial ground up river, or uncovered it around here somewhere. I bet its medieval armoury and the like. If so then I can add it to the collection I found in those dungeons I had discovered." he said as he chuckled to himself at the thought of finding a hoard of buried 'National Treasures'.

"So who needs a metal detector Peter? Just look at all this. Full suits of armour complete with some of the bones of the owners. I wonder if the skull in this magnificent helmet is poor Yorick! Maybe it'll speak to me." Was his jubilant whoop and witty remark at his fortunate discovery.

He had found and handled too many old bones across the valley in recent years for him to feel queasy and thought nothing more about them.

Peter gathered up all he could find, then washed them as best he could, before placing them carefully on the back of his flatbed wagon and concealed them again with tarpaulins from any would be prying eyes. He kept one long object to examine more closely and left it nearby whilst he continued with his building.

He worked hard until he judged the sun to be overhead and time for lunch, when he stopped and cleaned himself up for his mouth watering meal of 'Mothers Special'.

Meaning, two extra large home made oggies with lashings of onions, and a quart flagon of cider to wash it all down with. His horses had the lush green grass to eat that was growing along the river-bank, and he had some apples and carrots to give to them as their little treat.

Peter drained his flagon and gave a loud burp that made the horses lift their heads up and look over to him.

"That's better! Now I can have a look at this thing." he said to the horses, as he started to examine the object that took his eye.

As he looked at it, he felt there was something about the feel of it, which told him it that perhaps it was special, and thanks to the river mud, well preserved. He decided that it needed careful handling and time to look at it.

"There must be at least half a dozen suits of armour in among this lot. I wonder if this item and others here belong to one the ex-owners'. I must dig around and look to see if there's any more stuff in case the water washes some of it away for good. The twins will have a field day with their project to, never mind the Museum's Archaeologist." he whispered to himself.

Suddenly this find of a rich seam of ancient battle artifacts became Peter's work, as he searched quickly along that whole stretch of the river bank for any more treasures. By the time he had finished and satisfied himself there were no more 'surface' artifacts to be picked up it was nearly time for him to pack up and go home.

It took him several trips down to and from his underground arsenal to clear the wagon, before he could go for his shower and have supper.

The twins were finishing off their shower when he and Patricia arrived together for theirs.

"I don't think somehow Tom will be joining us. Maybe he'll have his shower after we've all gone." Patricia said laughingly as she covered herself with soft soap and let the water rinse her down.

"Maybe he's just shy, and not used to mixed bathing." piped the twins.

"Yes, probably got different values and upbringing. Still, each family is as different as you and me." Peter said.

"Oh no he isn't!" Tom whooped as he joined in the circle of naked bodies.

"Make room for one more, I'm a coming in."

"Well hello Tommy Sadler!" the twins said as they slowly eyed him up and down. "He'll do, we suppose." they sniffed approvingly, and passed him the bucket of soft soap.

"My family has virtually the same hygiene regime as your family. It's been that way ever since the foot and mouth epidemic twenty years ago that virtually wiped out all the village tanneries in the whole country." Tom explained.

As nobody was self-conscious of their naked bodies, he just soaped himself down like the others did and enjoyed his shower.

They all chatted and swapped notes about their day whilst they completed their shower and got dressed for the house.

As they went through the kitchen corridor, Peter told the twins that he had a couple of new artifacts he'd found and for them to come with him after supper to look at them, they agreed, but reluctantly.

Peter switched on the light of the tunnel leading down some steps to the two cavernous dungeon type rooms.

"It's all right girls, I promise!" he said reassuringly, as he led the way.

"There's nothing to be afraid of. It's just another part of the farmstead that's all."

When they arrived at the bottom, he pushed open the iron studded wooden door and switched on the light for the girls. He turned to them and with a wave of his hand said.

"See? There you are girls. I told you there was nothing to worry about. I've had it modernised with electric lights and it even has my work bench installed."

Jilly popped her head in through the door first and nodded to Jenny to let her know that Peter wasn't lying.

He showed and explained to them some of the old finds from around the valley, then went over to the large pile he brought back from the river.

"Look at all these I found. I reckon they're knight's armour in different styles and probably from different centuries judging by some of the markings and heraldry. I've found different types of weaponry too that I can recognise, but I don't know about these little metal tubes and these funny looking Z shaped metal things, though."

The girls started to sketch some of the armour, and took trace drawings from the etchings if they couldn't work out the words.

When Peter showed them a magnificent helm[*] and the mysterious object, he told them that they probably belonged to the owner of one of the suits of armour. "Peter! The words on some of the armour and on some of the swords, looks like French. Yet the words inscribed on some of the helmets looks like Latin, which puts them about a hundred years or so apart, or maybe on different sides of conflict. One of the swords looks valuable enough for it to belong to some Lord or even a royal Prince, but we'd like to see what's in this long object." Jilly informed him.

"Just as I thought. Then this helm must belong to an equal rank too." Peter enthused as he turned the helm over slowly and tried it on for size.

"Yes. Some of these rusty looking bits of metal could be pure silver, with some of the attachments made of gold according to the artifacts we had shown our teacher. Otherwise the rest are made of iron, and belong to the poorer knights." Jenny added, as she examined a piece of corroded metal.

The next hour was spent sorting the pieces into some sort of order according to their history lessons and memory.

"Well girls. It's time to leave now. We'll come back tomorrow and if we can make up some decent suits of armour, see what the real thing looks like. I have already found some assembled, almost ready to wear when I discovered this place. What do you say?" Peter announced.

"Oh yes please. But wait until we've gone through the public library to find out about these drawings and sketches we made. Maybe we can find some names of the original owners to give them." the twins said with great enthusiasm and nodded their heads vigorously and left the room.

"Hello Mother! We're back." The girls greeted in harmony.

"And so you are." Helen said.

---

[*] A Medieval name for a knight's helmet.

"We've had an excursion along the access corridor and Peter showed us his little collection. We seemed to be gone ages though." They continued.

Peter looked at the big clock over the mantle piece to see the time.

"Is that clock right Mother?" Peter asked, as he disbelieved the time it showed.

"Yes Peter. Wound it up this morning after the girls went to school. Why do you ask dear?"

"Oh nothing Mother. Just curious that's all." Peter lied and sat at the table whilst Helen put a mug of tea in front of him.

He drank his tea in silence and didn't even hear Patricia asking him a question until she called his name several times.

"Peter! Calling Peter Plumstead, are you there?" Patricia teased as she saw a blank look on his face.

"Hmm! say what? Oh sorry big sister, I was miles away then." he replied as she shook his shoulder.

"Thinking of Susan again I'll bet." Helen offered.

"I asked you if you're coming over to the tannery with me to get the new saddles. But obviously you've got your mind elsewhere instead, so I'll go on my own then." Patricia said quietly and left the room.

"No! I'll come with you. Just give me a minute will you." he said as he gulped down the rest of his tea and followed her out.

Peter worked hard and completed the building of the landing stage over the following few days, much to the satisfaction of everybody who passed by on the river. He also managed to find a few more bits of artifacts again during his lunch break, which he cleaned up and gave to the twins for their project.

As the days went by he spent more and more time with his collection of armoury and artifacts, so much so that Ken or Helen had to come and tell him leave it and do some much-needed work.

Each time he went down the tunnel and entered his den, he felt that there was something keeping him there, as if the suits of armour he had assembled were trying to tell him something. There was also a coldness pervading in the chambers even though he had some central heating pipes diverted to run through the place.

All was well apart from the times he wore that special helm, which seemed to hold him in some sort of suspended animation.

"Peter! Ever since you finished working down at the landing stage, you seem to be withdrawn, with signs of lapse of memory or hearing. Is there something wrong?" Helen asked as Peter was eating his lunch.

"I don't know what you mean Mother. Is there something I'm supposed to do that I've forgotten?"

"The twins keep asking you about the battle sights you promised to show them, and asking you questions about their project, but you appear to either ignore them or don't reply."

"I'm sure if I'd promised them then I will. It's just that I have other things on my mind at the moment."

"What could it be for you to be almost in a trance then Peter? Even Patricia and your Susan have noticed a change in you."

"I really don't know what you mean, but whatever it is, it's sure to be nothing to worry about."

"I think there is Peter. You're as white as a sheet and look as if you've fallen into Charles's flour sacks." Ken interrupted, as he sat down for his dinner.

"He's probably been too long in the cold water, and hasn't warmed up yet." Patricia added as she too sat down for dinner.

"Yes! That's probably it." Peter concluded and left the table to go out into the washroom tunnel.

He finished off his chores for the day and made his way back to his workshops. When he arrived he heard noises coming from inside, which made him think that the twins were messing around in there.

As he opened the door the noise stopped suddenly, then when he switched on the light, he saw that two of the suits of armour he made into a standing pose, had been smashed and knocked all over the place. One of the swords was pierced through a helmet that was skewered into the earthen floor.

He looked over to the helm he wore when he was down there, and saw that instead of being where he put it, it was next to the mysterious object that he still hadn't had time to look at.

'So that's the noises the twins were hearing. I wonder just what is going on?'

"Right you lot! I am taking some of you out onto the range and putting you to good use. I have some scarecrows that need protecting, maybe you'll lend your swords to do just that, instead of making scrap metal of each other. But first I'll have to wait until I find out which of you gentlemen belong to which army and which century. I'll not have fighting in my castle." Peter said in a commanding voice to these imaginary knights.

He bent down to pick up a fallen helm when he saw a dagger fly through the air just above his head, which stuck itself into his wooden workbench.

"Okay then who threw that?" Peter asked, as he stood up slowly and reached for his rifle.

"The next gentleman who does that will end up with this special stick shoved up his arse, tin plated or not."

He really didn't expect any movement or reply or for these 'gentlemen' to understand him as they were from a different century and language.

"I must be getting soft or something. It's just my imagination someone threw that dagger. Probably fell off its hook on the rafters above me." he said to himself just as the twins came through the door.

"Peter. We've discovered some of the knights these suits belong to. One of them belongs to the Earl of Bymouth's ancestors dating back to the Twelfth Century, and that helm you're wearing might be part of it," they said swiftly as they took in the scene before them.

"What have you been doing with our tin men Peter! We know some of them are mismatched, but we're trying to put them into their proper order." Jilly rebuked him, as she started to pick up the strewn pieces of armour.

"Yes Peter. We have been given several drawings. One of them is from a battle that took place down at the dyke, around the Eleventh Century, and this one is possibly off a crown prince from the same time. Look!" Jenny said as she showed him two of the pieces of paper.

"That's great, girls! We can try and make models of the soldiers out of these bits of tin and place them for real, where it says on the battle plans." Peter said earnestly as he took the drawings from them.

They spent the next few days putting the pieces of the jigsaws together, and discovered that from the list of knights they made up, they had knights from four different centuries, but they could only find enough evidence for three (of the known) battles that had taken place in the valley.

"It looks as if we've got suits of armour left over, and we've possibly stumbled upon another battle, probably long forgotten. Maybe you can discover which period and which of our gentlemen here were involved." Peter announced to the twins.

When Peter donned his helm again, and started helping the twins rebuild the suits of armour, he felt a tingling sensation on his forehead and at the same time heard strange voices.

The voices started as mere whisperings, and seemed to accompany eerie shadowy figures he saw inside the suits of armour.

He dismissed these shadowy figures as a trick of the light, and thinking it was the twins whispering, asked them to speak up.

"But we're not talking Peter. We've not spoken for a while now." Jenny said as she tried to put a sword into a scabbard and hang it around a suit.

"It must be that helmet you're wearing. It is going to your head and you're imagining things." Jilly added. "Oh never mind, girls. But what does 'Honore Pax' mean?"

"That's Latin Peter. We'll look it up in the French and Latin dictionaries we've borrowed from the school library to help us." Jenny stated.

He suddenly realised that only when he wore this helm, it was trying to show or tell him something, but suddenly disappeared and for everything to return back to normal every time he took it off.

Later on that evening when the three of them returned to do more research and work, Peter decided to do a little experiment.

He put the helm on and stood still for a while until the voices and shapes started to appear from the armour they were wearing.

There was a blinding flash of white light that came from seemingly nowhere, and in that moment Peter could see exactly who the original owners were and the armour they wore.

It took a little while for Peter to hear properly but they all seemed to speak in different languages. He could make out a few words but not enough to understand them. It was as if they were talking among themselves but taking no notice of him.

"Well good day gentlemen. Please introduce yourselves." he said as if to himself, and was totally amazed when one of the suits made its way from the back of the room and stopping in front of him, spoke to him, and to his amazement, Peter understood each word.

"You sire are undressed! What manner of clothing are you wearing? You must be a foreign, but who are you and who is your master?"

Peter was so amazed it made him sit down heavily onto a stool, which made the helmet topple from his head and fall into his hands. In that split second the light disappeared as did the voices and the figures.

"So that's it. I put this helmet on and hey presto I'm taken back to the days of these metal gentlemen," he said to himself in great excitement.

"I'll tell the twins which piece of metal and weaponry belong to which century and exactly who wore what."

"Right then girls. Take this piece of armour off this gentleman and put it on that one over there. This type of sword belongs to." he began to direct them.

"But how do you know Peter?" Jenny asked.

"Quite simple dear sister. The list of knights tells us which year they lived, and the armour tells us which period they belong to, apart from some of the foreign ones that is. All we do is match them up." He lied, so as not to give away his little secret just yet.

It took them a few more sessions down there to re assemble their tin men until they were ready to show them to their parents.

"Would you look at this Ken!" Helen said in amazement.

"A whole army of tin men."

"Don't tell me that you've neglected your duties just to play with all these bits of tin Peter?" Ken asked angrily.

"What do you mean Father?" Peter replied defensively.

"It's one thing helping the twins with their history project, it's quite another to start building real models for them. Where did you get all this junk anyway? I want it shifted immediately, and you back to work." Ken ranted.

"But dear. The girls have told me that their teacher reckons that some of these could be quite valuable." Helen responded quickly.

"Valuable you say! It's just a load of junk metal. Who'd want to buy this lot?" Ken said loudly, as he started to calm down.

"If I'm correct about that suit over there Father, the Earl of Bymouth would be most interested because it belongs to his ancestors, as do some of the others that were his fellow knights." Peter said calmly as he pointed out to the suits.

"Yes, and the Bymouth museum would probably be interested in the rest but we're going to use them first, for our exams next month Father." The twins said enthusiastically, enough to placate Ken's anger.

"Well if that's the case, all right then." Ken conceded.

"Some of these knights must have been very small judging by the size of some of the suits. Maybe half time knights?" Patricia joked to relieve the tension, which it did.

Peter told them that he was going to put the left over bits onto the scarecrows for his shooting practices. If all went well, and the twins passed their history exams then the tin gentlemen could be taken for disposal.

"Well, okay Peter! I'll give you until the end of the twins summer term to complete all this, after that, then its scrap heap time." Ken said firmly as if to put an end to the matter.

"Yippee!" the twins cried as they started to rub and polish the bits of metal. "C'mon Peter. We've got a lot of polishing to do to make them all nice."

When Helen, Ken and Patricia left, Peter shut the door quietly behind them and turned to the girls.

"I have a big secret to tell you both, but you must promise not to tell a living soul. This secret will be your weapon to get top marks for your history lesson as it will show you exactly what was what, who did what and to whom. Promise me? "

The twins looked at each other for a moment then nodded their heads.

"We promise Peter. If what you say is true then we'd have to start writing down all that happens." they said in unison.

Peter told them what happened to him every time he put the magnificent helm on, what he sees and what he hears. But he wanted to try a couple of things before he did any more.

"When I put this helm on, see if I disappear. Then use a watch to see how long I appear to be away, and if you can hear me speak, write down anything I say or describe." Peter instructed the twins, who got themselves ready for his little experiment.

He donned the helm again and in no time he was in the bright light again, looking around at what he saw. He heard some voices, which he tried to repeat, and for a while just described out loud what he saw, before removing the helm again.

"Yes Peter, you did disappear. But yes, we heard very clearly every word that was spoken, and some of the sounds around you." the twins said excitedly and showed him what he said.

Peter looked at what was written, and told them that he had to walk around the place to get some of the descriptions, and asked how long he was 'gone'.

"You've only been gone five minutes." Jenny said as she showed him the time on her watch.

"Well it seems that I can walk around and be in that time zone for hours without any harm to myself." Peter said slowly, as he examined the helm closely again.

"It appears that if I wear something such as this helmet, I can be taken there. But what if I take something more modern. Hand me my long bow and rifle, Jenny. Jilly, you stay back and write down all you hear again." Peter directed.

He slung his quiver across his back along with his long bow and held onto his rifle tightly as he replaced the helm on his head.

Once more he returned to this place, to find that he still held his rifle in his hand and his longbow still slung on his back.

He noticed that a man was walking slowly towards him who called to him.

"You sire! Who are you? I noticed you coming out of the woods. Is that where your quarters are?" the swarthy, medium-sized man asked as he came right up to Peter.

Peter didn't reply in case he said something wrong. Instead he just nodded and pointed towards the wooded slopes of the low knowle.

"You must be one of the foreigns, judging by your weaponry." the man stated as he walked past, ignoring Peter as he went.

Peter looked all around again and took the time to describe more of the place for the benefit of the twins, even though there was a lot more trees around, he instinctively knew it was the By Valley and his own hunting grounds as it perhaps used to be all those centuries earlier. This knowledge made his pulse race at the very thought.

"It worked a treat girls. But my next visit had better be a good one, because the place is getting crowded now, and I'm starting to be noticed by some of our gentlemen. It looks as if there are two opposing armies on the move towards each side of the valley, so there's going to be a big scrap down in the valley soon." Peter informed them.

"From what we've written down it sounds very exciting. Where is this place anyway?" Jenny asked.

"Believe it or not, but it's our very own By valley. Think of the valley as I've just described, then think of it now and see what the changes are to it." Peter replied excitedly.

"That's not fair Peter! Why can't we see what you saw?" Jilly pouted.

"After all, it's our history project, not yours Peter." Jenny sniffed.

Peter told them that before he took them with him they would have to work out what to say, and what armour they would wear, bearing in mind that all the armour would be spoken for when the big battle day came.

He also added that it would be extremely dangerous even for him to be there and anyway, there would be no place on a battlefield for two healthy, attractive looking girls.

"Ha! Sexist!" they taunted.

"Remember girls. It's the Twelfth Century not the Twentieth. It's strictly men only out there." Peter reminded them.

The twins looked at him, and realised what he said was pretty much the truth, but still were not satisfied.

"How about a quick look. Just see around and back again Peter? Oh please!" they pleaded, but he remained adamant and told them he didn't want them hurt in any way.

A few days later when the three of them had everything polished and in the correct order, the twins told Peter of a plan they were hatching so that they could go with him on an 'away trip'.

Peter listened quietly without interrupting them, until they were finished.

"It sounds quite feasible. But you'll have to wear very loose clothing to disguise the fact that both of you are very much female. You'd both be my squires, as those are the ones who carry the knight's swords and baggages, so your costumes would have to be the same and almost match mine." Peter enthused at their plan.

"But the only fly in the ointment would be that I'd be a knight without a horse."

"If there's going to be a battle, then there's bound to be the odd horse running around for us to catch." the twins suggested eagerly.

"Sounds fine by me. But you'd have to stick very close to me. I'm the one with the helm. If it gets knocked off and you two aren't close by then you'd be left on your own. If either of you got hurt, Mother would kill me." Peter said, acting the devil's advocate.

"We'll stick to you like glue Peter. But maybe if we had something belonging to you then we'd go with you if you did leave." they replied eagerly and determined not to be put off.

"Okay then girls. Its history lesson time." Peter conceded as he started to get things together for their 'away trip', whilst the twins hummed to themselves preparing all the costumes, and the equipment they were taking with them.

Their away trip was set for the coming Saturday when everybody would be going to By Bys for the monthly market day, and made excuses to everybody to cover their absence.

"Right then girls! You can open your eyes now." Peter whispered to them. "Remember, stick closely by me and do exactly what I tell you, and Jilly is the only one to speak."

The twins opened their eyes and were open mouthed to see everything that Peter had described was exactly as he said, and even much much more for them to behold. They just stood there for a moment trying to look everywhere at once when Peter whispered to them that the show had just commenced.

"Are you ready girls? Then let's go!" Peter commanded.

He strode boldly out of the woods and into the open with the twins following very closely behind, carrying his weapons and equipment.

He held the improvised standard in an upright position so that the breeze fluttered his St George's banner for all to see.

The trio were met by a tall man with long hair flowing down his back, dressed in magnificent armoury and carrying a very large sword.

"What standard are you carrying knight? Who are you and to whom do you owe your allegiance?" he demanded belligerently.

"I'm Pierres D'angleurs from Charlemaigne. My allegiance is to whomever pays me the most, and these are my squires. I understand you are under manned and in dire need of a good sword for a good days work." Peter replied slowly with the hint of a French accent.

"Where is your horse and quarters?" was the next question.

"My horse was slain from under me during an ambush to get here. My quarters as you say, are but the woods or whatever shelter I can find."

"What do –" the man started.

"Tut tut! Man. You ask too many questions. Put up your sword and let us pass unhindered." Peter commanded gruffly, which did the trick and saved him from answering much closer questioning.

"My liege does not take kindly to people coming ungentlemanly behind his back when he is about to do battle. You may pass." the man conceded and lowered his sword.

Peter rammed home his advantage and lashed the girls with his leather whip, cajoling them to get a move on. This was obviously some sort of standard happening of the day that pleased the stranger, for the knight kicked Jenny on the bottom, making her sprawl into the mud, whilst he laughed at what he did.

Peter turned to him

"Nobody but me chastises my squires. Don't try that again. You're advised to keep your strength for the enemy over there not for friends over here." he growled and gave the man a very menacing look. The stranger simply nodded in acknowledgement of the underlying threat imposed upon him and went on his way.

They arrived in among a large group of knights who seemed to stand arrogantly around the central figure of Peter's gaze.

Peter saw the sumptuous and resplendent suit of armour and remembered from some of the photographs that the wearer of such a suit would be a royal, possibly a king.

"Your majesty. I'm at your service." Peter said calmly and bowed deeply to this man sitting on a wooden barrel.

"Who are you? How do you know me, are you a friend?" he asked.

"Everybody knows and loves you and wishes to serve you. I'm Pierres D'angleurs." Peter said as he stood up to see a giant of a man that seemed to be squeezed into an armoured suit several sizes too small. His neatly trimmed beard and jet black hair surrounded the bluest of eyes Peter had ever seen on a man.

"Pierres D'angleurs! Never heard of you, but you're more than welcome. And for your information, not everybody is grateful to me nor wishes to serve me, else we'd not have that rabble of an army over there facing their king. A collection of barons and other ingrates who have forgotten who made them." he replied with a deep gravelly voice.

"We'll lick all of them, even though we appear to be outnumbered. But that's just how I like it. Don't I sir knights!" he declared, which brought a swift bow and a

"My liege!" From each of them.

"Cutler tells me you've travelled far and got ambushed to get here. It also looks as if you've lost most of your armour, but your weaponry looks decidedly foreign and very strange to me. Still, as long as they keep you alive to slay those ingrates over there, that's all that counts. Take yourself and your servants over to my quarters and refresh yourself. Sir Percival! See this man gets a decent charger and anything else he needs. Be off with you now, I have a battle to plan." the King said magnanimously and dismissed Peter with a wave as he turned his back to him.

Peter and the twins followed Percival until they came to a large marquee with people darting in and out of it.

"Rest yourself at the back. See the man in the funny looking hat; he'll give you victuals to sustain you through the day. Tomorrow we die for our King." Percival stated as he pointed to where Peter was to go.

The trio sat on some straw bales and started to eat the food given to them by a buxom wench, but keeping a wary eye on the others in the large tent.

"I'm the victualler to the king but my trade is coopering. I make the wine barrels for the king and his court. Fine wine it is too. Here some for you. A man must not go without his wine." A squat man stated as he offered Peter a small cask.

"Thank you victualler. I'll have my servants pour me some directly." Peter replied civilly as the man left and disappeared into the gloom of the tent.

The twins were hiding their faces trying to smother their giggles, when Peter whispered to them to shut up.

"Squires do not giggle like girls." he said, trying not to smile at the very truth in the matter.

"Yes but why that French accent and carrying an English flag, never mind the bit about your dangly bits?" they giggled again but got a stern look from Peter that silenced them.

It was getting near dark in the camp, with everybody settling down for the night, when Peter shook the twins to tell them he had to go to the loo.

"And about time. We're absolutely busting. From what we gather, the loo is behind the second tent, in among the woods." they whispered back.

All three got up slowly and made their way out of the back of the marquee towards the woods and relieved themselves with eye watering effects.

"Ahh thank god for that!" the twins said in unison as they managed to make themselves decent before some men exposed themselves and took their toilets in full view of the twins.

"That's the blessing in mixed bathing and living on a farm, dear sisters." Peter whispered as he led them onto the track leading back to the camp.

Peter heard something close by, and stopped for a moment before slipping his night sights out from under his cloak, to have a look around.

He saw Cutler creeping through the woods and making for the bottom of the valley.

He followed Cutler with his sights for a while, enough to see him meet up with two men on the other side of the stream who must have been waiting for him.

All three men moved off and up the wooded slopes of the high knowle, to re-appear at the large campsite bonfire of the enemy.

"It appears we have a traitor in our midst girls! The knight Cutler has joined with the enemy and is probably giving the kings' plans away. We had better warn him immediately, so keep close." Peter whispered to them.

Peter announced himself to the king and told him that he'd followed Cutler to the stream and saw him go over to the enemy camp.

The King screamed Cutler's name several times, but only Cutler's squire showed up.

"My sire has gone for his daily walk your Majesty." the squire said apologetically, as he gave a deep bow, but it did not satisfy the king.

"Then bring me his standard and weapons." the King demanded.

The squire came back telling the king that they'd all gone and pleaded for his own life to be spared.

The King took no notice and ordered him to be taken away.

"I'll have no traitors in my camp. Have done with him and all who still take my kindness." he said coldly, as the hapless squire was dragged away, begging for his life to be spared.

"Sire! If I may be so bold!" Peter started.

"You sir are bold indeed. You have my ears." was the sharp reply.

Peter told the King that he had encountered several different enemies and had learned some of their tactics that he, the king, could benefit from them.

The King sat down heavily on a tree trunk that served as a bench, and listened to what Peter was saying, all the time stroking his beard.

Peter told him about some of the tactics, and dirty tricks that he should use, as they worked well and were performed over the centuries, but pretended he learned about them during the foreign battles he had taken part in. In truth he had read and studied them in his own history lessons at school.

"You dare to change a King's battle plan just for one puny knight?" the King asked bluntly and belligerently.

Peter had the measure of the man and refused to show any sign of weakness, had he done so, all three Plumstead's could end up with their heads chopped off. Nobody dared argue with this monarch.

"The thing is your majesty, Cutler is now telling your opponent all about your battle plans, and when the time comes for it he will use this knowledge against you. Now if you do as I ask, he will never be able to outguess you nor will he win this battle even though he outnumbers you by far."

"How would I know if all these strange ideas of yours will work?"

"It is simple your majesty. Your opponent will prepare his army according to what he has been informed by Cutler. That is, he will assume that half of your men will be out protecting your rear and your flanks leaving only a couple of phalanxes to face them, until your reinforcements arrive to take up the battle. So he will not bother with your flanks but gather most of his troops to take up a frontal assault on you in one big massive thrust for a quick end to the battle before your reinforcements do arrive on the field." Peter stated, by drawing a picture in the ashes of the wood fire for the king to see what he meant.

The King saw what Peter meant and spoke about his tactics to counteract it, but Peter advised him of other more bolder moves and tactics that had the king almost in awe of what was revealed, and only questioned something that he did not understand.

Only when Peter had finished showing the King by his drawings on the ground, did the king lapse into silence for several minutes, as if to weigh up all the information that Peter had given him.

"Forsooth Pierres D'angleurs! You appear to be an educated man for tactics that only I can outmatch. If those ingrates and upstarts over there, think that they can win the battle in one big attack then we shall force them to fight until we outnumber them, even if it takes us another sunset. Maybe we don't need our re enforcements if all my tactics work." the King exclaimed heartily, and sat once more in deep thought, stroking his beard all the while.

Peter managed to control his delight by not showing any outward signs, but was satisfied that the king took what he had said and claimed it all for himself, as if it was he, the King, that had made all the battle plans.

"Bring me my sword." the King commanded aloud, which appeared seemingly out of nowhere.

"Kneel Pierres D'angleurs," he commanded, and Peter obeyed instantly.

"I dub thee Sir Pierres D'angleurs." the King said and tapped Peter on both shoulders with his heavy broadsword.

"Let it be known that although he is of French origin, he will be accorded the title and privileges bestowed upon him as an English Knight of the realm." he added in a loud condescending voice, then completed the impromptu ceremony saying.

"Arise! Sir Pierres D'angleurs."

Peter stood up slowly to receive the King's wine reeking breath as he kissed Peter on each cheek. Then he offered Peter a swig from a golden goblet, who drank it all down with a flourish and made a loud burp which pleased the king even more.

The twins were given a gourd of wine each to drink from, to celebrate with their master, and did so with equal flourish as they were used to drinking farmhouse cider to care otherwise.

Their new status brought them almost to the fore with all of the other knights, who received Peter and his squires with mixed responses.

Peter kept the twins in close attendance as the King kept him up most of the night, mulling over the new tactics and plans with the other knights. The dyke to be dug deeper and wider with the hidden spikes to counter any dragoon or cavalry charges; the flooding of the field below that to slow the enemy down, and even a wide belt of straw above that to be set alight when the enemy infantry marched over it were deemed to be good ideas, but they had to be completed before the sun came up.

Peter managed to extricate himself from the King's presence stating that he had to prepare himself for the day's rigours, and took a stroll into the woods with his sisters.

"Listen now girls. We have to nip back home to see what armour has vanished, because I spotted at least one of the suits here, which means that they're going to get killed. So hold on to me now as I remove this helm." he whispered.

They arrived back into the rooms again and to their amazement, most of the suits of armour had vanished without trace.

"It's just as well you cataloged them all girls. Now we know who our opponents are and who will survive the day." Peter said calmly as he looked at his two sisters.

"You both had better stay here now and listen to all I tell you. You have a lot of writing to do, especially with the new battle plans. No wonder nobody knew about this battle. The historians had it all wrong, probably based on the chronicles of the King's original plans as betrayed by Cutler. It also means that Lord Walters is the Earl of Bymouth who was one of the barons that turned against the King, and must be part of the opposition. He must get killed for us to find his suit, which has now disappeared."

"We will hear all the sounds and voices around you, but will you describe some of the action and tell us who gets what

Peter?" Jenny asked swiftly, sensing that Peter had to return very quickly in case he was posted as yet another turncoat.

Peter nodded and received a kiss from the twins before he put his helm back on.

He arrived back exactly in the same spot as he left, then climbed up into a tree to get a good look over the battle field. He was there quite a while scanning the opposition with his scope. When he was satisfied he climbed down and went back to camp to prepare himself and his weapons.

"Sir Pierres! There you are." the King's voice boomed as he beckoned Peter to come and join him.

"Your majesty?" Peter acknowledged and bowed deeply to the King before coming over to him.

"We have had a deposition from our opponents who wish to start battle on the morrow when the sun comes over the valley. Which means we have plenty of time to get our final plans made in time to let the battle commence."

"No sire do not do this! The Saracens and even the Persians were famous to offer such an undertaking but went back on their words and attacked our army before we were ready for them. Hasten your plans as I tell you then just you wait until the battle commences, for him to see that he will be outfoxed by you at every turn. At a guess, you have until the sun rises over that bluff to get ready." Peter explained, then went on to tell him just whom he was fighting.

The King looked at Peter and started to laugh at the names.

"That pretender to the throne, Prince of the Anglians you say! His full court of knights you say! Forty thousand men at arms you say! You appear to be well informed Sir Pierres. Are you sure you're not the traitor? Next you'll be telling me who won before an arrow is fired." he joked and slapped Peter around the shoulders heartily, nearly knocking his helm off his head.

'I wonder if you'd stake your kingdom on that knowledge.' Peter thought, but just humoured the King by pandering to his egotism and ebullient manner.

One of the knights who took umbrage of being ousted by Peter, as the King's favourite knight, sidled up to the King and said.

"My liege. Sir Pierres might be well informed and his ungentlemanly tactics in battle are outrageous, but how well does he fight? We have never seen some of his weaponry before and he doesn't even carry a sword or own a war lance. He probably does not have jousting experience enough to subdue his opponents."

The King listened intently, stroking his beard once more, then turned to Peter and asked if he heard what the knight had said.

"Yes your majesty. I do have strange weaponry, but if the knight wishes to challenge me to one of the new fangled whiz-bang weapons some of your personal guards and a few knights have instead of a traditional joust, then I would welcome it. In fact I challenge him to a duel with a longbow at five hundred paces." Peter said crossly for he was not a world class marksman for nothing.

The figure of five hundred paces drew gasps from all the knights, who said it would not be possible, it was never done before, and anyway they needed all able-bodied men for the show.

The King looked at Peter and his rival and declared.

"The one who kills first, with just one arrow at the furthest man, will win. The other one will meet disgracement and be banished from my court. Do you both accept?"

Peter nodded his approval knowing that this knight would lose not only his place in court, but his life as well.

He thought no more about it and dismissed it from his mind, as he went and stood looking over the valley below him, quietly describing the scene of how each army was drawn up.

The opponents on the high knowle, had four phalanx boxes of a thousand infantry in each and in three rows, with three blocks of five hundred heavy dragoons lined up in front of them, with another two phalanxes of the same size of cavalry behind them. Some hundreds of archers were positioned in a group on each flank, who had two units of about one hundred light cavalry behind them. The knights lined up in front of the lines of troops on the high knowle numbered about thirty. Coloured flags fluttered everywhere, drums were beating and fanfare trumpets blaring out. The shire horses on the farm looked much like those the heavy dragoons had. Their General sitting on his horse, wore a magnificent helm that appeared to be covered in jewels.

His armour shone in the sunlight and a bejewelled sword was in his hand. He was guarded by several more knights, some of whom were on foot. A large banner that fluttered in the breeze had a red lion standing above three black scimitars on a yellow background. His army had covered virtually all of the high knowle and presented a several hundred yard frontal assault on the King's army.

He described his army on the low knowle, which was much less than half the size of the other one and looking much the poorer, and definitely outnumbered considerably.

He knew that the King's plan was to entice the opponents to come up the slope to engage his troops, by offering just a few of his troops as a bait. The Prince did not know that several stakes were placed on the low knowle side of the river that would be hidden by the rising water that was caused by damming. The King also had a twenty foot wide belt of trip ropes that were hidden under a layer of straw, which stretched right across the open ground that was to be the battlefield. The ruse being that any pursuing rider or infantryman running up the slope would trip on the hidden ropes, therefore rendering them temporarily out of action, that would delay the onslaught and for the aerial bombardment of arrows to strike them down as they struggle up the slope to the next obstacle that faced them.

He also had several traps and snares put around the perimeter of his army to protect them against any surprise attack by cavalry or even foot soldiers.

The dyke hid the spike holding men that would shield the infantry troops from the any mounted attack, and a thousand heavily armed infantry men to pounce on any attacker that did manage to reach this formidable redoubt. He also had large bales of straw placed along the entire length of the base of his knowle for yet another ruse.

Peter (remembered the famous battle whereby the English army won the day through the sheer fire power of archers), told the King that if he had command of the archers, then he will win the day for him providing he listened to the instructions that was given. The King agreed to Peter and gave the necessary instructions that most of the front facing infantrymen, were to be given longbows that would fire in salvoes so that there would be a constant rain of arrows falling down upon the attacking forces. But his own two groups of mounted archers would be used to move up and down the battle field to provide a crossfire of arrows.

The static archers were protected by a cordon of heavily armed infantry and backed by a contingent of cavalry. The King had his archers move forward or back at will and to keep up the bombardment of lethal arrows into any opponent re-enforcements that moved towards the dyke. The wide belt of straw would be set alight once the enemy phalanxes were moving over it.

Two units of Lancers were on both flanks to counter any opponent's cavalry charge, and to attack the opposing unguarded archers who were isolated and static. He counted only ten knights on horseback out in front of the infantry, with a further three in front of the reserve troops. The kings unit of two knights and bodyguards were placed around him to protect him.

Peter told the twins that the slaughter would probably start in about an hour from now, for the twins to have the chance to draw the scenes and listen to Peter's running commentary before he finally got embroiled in the fighting.

He took up his position so that he could command the archers, but just a few yards away from the king who was animated in his orders to his troops.

"Sir Pierres D'angleurs. You appear to exclude yourself from this. Why do you shirk your duty?" he asked angrily.

"Your majesty, I am here to command your archers and to protect you from your ingrates over there. I shall exact more men from them, than all of your other knights put together. Mark my words well.

"They will surprise you with their heavy dragoons and attack your men at the dyke like a heavy hammer with probably the first two waves of phalanxes in behind them to ram home their attack.

"Your men are not ready to engage them yet, so you had better get them to work and provide the finishing touches to your plans. The enemy will be struggling to come through the deepening and widening stream that we have created with the dam further down the valley. But as soon as they meet the trip ropes covered in the hay we would slow them down even further. Once the enemy manage to get across the hay we've laid down, then the long range archers should commence firing." Peter stated and took his longbow off his shoulders in readiness.

He walked his horse down to a group of knights on horseback, pointed towards the heavy dragoon and told them the same. But got the same negative response, and was derided for suggesting such ungentlemanly conduct from fellow knights across the valley.

Peter had just returned to his chosen spot again when his predictions started to come true. The King turned around and looked at him with surprise.

"I mark your words Sir Pierres!" was the shout as he ordered his archers to engage, then waited until the crucial moment when eventually what heavy dragoons managed to reach the dyke, for him to order his pike men to show themselves.

Peter did not hear him as he had left to go down to the right of the infantrymen to use his longbow. He waited until they came within his five hundred yard range before picking his target and shooting at the oncoming dragoons.

The sky was full of arrows that were falling like rain onto the dragoons causing a serious threat to them, given that Peter had the archers have their arrows tipped with steel as opposed to flint or simple wooden tips. The weight of the oncoming heavily armed horse and riders met the spikes, which caused mayhem and carnage as they got impaled upon them. The fallen riders were literally chopped to bits by the King's axe wielding infantry men. Whilst the lancers who were much faster and more maneuverable than the heavily armoured dragoons slew the remainder.

It was a debacle that quickly followed with the fate of the advancing infantrymen who were too far behind to take advantage of this initial assault. Peter did a pincer movement with his archers, and had them fire into the flanks of the oncoming infantrymen. He targeted the oncoming knights, and with each arrow he watched as one by one they fell dead off their horses.

The fire arrows were then sent out to torch the dry straw, which started to incinerate the opposing army as they crossed the area. Any soldier that managed stagger clear of the inferno, were picked off by the King's lancers and his cavalry.

The King's men that were not involved with the opening attack from the Prince's men simply stood and watched until the crescendo of screams from the burning field had stopped. The King nodded with satisfaction that he witnessed it all as the Prince could not, save to listen to the pitiful screams of his men, due to the smoke being blown by the wind directly onto the Prince's side of the valley.

Peter raced over to the King and told him of this fact, and told him that this was his chance to go onto the attack.

"I will bring the archers down to the waters edge and have them fire into their waiting forces opposite. They won't be expecting us as they can't see us, or the arrows that will fall down upon them. That way can wipe out or destroy at least another two of their phalanxes, or at least force them to retreat, without you losing a man." Peter advised quickly, as he pointed to the thick smoke billowing across the valley and almost obscuring the entire opposing army.

As the battle wore on, so did Peter keep up with his running commentary for his sisters' benefit.

Unbeknown to him, the King had been watching Peter's accurate shooting, and sent a messenger to bring Peter back to speak to him.

"Your majesty! What is it you want with me? First you want me to engage now you want me to run from the enemy." Peter said with mock indignance, but gave him the customary bow.

"I've been watching you use your bow and arrows. Maybe you've had your training as an archer. Be that as it may, you have definitely won your spurs. Your tactics and personal actions have accounted for quite a number of the enemy and it appears that you have acquitted yourself well.

You may leave now with honour and with my blessing as this is not your war to be fighting." he said gruffly, and held out his hand as if for Peter to kiss it.

Peter refused to give way.

"You will need me again before this day is over your majesty. You have already lost half of your knights and we're still heavily outnumbered. It appears they have all the champions and you have none. It is my pledge that I will stay to protect you and make sure that you win the day over these traitors." Peter said somberly.

The King looked gravely at him and then cast a quick glance over the battlefield.

"Hah! Well spoken Sir Pierres. A real man with a stomach for a real fight. That's what I like." the King shouted over the clamour of the fighting below them.

"That field of fire had their first two waves of phalanxes consumed and killed off by your pincer movement of archers and my lancers, and although we took advantage of the smoke to wipe out another, they still outnumber us. But we'll show them that they are fighting against the lawful King of the land, as I intend to hold our ground to the last man!" he added defiantly.

The battle ebbed and flowed for a few hours more, until there seemed to be a lull in the fighting to clear the dead and war litter from the battlefield, when three knights rode slowly towards the King. All of them unarmed and from the opposing side, carrying a lance that had a large white flag of truce tied to it. When they finally arrived in front of the bemused King, they spoke slowly and with a loud voice.

"Sire! We are an emissary carrying a flag of truce to parley and speak with you.

My liege has accused you of not fighting in a gentlemanly manner, and that you do not fight fairly. Your dirty tricks and ruses may have bought you a little reprieve but you are still no match for us.

Look around you sire! It is beholding of you to desist and surrender your weapons. We still outnumber you two to one and we have still not completed our battle plans with you. It is plain to see that you sire, have lost. Your honour shall be satisfied if you leave the battlefield to us and retire from it. If you surrender your arms, we will grant you quarter. If you do not, then the Prince of Anglia will slay all, including all in your baggage camp."

Peter whispered this ultimatum to his sisters, what the phrase 'quarter' meant and described the two knights, for their records. Then trotted slowly across to the delegation, drawing his rifle out of his scabbard ready to shoot any hostile movement.

"So a cowardly traitor comes to lay the law down on his King, eh Cutler? What about you Walters?" the King taunted.

"How long do you think you will last with the Prince of Anglia, a week maybe a month, especially as you had misguided him on what my tactics where? I had suspected for some time that you were a traitor Cutler, that's why when you left as a turn coat, I had hatched my real battle plans." The King taunted.

Cutler looked a round at the bloody battlefield where the bodies of the Prince's dragoons, cavalrymen, and where the slaughtered archers and four phalanxes of infantrymen lay, whilst the King still had his cavalry, archers and the main body of his army still in position awaiting orders.

"Sire we wait your answer." Cutler replied curtly, as he dismissed the scene with a shrug of his shoulders.

The King looked over the battlefield again and saw that despite his brilliant successes on the field to reduce the odds against him, his army was still outnumbered, and that his re enforcement troops had not arrived to help him.

"You have no choice but to retire or surrender." Walters said with a sneer.

"It appears that Duke Deboise and his army who you were relying on came over to our side for a mere bag of gold, your majesty. As you can see, his army is already forming up to form our final battle plans." Cutler said with relish.

Peter saw that the King was about to rush forward to strike the knight, but quickly grabbed his arm to prevent him.

"I think gentlemen, you'd better leave before you outstay your welcome. But we shall meet again." he said as he moved his horse in between the knights and the King.

"Who are you sir? I don't recall your name." Walters asked Peter.

"Never mind him, he's just some foreign upstart trying to earn himself a purse. He obviously picked the wrong side." Cutler stated.

"This foreign upstart as you call me, will slay all three of you right now unless you yield and go back to your crony master." Peter said with venom and raised his rifle at them.

"Oh look, he's got one of them useless whiz bang gadgets tied onto a stick. There's three of us, what then upstart?"

"Then who will be the first among you to die first? You Cutler? You Walters? How about you? I can kill all three of you in the blink of an eye, just try me." Peter snarled, as he pointed his rifle threateningly towards each man in turn.

Cutler sneered at the challenge and re stated his ultimatum before he backed his horse away and left with the others to go back to their side of the valley.

The King had his trumpeter sound the recall of his surviving knights and soldiers, who arrived in dribs and drabs, all in various states of dishevelment and looking despondent and glum, not knowing that in fact, it was they that were on the winning side

The King announced the deposition and told them that they could either fight or just go home and try to live in peace. It was their choice but to give him their answer. Almost to a man they decided to end the day with their spurs on and a lance in their hands and gave the King a rousing cheer as their reply.

"You see and hear this! That's what makes this nation famous, Sir Pierres! We might be outnumbered, but with men like that, our enemies should tremble in their shoes." the King beamed, and returned the salute to his stalwarts that remained, before sending a messenger over to the opposite camp with his decision.

Peter managed to have time alone to talk to his sisters, and also to look through his telescopic range finder to see what was going on over the valley.

He spotted the Prince sitting enjoying a goblet of wine and laughing at something, which turned out to be the head of the poor messenger.

Two hours had passed for the battle to re commence, with Peter down at the dyke killing at will with his longbow.

"It seems that we're getting nowhere fast, so there's only one thing left to do and that is to shoot those men up there enjoying their wine. I'm forced to scavenge my arrows from the dead to maintain my archery attack. I have only twenty rounds of bullets left and there seems to be about ten times that amount to shoot at." he muttered to himself, forgetting that the twins were listening to all the sounds around him.

He got his rifle out of its scabbard, and pointed it at the enemy. The first person he saw was Cutler, who was riding towards him at a fast gallop and his war lance ready to strike.

Peter sighed, put his rifle down and waited until he came into a decent range before he shot Cutler through the throat with one arrow. On seeing that, another knight decided to run Peter through, but he too got the same treatment. Then two more assailants tried their luck and paid the same penalty, before other knights had realised that this archer was too good for them to tackle and stayed away.

Peter looked through his telescopic sights again to keep a close eye on the Prince and his men, and guessed that the Prince must have seen his deeds and sent two more knights after him.

Peter lined up the first one in his sights and shot him straight between the eyes, then the other. The noise of his rifle was lost in the noise of the battle and almost indistinguishable from the pops of the 'whizz-bangs' that were fired off from time to time. Peter had another look at the Prince and saw that he was now sitting on his horse with his visor up, getting himself ready to join in the affray and gathering up his remaining knights. He took careful aim with his rifle and gently caressed the trigger that sent the bullet on its way towards its target.

He looked at the gold helm with the large red and white feathers sticking out of the top, and at the large banner with the lion on it, then saw his bullet strike home.

"Bulls eye, so to speak," Peter whispered as he witnessed his handiwork

The Prince's face was of total surprise as he clutched his chest and looked down to see his blood pouring from a small hole in his armour, before toppling over backwards onto a pile of horse dung.

His knowledge of marksmanship told him it took three seconds for the bullets to hit their target from such a distance, and fired twice more in succession at the group of bewildered knights that were supposed to guard their general, killing another two of them.

He looked through his sights again and saw that the others were looking around in the bushes as if to find the pistol-wielding assassins. But after he shot three more, they just ran away, leaving the dying Prince and his army turning into disarray and already running full pelt into retreat.

The King had heard the strange noise and guessed it came from Peter's strange weapon. So he went down to the dyke and stood behind Peter during all this time, until Peter stood up again when he was satisfied enough was done to stop the battle.

"Always kill their generals and captains first, or in your case, the odd Duke, Prince and their champions, your Majesty.

That way there would be nobody to give the orders. No orders, therefore no more fighting. It's easy as that!" Peter said with relish, as he pointed to the fleeing army that seemed to melt away into the high knowle woods, as the Kings troops scrambled after them and slaying all those that were caught.

"It appears Sir Pierres, you have won the day for us. Let's go and receive the surrender from whomever is left to stand and fight." he commanded.

"Not I your majesty! T'was your brilliant strategies that won the day." Peter responded gallantly and gave the King a deep bow, before he returned his long rifle back into its valise again.

"Hah! Well said sir! You sir are definitely my best champion." the King exclaimed, and left Peter to his own devices again.

Peter sighed quietly then picked up his longbow, and started to walk up towards the high knowle, when a Herald leading a horse, came running up to Peter and gave him the reins.

"His majesty wishes you to ride with him." Was the simple statement, which he simply obliged.

They found that there were only four opposing knights left to surrender, one of them was Walters, who swore at Peter when he arrived.

The King had them and their HQ marquee surrounded with his lancers, before he emerged through the encirclement.

"It appears that we, not you, have won the day, Walters. You will not be offered quarter, as you're traitorous ways permits me to withhold it from all of you." the King started.

"But we gave you quarter. This is very ungallant of you sire" one of the knights protested.

"Where I come from, any person who goes back on their word, gets shot. Especially those people who turn traitor, and on those who murder an unarmed man. Now that really was ungallant of you." Peter said menacingly.

"But it was the Prince of Anglia," the third one said as if to shift blame, but only succeeded in making the King more angry.

"Render the Anglian sword and crown and that of the ingrate Duke DeBois unto me before I have you all run you through." he barked, and signalled his lancers to level their weapons at these knights.

Peter went over to the fluttering standard and snapped the flag pole in two before he carried the flag over to a wooden table, laying it roughly on a wooden table so as to form a table cloth.

Walters glared at his captors, but reverently sheathed the magnificent Essex sword back in its scabbard and placed it in the middle of the table.

One of the other knights had retrieved the Prince's magnificent plumed helmet and it too was placed on the table.

"Now your swords and heraldry if you please." the King prompted Walters and the other prisoners.

Whilst the other two were struggling to remove their weaponry and heraldry with everybody looking on, Walters somehow took advantage of the distraction, and by grabbing the flag quickly wrapped everything up that was on the table, before he leapt on a nearby horse to make his getaway.

He was too quick for everybody and by the time Peter got his rifle back out again, Walters had reached the stream at the bottom of the valley.

Peter clipped on his night sights, ranged his target, then calmly shot the fleeing man. "Someone go and fetch that dead traitor and all that he carried." Peter announced.

But as it was dark and there were still hostiles lurking about, nobody ventured out of the light of the still blazing campfire in front of the Prince's marquee.

Peter saw this hesitation and stated to all that everything would be collected in the morning.

Peter took his leave to rest for the night and slept well. In the early morning as he woke, he saw through the early morning mist that the valley was still littered with dead bodies of men and horses, and the debris of war all over the place

He watched the scavengers out robbing the cadavers, before gathering them up and piling them unceremoniously into large heaps, and decided it was now safe for the girls to return to the battle sight.

Peter took his helm off and was surprised to find that they were eagerly waiting to return to see this scene and record it. It was their reward for listening to him all this time.

During that time, the twins told him they heard all that was said, the screams and the noise of battle, and wrote it all down. Also that as each knight got killed their suit of armour appeared back into the room, as did the mysterious object. But there was one item missing and they told him that it was the helmet he was wearing.

"If all has returned except this helm, then something is going to happen to its owner." Peter whispered, and took it off quickly, to bring them back into the room.

After discussing all the possibilities, it was decided that Peter would return to try and solve the mystery of the helm, but needed someone with him to bring him back again, but who?

"Ah there you are Sir Pierres. I see you've managed to find your squire again." the King's booming voice greeted as Peter walked into the King's tent.

"Your majesty wishes to see me?" Peter asked civilly but whispered aside to Jenny to stay very close to him.

"I wish to bestow a crown on your head, as a mark of payment for saving your King from ignominy. This crown will be worn instead of your helm." the King stated and went to remove the helmet. Peter stepped back to prevent the King, who looked astonished at Peter's reaction.

"Sir Pierres, why do you refuse the gift from a King?"

"Your majesty! My helm is that of a crown. The crown of a Saracen King whom I slayed during the crusades to the holy lands."

"Pah! You favour a tin pot crown over a real one? This is the crown of a northern King whom I slayed only last month." the King persisted.

"I would have it that you place it tightly upon my helm. That way I can wear both at the same time and preserve the honour of each brave King who died under them." Peter said diplomatically.

The King started to stroke his beard and gazed at Peter for a little while.

"For God's sake, be careful. Peter." Jenny whispered.

"Be Gad! Hah! A man after my own heart! Well said that knight!" the King said jubilantly, as he placed the crown on top of Peter's helmet.

"There Sir Pierres! You look almost like a King now." he said as he bowed to Peter who returned the compliment.

"Let's make merriment Sir Knight! Where's the wenches? Bring on the victuals! Let's celebrate a well fought battle!" the King laughed loudly as everybody except Peter ran around doing the King's bidding.

It was early morning when Peter went back into the woods, with Jenny in close attendance.

"Sorry to keep you waiting again Jenny. But we've got to go again." he said as they relieved themselves at an open ditch that served as the loo.

When they were finished they strolled back and started to gather up their things, explaining to the inquisitive King as to where they were going.

"You have done your duty and are a free man to go now Sir Pierres. But you take with you, the gratitude of a King and this." he said, as he threw Peter a large leather pouch.

"It is the King's gold, that will help you raise your own castle and you own army from the northern lands. You will be loyal to me and keep my borders safe. If I need you then you will come prepared to help your King like as of this day." he said, as he embraced Peter and kissed him on both cheeks.

"Fare thee well your majesty. In faith and my allegiance to you, your northern lands and borders will remain at peace and safe." Peter replied bravely, and gave the King a deep bow before straightening himself up and mounted his horse, with Jenny holding the reins for him.

"Well said Sir Pierres D'angleurs. Wished I had more champions like you than the chicken livered scum I'm forced to put up with at my court. You will not be forgotten, my champion!" the King shouted back as Peter left the group of soldiers behind.

Peter and Jenny went through the woods to get out of sight in order to get back to Jilly. But something caught Jenny's eye that glinted in the dapple sunlight of the woods.

"Peter, I think there's somebody watching us." she breathed.

Peter kept walking his horse but casually looked around and at the same time drew his rifle.

"I see him about one hundred yards ahead and to our right" he whispered

"Get on the other side of me, the horse will protect you, but hold on tight." he added.

They had gone just a few more paces when Peter saw Walters coming slowly at them on horseback with a lance pointing towards them.

"Hah! You thought you'd got me last night. You nearly did for me, and I've lost my liege's sword and heraldry. Now I will pay you back. Prepare yourself, knight!" Walters said as he turned his horse around and went off to give room for the battle.

Peter saw the blood-smeared holes in both sides Walters armour.

"Look, the bullet must have gone straight through him. He's seriously wounded. Just to knock him off his horse should finish him off."

"Be careful Peter. Remember the helm needs to be returned as well as us." Jenny said fearfully and held onto Peter's leg.

Walters turned his horse and started to gallop towards them, levelling his very long lance at him. Peter just sighed, raised his rifle, took careful aim and shot Walters right between the eyes.

But what he forgot about was the momentum of Walters' body being carried forward by the charging horse, as Walters' war lance somehow managed to fall and strike Peter's crown off his helm. The force of impact knocked him unconscious, which made him fall from his horse. As he landed heavily onto the ground at Jenny's feet, the helm fell off and rolled into the bushes.

When Peter regained consciousness again, he found the twins fussing over him with bandages and antiseptic creams.

"What happened Jenny? Must have taken a knock from that lance." he asked slowly, trying to focus his eyes to his surroundings.

"We've done it Peter! We've got the helmet and we're back home again." Jenny said happily as she kissed him.

"Yes we've managed to solve the mystery helmet and this strange object. Mind you it was strange to see all our tin men vanish and return again with fresh blood and caked in fresh mud." Jilly added, giving him a kiss on his cheek.

"The object consists of the Prince of Anglia sword, scabbard, and his helmet all wrapped up in his standard." Peter said slowly as he raised himself up painfully to a sitting position on the wooden table.

"We will go and look for the Northern Crown later, but I'm famished. Is it supper time yet girls?"

"No! It's only tea time Peter. For all the time we spent back there, we've only been gone two hours." the girls said excitedly and hugged him again.

"Well, my head hurts real enough, that's for certain." Peter protested mildly and laid back down onto the table to receive more tender attention from the twins.

The next few days went routinely for the Plumstead's, with the twins feeling satisfied with their history project they gave to their head master, and Peter catching up with his fence and wall repairs.

Peter had just come back from the sawmills when Helen told him that there were two men coming to see them, something to do about the twins project.

When the two men eventually arrived, Peter was surprised to see John's father, the Earl of Bymouth standing inside the front parlour.

"Hello young Peter! Heard you bagged another rabid dog last week, well done." Bymouth greeted as he shook Peters' hand firmly.

"Well thank you! But I understand you've come to see me about something else." Peter replied as he looked at the other person.

"Ah yes indeed. This is Professor Johnson from the National History museum." he said as he introduced the professor.

"Good afternoon professor. What can I do for you gentlemen?" Peter replied firmly.

"We've had a phone call from the history teacher of the Bymouth High School where your twin sisters did a project." Johnson commenced. He explained what the extremely high significance of the sketches and drawings the twins had made, and wanted to know how and where the twins got their information and research material from.

"It's quite simple professor. Anybody plowing their fields in this valley or even walking along the river could pick up lots of items just as I did. All they did was make up a story around the finds."

"Yes that's all well and good. But how did they know to describe a battle that was, up to now, unknown? They appear to have discovered a forgotten battle fought in this valley in the Twelfth but possibly in the Thirteenth century, and we think between the King of Mercia and the Prince of Anglia." Johnson persisted.

"Maybe if I were to show you two possible burial grounds I discovered which got unearthed after that last big storm over the valley; would you be satisfied?" he asked

Both men raised their eyebrows in surprise at this fact, and asked if Peter would take them and show them, to which Peter agreed.

On the way down to the landing stage, he told the men that he took some items for the twins to use on their project and was going to hand them over, but due to farm work commitments, he still hadn't got round to it.

He showed them the hollow tree and the other burial mound telling them that the river probably wasn't as deep during that time, therefore some of the water meadow would contain a lot of battle remains in its mud.

Johnson looked around for a while, taking several photographs, and picking up odd fragments.

"Yes! There is a burial ground here. It looks as if there's a lot under that old tree and further down the river about two hundred yards. I need to get a dig organised. But first we will have to cordon off the sites, to prevent ham fisted amateurs spoiling them any further." Johnson said finally, but with excitement in his voice.

Bymouth found the remains of a sword, and some small cylinders just like Peter had, and showed them to Johnson.

"If my memory serves me correct, these are the barrels from the remains of the first hand pistols ever to be used. Which means this area is a very important site." Johnson informed them.

The two men looked around whilst Peter pointed out the different places he had found some of the things the twins used.

By the time they got back to the farmstead and decontaminated their gumboots, Ken was in the front parlour waiting for them.

"Ah Mr. Plumstead!" Lord Bymouth said, as he shook hands with him then introduced Johnson to him.

"It appears that you own a very important piece of land, and thanks to the very plausible story your two girls made up for their history project, we've discovered an important chapter in our national and local history." Johnson started, then went on to explain what he would like Ken to do, to help them.

Ken and Peter asked many questions on the various aspects of this proposal before all were satisfied enough to call the meeting to a close.

When the men had gone, Ken turned to the twins with excitement and a large smile on his face.

"Whatever cock and bull stories you girls have told, you certainly have started something that will make this farm famous." he said and embraced the two of them at once.

"You clever girls. If those bits of tin you've made up become as valuable as Johnson said, then we'll be able to get the farm back, and onto an even keel again. Just think! Instead of plowing fields for a living, we'd take tourists around the place and sell off a few artifacts to them." he enthused.

Helen looked at Ken's face, and realised that it was the first time in ages her husband seemed to have something to smile and laugh about.

The twins' story hit the local news headlines, and was the talk of the town and especially in By Bys. Before long the normally quiet river was full of river craft of all types, trying to find their own artifacts along the river.

Peter was employed full time to keep away the metal detector wielding hordes. In the end Sergeant Phillips had to put a police notice up warning everybody to stay off the PRIVATE land.

Eventually, Johnson reappeared one fine day, with a small crew of archaeologists who spent the next two weeks on the sites, thus relieving Peter to do some other much needed work around the farm.

Walters, the Lord of Bymouth, also made an appearance to see the pile of armour and weaponry that was recovered, but was to be disappointed that none of it belonged to him.

Peter was on hand to see Walters about to leave, and called over to him.

"Lord Bymouth. Remember I told you last month about the bits I haven't had time to see to, and some of which turn out to be important?" Peter prompted.

"Yeees!" Walter drawled then remembered the conversation.

"Peter if you have anything belonging to the crown you are to surrender it immediately or you'll be sent to jail. Any important finds belong to the crown." Walters said coldly as if to badger him.

"Be that as it may Lord Bymouth. But I think you'd better come with me and see for yourself, whether certain artifacts should leave the area. It was from these items that my sisters made up their, shall we say, almost uncanny and accurate story." Peter said to entice him to be less belligerent and more amenable to him.

Walters stood looking at the tin men in total amazement, with his eyes bulging and his mouth agape.

'But! But!" he stammered.

"But where did you find all these." he managed to ask after a while.

"Exactly where the professor is digging. Do you see that suit over there? It has your family crest on it. Oh and by the way, so does the helmet, and the shining steel sword next to it." Peter informed him off handedly.

Walters walked swiftly over to the suit and examined it closely.

"There's a hole right through the chest plate. Made by an arrow, or even a lance, by the look of it. Yes that must be it." Walters muttered, as he stroked the armour.

"Actually Lord Bymouth. It is a bullet hole. I know all about arrow and bullet holes. You know that of course, and I say that this person had definitely been shot." Peter stated knowingly.

"I have never seen such a magnificent suit of armour so old that has a bullet hole in it. Believe me, I've searched all over the nation for just that. Now you hand me one on a plate." Walters said as if in a trance.

"Well take it from me. The professor will confirm all this if you let him. But I'd say this would be the first Knight to be shot in battle. It would be a unique piece of armour any decent knight of the realm would desire." Peter said softly, giving Walters more ammunition to the greed that was shining in his eyes.

"You say that Johnson doesn't know about all this?" Walters asked.

"Absolutely not. Except for what my sisters wrote in their story." Peter confirmed.

"In that case Peter. I will buy this suit off you." he said after a moment.

"Sorry, it's not for sale." Peter replied, testing Walters' greed.

"You do realise as an Earl of the realm, I can confiscate all of this and you won't get a penny." Walters responded swiftly.

"Ah yes Lord Bymouth, I'm glad you brought that up. According to the recent chronicles, it appears that your forefather, the one that wore this armour, was a traitor to the King and was shot for it. There was no royal pardon given or recorded to your family name of Walters and that of the estate of Bymouth, which means that it excludes you from claiming any further chattels or baggage from the estate that you profess to own. Therefore all this that I found and your already great collection of armour, let alone your entire estate would also be forfeited. So really speaking, it's all down to a descendant of a traitor to make amends, and it appears that you're it!"

"The hell you say! My forefathers were loyal citizens through and through! Those chronicles must be a fake!" Walters shouted angrily as he advanced menacingly towards Peter.

"Not according to the recent discoveries and apparent truth in what they portray. On the face of it Walters, it seem that your family have been living a lie for all these centuries. Which means that I can demand anything I want from you!" Peter said quietly and in an off handed manner.

"That smacks of blatant blackmail to which I will have no part in." Walters retorted, but found that his statement cut no ice with Peter.

"Look, let's not beat about the bush. I'll offer you five thousand pounds cash for it and the other one with the arrow sticking out of it." he said nervously.

"Come off it! The sword and helmet is worth that alone. Besides, your family name must be worth much, much more. So think again! And I suggest at least four times that amount just for starters!"

"Okay then twenty five thousand pounds, and that's my final offer!"

Peter kept quiet for a while thinking over this final offer but decided to up it one more time.

"Okay, here's the deal! You hand over to me the full fishing and hunting rights from By By to Mutch Pitm. Sign over the farm deeds and river lands back to my father, plus a cash payment of twenty-five grand for good measure, then you'll have got yourself a good deal."

"Twenty five grand in cash as well? Why that's outrageous!" Walters stammered.

"The farm alone is only worth ten thousand, and the game and fishing rights worth only a further two thousand a year." Walters protested angrily.

It was Peter's turn to be surprised at Walters outburst of information, which suddenly hit him hard with the realisation as to why his father was struggling all this time to make ends meet.

"So that's it! All this time you've been bleeding us dry with your pleas of poverty! You've had the deeds to our land for over five years for a miserly debt of only five grand, yet we've paid you over five times that amount during that time. For that, the price has just gone up a further ten grand, and that constitutes my final answer. Take it or leave it." Peter said coldly as he glared into Walters face.

Walters whinged and moaned about the steep price he had to pay, as if to sway the resolve of this much younger person before him.

"Look Lord Bymouth!" Peter said, as he sarcastically emphasised the word 'lord'.

"Either you get sent to jail and have all the trappings your family have grown accustomed to for generations taken away, or you agree to my terms! You have 10 seconds to answer!"

Walters started mouthing obscenities and mutter to himself as he tried to contain his feeling of defeat and anguish. It took him the ten seconds to regain his composure before declaring in a hoarse whisper.

"Oh very well, you win. But I get all the armour and weaponry in your possession, and claim exclusive rights to any further such finds. Mind you, nobody gets to hear about this and you must sign on oath to that effect." Walters conceded.

Peter kept a straight face but inside he was overjoyed at the idea of his father getting control of his own farm back again.

'After all, what's a few old bits of armour in comparison?' he thought quickly, then held out his hand to shake on the deal

"Lord Bymouth! Not only have you made the right decision, but you strike a hard bargain as well. At least you will continue to be the Lord Bymouth and live up at your family manor. And on top of that, you'll be the proud owner of the first suit of armour to wear a bullet hole and its one of your ancestors to boot. In fact, judging by the accuracy of such a bullet hole I would say it was done by a professional on a professional." Peter agreed, and smiled briefly at the truth in that statement.

Both men shook hands to pledge their new agreement, and their private deal was struck in the understanding that nobody else would ever hear what went on.

It was only two days later when Professor Johnson made an appearance, demanding that he be shown the collection of armour Peter had taken from the burial site and kept for himself.

"It appears that Lord Bigmouth, or should I call him Traitor Walters, has been speaking to you Professor, he is definitely not a man of his word." Peter said crossly and led the way down to his workshop.

Johnson photographed everything, made an inventory of the collection, telling Peter that these were just what they had been looking for, also that he was confiscating the lot immediately.

Peter got angry with him and told him of his so called deal with Walters.

"It appears that he had no business to offer you anything, and if what was discovered is the truth, then he too will have some handing over to do, as well as explaining his present existence as Lord Bymouth. That title, by the way, has just been suspended pending royal judiciaries and enquiries."

"Now that is history repeating itself as far as he's concerned, and he deserves all that is coming to him. But for me, I found all this lot, and as the finder plus the fact that they were found on this land, it is mine by law and nobody is allowed to take these from me! Besides, according to you experts all this never existed until my sisters' history project was handed in to their school teacher."

"In ordinary circumstances that would be true. But it was the Prince of Anglia's sword and regalia and all the other very important artifacts that makes you liable to render them as treasure trove." Johnson said softly. Then to cushion the blow he had given the now very downcast Peter he added.

"Think of it this way Peter. Such a valuable find will attract a high value reward from the government, and also it rewrites an important chapter in the history books. That of course would make the Walters offer pale into insignificance. Also, the special helm you are fond of will be bought for a handsome sum by the national museum of France, and all you and your family need do now, is just wait until it all comes through the right channels. If there's small comfort to be gained from your betrayal by Walters, it is that you now have a much better deal.

By that, I mean you can get on with your life, but as I've just said, he has to wait for official and constitutional guidelines to be ratified before he can claim his titles and property back again."

Peter nodded his understanding of this implication but still felt very much bewildered, downhearted and disappointed at the thought of how close he had come to solving the family's farm debt problems for them.

"I expect it will take about a couple of months to get all this sorted, but I will keep in touch with you. If you have any problems with Walters, just call the local history museum Peter!" Johnson said as he shook Peters' hand in farewell before climbing into his car and left

When the day came for the Plumstead's to be officially notified, the Low Knowle farm underwent a rapid change, as did its occupants, thanks to the several hundred thousand pounds reward for Peter's tin men, the Northern Crown, and other important artifacts.

It went from an arable farm to a dairy farm, as Ken was not allowed to plow up any more fields, but had to increase his dairy herd to help keep the grass down.

The whole farm was designated by the National Heritage trust as a special Battlefield sight, and the hexagonal farmstead was also given national importance as a Grade I listed building.

Ken was also given a government subsidy to maintain his Shire horse Centre to compliment the whole ambience of the valley.

Helen runs a little tea-room with Clive's new girlfriend Sandra, that Cousin Frank had built for them on the landing stage, and where lots of river craft now use as a special sight seeing trip from By Bys to Mutch Piddling in the Marsh.

Clive returned from the hospital, much taller than he went in and is busy mastering his new legs. He is about to marry his Sandra, and take over from Ken in the running of the entire home farm and its estate.

Lord Bymouth was publicly stripped of his title to become just plain Mr Walters. He had to sell off most of his five thousand acre estate and chattels to pay for 'back taxes' but was allowed to keep the manor and just twenty acres around it, albeit in his son's keeping, and now lives as a recluse in a small gate lodge on the edge of his old estate.

John made an honest woman of Patricia with a summer wedding, and took over the Bymouth manor to maintain it as part of the national Heritage Trust, whilst Susan became a well respected By Valley vet.

Peter was given the lofty job of Park warden to add to his Land Ranger duties, which is mainly to keep rabid dogs, poachers and metal detector nuts off the river and out of the valley. He is also the chief tour guide around the battleground and farmstead.

He married Susan who is feeding him well now, and both live at the Low Knowle farmstead.

The twins had been awarded an Honours Degree in History from the County University. Jilly is now courting Tommy who resurrected his father's old tannery business, and with Jenny, both girls enjoy life as University lecturers.

Claire and Charles had twin boys, and hope that one day they will take over the mill from Charles.

As for Sir Pierres D'angleurs? This fictional story you have just read, is all down to the imagination to create such a story from a very little known fact gleaned from the annals of history.

For the truth is dear reader, there really was a knight who was given the dubious distinction of being recorded as the first armoured knight in British history, ever to be killed in battle by a single bullet and not by any other means. And that his suit of armour is still being displayed in an appropriate museum somewhere, even today.

Which means that there are a few questions that you might wish to seek the answers to:

Just who was that bygone mysterious knight? Where and when was this battle fought? And, in which museum or private collection would you now find this suit of armour?

If you find out the answers then you 'have my ears', and 'by your leave', kindly let me know!

Moreland & Other Stories

Lucky Creek

Ben and Frank were brothers, working for the Ordinance Surveyors Department in the North West Territories of Canada, and situated near the Pan American-Soviet North Polar region.

They were sent out as part of a team on an expedition to survey uncharted terrain, and bring back several different sets of data that would then be made into detailed maps for the Canadian Ordinance Survey Dept and various interested world wide organisations.

Of the four man team, two had left some time earlier with most of the data that they collected, but as Ben was the team leader, he and his brother opted to continue on and do the last section of the area, before the winter came in again. The area left for the brothers to survey, was a vast one that no sane person would dare to be in, and they were given a limited time before they were to be picked up by sea plane, at a certain rendezvous point several hundred miles away.

After several weeks surveying and trekking up into the mountains, crossing glaciers and lakes, through dense forests, and living off the land, they were forced to make their way back on a different route towards their pick up point.

"We've covered several high mountains on this trip, but this one was some dangerous mountain we've just crossed. Cracks and loose boulders everywhere. At least we have a good camping area for any return trip. I think we will designate its name as Boulder mountain." Ben spoke quietly as if to himself.

"By the look of it Ben, we still have one maybe two lakes to traverse and maybe a few low foothills." Frank said after a while, as both of them did not speak for hours at a time.

"Yes, I reckon that. We may as well break camp now and move further down this lake here. Its about twenty miles long, but we may have another lake on the other side, as God knows what's hiding behind the bottom of that mountain. So let's get going." Ben stated, as he finished panning his terrain scanner along the route they were to take.

"Yes, I'll pen the designated name for this one as Lake Long." Frank stated.

They loaded up the last of their gear into their long two-man canoe, climbed in and paddled it effortlessly through the calm inky waters.

After a couple of hours of steady paddling, Frank who was in the front, called Ben to stop for a moment.

"There's several logs up ahead blocking our way Ben. We'll just have to pick our way through them."

After several minutes trying not to get tangled up in the hazard, Ben pulled the canoe alongside one of the logs to see what type of tree it was.

"Frank, this one is a whole tree with roots and all. I wonder what happened for all these to get here. Avalanche probably!"

"I don't know, but I've got one of my uneasy feelings again. I suggest we beach for the night."

"No, we'll keep on going at least to the end of the lake, Frank. We have only got three left to get back to our pick up point, otherwise the plane will leave us behind."

They took their time and picked their way slowly through the hazard, and after a few more hours they had finally traversed the length of the lake.

"Just as I thought Frank. This promontory is the start of another lake."

They paddled up to it and saw that the water curved round it to reveal an even bigger lake for them to go up.

"Designate this one as Lake Surprise."

Frank never replied, instead he stopped paddling and looked all around him.

"Listen Ben. Do you hear that?"

Ben listened for a moment.

"Nope. I hear nothing."

"Exactly. There's not a breath of air. Not a chirp, or sound anywhere, not even a ripple on the lake."

Frank whispered.

They started to whisper to each other as if trying not to break a silence, which was deafening to them.

When you touch the deafening sound of silence your ear drums ache for just one beat of noise, though you hold your breath in case you violate that unique moment.

"Remember when we were kids, and I stopped you going ice skating on the river. I tried to stop your pals too but they didn't listen?" Frank asked quietly.

"Yes, spooky that! You told us you had a nasty feeling, and we all laughed at you. That was until the ice broke and most of my friends drowned." Ben recollected.

"Yes, and everybody thought it was a coincidence until the next time I had one. The time when I told Dad to stay at home instead of driving the camper van over to Aunt Glenda's place." Frank continued.

"Yes. Uncle Charlie drove it instead and got killed when it crashed because of brake failure." Ben said as he remembered the incident.

"You know that I've got that sixth sense and it always comes as gut feelings. Well I've got it now and the more powerful the feeling the bigger the trouble. We'd better get off the lake, and sharpish too. Besides, I can't see much in front of me until the moon is up and full."

Ben thought of other incidents involving his brothers feelings and warnings, too numerous to mention, so decided on safety as the best policy.

"Okay! Let's make camp up on that rocky promontory on our right, over there. We can get a good view of things in the morning." Ben agreed.

It took them several trips to get their gear and canoe up off the shoreline, and make their camp for the night.

It was an uneasy, almost sleepless night, but when the dawn broke, the noise of the dawn chorus woke them up to a bright and breezy morning.

They lit their fire, and having eaten a cooked meal of freshly caught salmon, they decided to start the survey point from their camp.

"On this point, we're about two hundred feet above water level, so if I adjust the scanner we can pan round to get a good view of both lakes." Ben advised.

"I have the scanner set up and running for ten minutes. I have the other end of the first lake sketched and ready for filing. Maybe you can give me a hand with the chronometer and gyroscope Ben. There's a lot of magnetic activity in these rocks, so we might need an extra calculation or two to fix our positions."

"Sure thing!" Ben replied.

"What was all that about last night Frank?"

"I don't know. But we ran into those trees didn't we? So it must have been that." Frank said matter-of-factly.

It was getting near noon when Frank told Ben to stop and listen again.

"Ben! Listen! That silence is back and my gut feeling is stronger this time, and I just don't know what it is."

Ben took his binoculars and stood on a rock at the very edge of the promontory and looked around at both lakes that seemed to pass either side of him.

"Everything seems as Mother Nature intended Frank. The snowcaps on the mountains are neat. There's no gap in the forests, so no sign of an avalanche. No sudden spume of water, and no apparent life on the lakes. Come and have a look for yourself." Ben offered, but Frank refused, preferring to work on his sketches.

They worked methodically through their tasks until they had finished before deciding to get something to eat.

"Too late to start back down to the shoreline and onto the lake, so we might as well settle down for the rest of the day. Consolidate our camp area if you like. Start off, first thing in the morning after a good nights rest. How's that?" Ben suggested to his younger brother.

"Suits me fine. I can get some more drawings and measurements added for the film records."

"We have that lake to go up. Do you see that narrow, low lying strip of land between those peaks? That's where we're heading for." Ben asked as he handed Frank the binoculars.

"From here it looks pretty straight forward. Up and over, into the next lake. Unless we can canoe out of here." Frank stated as he handed the binoculars back again.

"Well, according to our instructions, we've got to go through some sort of gorge there. White water rafting for about a mile or so before we reach an open tidal lake and our plane ride."

"Are you serious? White rafting in our dodgy canoe? We're lucky to stay afloat on a mill pond with all this stuff, let alone faffing about on white water, Ben."

"Aw c'mon, it's only about a mile long and only going down about fifty feet. We can do it." Ben chuckled as he assured his brother.

"Can you remember what's on the other side? Open sea water?"

"Not quite sure. Maybe another lake before we reach that one, knowing our luck. According to the terrain scanner, we have about twenty-five miles of water and land to cover by tomorrow evening. Else we're on overtime, search parties and the like, and the government don't like spending on that."

"Yeah, the tight fisted lot. Fancy not letting us keep the SABRE* to help us. The other half of the team took it back, but they were on the home stretch compared to us." Frank concluded.

That conversation was the longest they had had for several days. Soon they lapsed back into their silent routine again, listening for danger or tell tale signs of rapids, waterfalls, avalanches and even marauding bears.

Both men felt uneasy as the eerie silence crept over them once more as they sat looking over the lake from their vantage point.

"Quick, grab your binoculars and search your side on Lake Surprise!" Frank said hurriedly.

No sooner had they started looking, when there was a flicker of light as if from some distant lightning flash. That was followed shortly afterwards by faint rumbling that went into a crescendo of thunder before they heard an ear splitting crack and rumbling noise that shook the very rocks they were standing on.

"What the bleedin' hell was all that Ben? An earthquake or what?"

"I don't know, but get the videocam and point it up to that mountain at the head of the lake where we camped yesterday."

---

* **SA**tellite **B**eacon **R**escue.

Frank came quickly back with the video camera and set it up.

"Let's see what we've got then." Frank started

"Jeezus! Look at that! That seven thousand foot mountain has been cracked right down its middle and looks as if is about to fall. Look at the big cracks down its left side Ben." Frank said in awe.

Ben looked and was astounded at what he saw.

"Is this part of your gut feeling Frank?"

"No, something else."

"What else is there?" Ben moaned, but his question was lost in a rumbling noise much louder than before or what any natural thunder could make.

As Ben looked through his binoculars, Frank held the video camera and started to record what was about to unfold before their very eyes.

"Frank, if that mountain does fall, there will be one almighty splash. I think we'd better get higher up this slope." Ben shouted over the noise.

"You're right Ben! Even as you spoke, the mountain has just fallen into the lake, causing this ruddy great shock wave of water that's coming our way. And judging by its size, it's much higher than us too."

Ben looked quickly down Lake Long and saw the enormous wall of water making its way swiftly towards them.

"We've got about three minutes. Grab what you can and let's get the hell out of here."

Both of them ran back to the camp-site, and grabbed all what they could carry and scampered up the steep mountain slope.

They managed to find a small flat area where they simply dumped their stuff as the giant wave was almost upon them.

"Get the scanner going Frank, I'll record all this, live on camera."

They filmed the wave as it smashed its way along the slopes of the lake leaving a trail of devastation in its wake. The wave sloshed its way along and flowed right over their little camp below them, and even stripped the trees and soil almost up to where they were standing.

"There goes the camp and our belongings Ben."

"Never mind the camp, look at Lake Surprise. The wave must be sucking the water up, because its been almost drained."

Ben and Frank quickly swung their equipment round to point at the latest phenomena.

"Yes! It's growing higher as its going along, which means that it is shallower at this end. It's about three hundred feet now, and about half a mile thick. That will take some stopping." Frank whistled.

Ben trained his camera back onto the wave as it moved rapidly towards the end of Lake Surprise and the small bridge of land they were to cross over.

"Look at that Frank!" Ben whispered

They watched as the wave literally drowned the strip of land as it swept right over it and down into the next lake ahead of it.

"Once it hits deeper or open salt water it should cut itself down a lot. If it moves on a northerly direction towards the polar icecap, it will meet the mountains of the Salver Islands. That should stop it." Frank stated philosophically.

Both stopped their recorders and looked around at the total destruction the water had created. Whereas the noise was a deafening crescendo as the wave passed them, now there was an abrupt and total silence all around them.

The wave had stripped all the trees and soil off the mountain to expose solid rock, up to about two hundred feet above what used to be the water line. Now both lakes were almost empty save for a few puddles. The small land bridge was reduced to half its height and completely stripped bare, like an ugly gash in the side of the mountain.

The mountain that caused it, was just like a pyramid with a cliff side where the mountain's overhang had sheered off. Its remains lay in large piles of rock that covered almost a quarter of the top part of the lake.

The brothers looked down at where they had their camp and over to the other side of the lake from them.

Their promontory was just a column of bare rock standing on its own with a deep scar between it and the rest of the mountain.

Ben started to speak, but his mouth just opened and closed as he found that he could not utter a word. Frank found the same.

They were totally speechless as the realisation of what had happened and delayed shock set in on them.

Instead, they just stood there looking at each other, until finally, after several minutes, Ben slowly found his voice again.

"Brother! You and me are lucky to be alive. You saw the size of that wave? We could have camped over on the other side there. Those trees are stripped away much higher than we are here. The wave must have bounced off that side to go on down Lake Surprise." he said almost robotically.

Frank looked over to where Ben had pointed, and pointed his scanner to it

"The water splashed up to a height of six hundred feet. We're now at three hundred feet high, but our original campsite was only two hundred feet high." he said with a hoarse whisper as he shook his head in disbelief.

"Was that your gut feeling? Was that what you felt?" Ben asked anxiously

"Yes Ben, but its not gone away yet."

"Not gone away yet? What else can happen to us today?"

"Search me. I just know its not over yet."

Ben looked around the small place where they stood.

"Well, here we are campers. Stranded and perched on this effing nine thousand foot high mountain right behind us, a sheer drop of over two hundred foot below us, and the man says it's not over yet." Ben swore.

"If my memory is correct, there's a fishing village over there that was probably in the direct path of the wave." Frank volunteered, as he looked over and pointed in the direction of the destroyed land bridge.

"Poor bastards. Lets hope they survived." Ben whispered.

"Yes and we're lucky to get through it." Frank stated morosely.

"Let's see what we've managed to save. I got the scanner, video-cam." Ben commenced to reel off the equipment he had.

"I got our ground sheet, our dixies, the gun." as Frank reeled off his lot.

"Oh well, not bad. Pity about our personal gear, and the research material that we collected on the way. But at least we won't starve Frank. Look at all the fish that have been caught up in these trees below us. Anyone for salmon steak and chips?" Ben said as he tried to cheer them both up.

Two days later, still stuck on the mountain side, not able to climb up or down to get off their little perch, the stench of rotting fish wafting up from the dry lakes was sickening, forcing the brothers to mask their noses from the smell.

"Surely the seismologists must have picked up the tremors and will come looking to see what caused it. I mean, that was no ordinary avalanche. What about our pick up plane Ben?"

"Perhaps our back up team thought that we had perished in that lot if the scanner transmitter wasn't working. I honestly don't know Frank."

"I told you that we should have taken the SABRE. We would have been off this stinking place long before now."

"Never mind. We're alive, all thanks to your gut feelings. And to think I was going to take us along Lake Surprise, to the land bridge instead of camping on this shore line."

"Come to think of it, those trees we met. We were going down mid current but they were moving up lake along the shore line and against the current. And they were whole.

That's what puzzled me Ben, and that's what triggered me off?"

"What about now? Still got that gut reaction?"

"Yes, but only slight."

"Well Frank. If your last feeling threw half a mountain and a tidal wave our way, then god help us what else may come. You can have as many as you like, but make certain I'm miles away from you."

"Gee thanks brother!" Frank said in mock horror.

No sooner had Frank spoken, when was another loud rumbling noise took them by surprise.

They just looked at each other in amazement.

"Not again Frank! I hope this is your last one. Grab the video and point it back at that mountain." Ben shouted over the continuous noise, as he grabbed the binoculars and looked back at the damaged mountain.

"There must have been a loose part at the top that has now fallen, judging by the length of the noise created." Ben observed.

"Yes, it had a long way to travel down. Fortunately there's no more water to throw at us again. Anyway brother, if its any consolation, I feel nothing else now, that feeling has gone, so I think we are safe now."

"Thank god for that. I was beginning to think mother nature and gravity took charge this time round. To think that I had that place at the bottom of the mountain marked for another possible camp-site for later survey trips. The mountain is just a mere pimple compared to its former glory, we'll have to re designate it. What do you suggest. Pebble mountain?"

"What do you suppose caused that mountain to blow like that Ben? There's no volcanic history around here, only plate tectonic activity."

"Maybe the cam and scanner have the clues. Just have to wait until we get back to analyse the data." Ben replied as he scratched his head in wonder.

The brothers kept on looking and scanning the mountain for more possible avalanches, as the noise subsided to another ear shattering silence.

Frank, who was the artist and recorder, took several hours to record everything down on the last remaining pages of his journal. He also made sketches of the area to back up the films they took of the catastrophic event.

"We'll become famous if we can get all this data back to base. That's unless 'you know who' doesn't pinch our work off us again like last time. What do you say Ben?"

"I say, be quiet and listen. Do you hear that?" Ben answered.

Both men listened intently for a moment, looking through their binoculars and scanning the place where the noise seemed to come from.

"There it is Ben! Look down to your right. There's a red coloured sea-plane below us, coming up Lake Surprise"

"That's a Search and Rescue spotter plane. Quick, make some smoke on the fire." Ben said excitedly.

Frank ran across to their meagre fire and threw some green branches onto it, wafting it so that the smoke could billow much more.

Ben had a piece of glass that he used as a heliograph, to flash at the plane.

"They've seen us Ben. Look they're rising up to our level and coming right at us." Frank shouted, as he waved his arms at the pilot.

Ben took off his big overcoat and waved it frantically, as the plane seemed to waggle its wings back to them.

The plane circled around them a few times then left the way it had come.

"He's going away Ben!"

"Don't panic little brother. He can't land here, and there's not enough water down there for him to land on. They'll probably send an SAR helicopter for us later on this evening or even first light tomorrow."

"Not another night up this stinking pile of rocks. I can't face another fish now, I've had it. If anybody offers me fish in future, I'll shove it up their arse. You mark my words Ben." Frank spoke vehemently.

"Never mind Frank, we've only got one whole trout left. Do you want some?" Ben chuckled as he dodged a swipe from Frank.

The winchman buckled the safety harnesses around the brothers, as the helicopter sped its way over the empty lakes. Once he was satisfied, he started to fire a barrage of questions to them.

"Basically, a side of a mountain, at least some hundred and fifty million tons of solid rock decided to go walk about and dropped into the lake. The water that got pushed away in one go was about two hundred and fifty million gallons, forming in an instant, a massive wave that had only one place to go, and that was down the lakes and over the land." Ben concluded.

"No wonder the wave was over two hundred feet high when it reached the fishing village of Lucky Creek." the winchman whistled.

"That was some water displacement in one go. The rock hit the lake at its widest and deepest point. We reckon on about one mile wide and be over two hundred feet deep. When we see water, the darker the water the deeper it is." he explained.

"Lucky Creek did you say? A very unfortunate name don't you think?" Frank asked.

"A bad choice of name, poor bastards. Any survivors?" Ben asked.

It was their turn to ask the questions, which the pilot and the winchman answered in turn.

"No! All hundred souls perished. Everything just got washed away. One of their fishing boats was found some fifty miles away, perched on top of an iceberg." the pilot stated.

The brothers laughed at the thought of seeing such a strange sight as a ship that seemingly just parked itself on top of an iceberg.

That was the first time they had laughed since their truly narrow escape, and the release of the tension it gave was a relief to them both, as they embraced each other and laughed even louder, with the pilot and his winchman just looking on in amazement.

"What's those instruments you've got there. Your surveyors gear?" the pilot asked after the brothers laughter had subsided.

"We've got a video camera and a terrain scanner. Other bits and pieces, but all the rest was swept away. It looks as if our boss is going to charge us for the loss of government property." Frank volunteered.

"That's the truth!" the winchman agreed.

"Pop here, lost a Cessna out over the icecap last year. Ran out of fuel trying to get back through a snowstorm. He's still forking out for it." he added.

"Yeah! I've had to buy another one costing over 50 thousand dollars." the pilot agreed.

"Lucky we didn't have one of those SABRE's then, otherwise we'd be in the same boat as you. They cost mega bucks too. " Ben joined in.

The helicopter swooped over the bay where the fishing village was. Ben nudged Frank to look down.

"Bloody hell. Those poor bastards must have had all the soil from the mountain and most of the national forest dumped on their doorstep. Look at the barrage at the other end of the lake Frank!"

"Pilot, would you circle around this area so I can take a few feet of film, and pan my terrain scanner over it. It sure would save us a lot of time later if we had to come back and do it." Frank asked.

The helicopter banked and swooped over the stricken area for a few minutes.

"Must get back, fuel is low and I don't want to buy another aircraft again." the pilot apologised, as he straightened the craft up and flew straight to the airbase.

"It looks as if the bay is log bound with the rocks and soil forming a big barrier to stop water getting in or out." Ben observed.

"Thank god that's not our job, finding bodies from under all that, whatever. Anyway gentlemen, we'll be landing in 5 minutes, so fasten your seat belts. No smoking and watch the fat lady sing." the pilot said in good humour as he made his approach to land.

Before the brothers got out of the helicopter, they were warned by the pilot that a swarm of news and media locusts was about to descend on them, so they'd better hang on to their bags of equipment.

A large scrum of press and media descended on the brothers as they made their way to the Heliport control room.

"What's it like to be the only survivors?"

"Do you realise you've left over one hundred and fifty people dead out there?"

"Tell us your story!" were the demanding questions, as the brothers just pushed their way through the thuggish and loutish paparazzi.

"And now we see the McGill brothers, the only apparent survivors of the disaster area. You seem to have a habit of doing this. What was it like this time?" a trim and shapely but hauty female TV reporter stated into a microphone as she looked into a camera, then shoved it into Ben's face to answer.

"If you don't want that microphone shoved up where the sun doesn't shine, then get it out of my face!" Ben snarled

The female reporter blushed deeply, but persisted, saying "If you don't give me your story you'll be sorry you said that."

"Look lady! Just piss off and leave us alone. You lot already screwed us up last time round. We've just survived a mountain falling on us, and a two hundred foot tidal wave, so go frig yourself." Frank snapped.

"A four hundred foot tidal wave did you say? How do you know that?" another reporter asked.

"Yeah how'd you know that. You're both surveyors, show us the pictures you've taken. Give us your goddamn pictures!" a reporter demanded.

"They've got films of it." someone said excitedly.

"Somebody grab the films!" another shouted.

"Look at their sacks. Must be body parts!" another suggested.

"Are you carrying body parts and loot from the fishing village?"

The wildest suggestions and demands were flung at the brothers.

"Give us your films. We'll make you famous if you give us your films!" one reporter proposed, which started an even bigger scrum huddle that the brothers found hard to extricate themselves from.

A large man dressed in a military style uniform with a rifle in his hands appeared and ordered everybody to stand back or they'd get arrested.

"Make room for these men. Anyone still here in ten seconds will get a rubber bullet up them. Now get the hell out of here and leave these men alone. They've had enough trouble without all you pack of hyenas on them." he said in a loud booming voice.

The press and media louts swiftly melted away as the man waded through them and shepherded the brothers into a waiting van.

"We have been waiting for you, gentlemen. Glad you could make it." the stranger said with a big smile on his face.

"Glad you turned up mister. We were being eaten alive just then." Ben said as he offered his hand to the man.

"Glad to be of service." Was the reply as the man shook hands with them.

"This van will take you back to HQ for debriefing, and a formal press report will be issued later on." the man concluded as he saluted the brothers, who then piled into the back of the large van.

"I hope you two have brought me some lovely pictures. I have been waiting for your return so that I can tell the world how I discovered a scientific phenomena." It was their boss Stanton, the head of the Geographical Survey and Scientific Institute.

"Where's all your equipment McGill. I'll have it all docked from your pays." growled another voice.

"Yes, we want to know exactly what you saw." said some foreign sounding person.

Ben turned to his brother and said sarcastically

"Oh no! Its not welcome home Ben and Frank McGill. Glad you survived McGill! How would you like to take a few weeks off Mr McGill! Oh no! It's more like, come here McGill! Give us your reports McGill and let's screw you for everything like last time McGill."

"When you're quite finished McGill, it's us that sent you on that mission. Now just tell me who you spoke to about all this." Stanton demanded menacingly.

"Hang about now Stanton. If I remember correctly, you wanted all the team off the mountain area. I was the one that decided to take on the second part. We were forced to take a different route back, and it was my brother and me that made all the decisions out there, not you. Why are you trying to steal from us yet again? What have we found that you want all to yourself?" Ben demanded.

"The thing is, you two should not have been in that last place. It is a restricted area, and any pictures or data coming from it are to be confiscated, and handed to the Ministry for Defence." the mysterious voice said gruffly.

"Who said so? Just who the hell are you mister?" Ben demanded from this foreign intruder.

"This is my Soviet counterpart here to pay us a little visit. Mr Silienko meet the McGill brothers who produced your last survey." Stanton said off handedly.

"Ah yes! The McGills." Silienko said softly and nodded his head.

"You see Mr McGill, when you, shall we say, strayed into a certain area, you then became subject to the Soviet Military regime. Your boss Mr Stanton and I have a special understanding that circumvents these procedures that benefit us all. And in the process, help keep the status quo between our two nations. All you have to do is hand over your equipment and records to us, we'll see that they get used wisely." Silienko said in almost perfect English.

"I saw you speaking to a couple of the reporters. What deal have you struck with them?" asked Fanshaw, the organisation's accountant.

"Deal? Oh yes! A deal with the press!" Frank started, and nudged Ben to alert him.

"We've signed up with the reporter from the National Waterways Board, I think they called themselves."

"Yeah, and someone borrowed our video-cam, but we've got it back now. So as far as you're concerned Stanton, you can take a running jump." Ben said as he switched on to what Frank was up to.

"Why you stupid idiots!" Fanshaw exploded.

"Those were special films we gave you. You'll just have to go back and make some more out of your own pocket or I'll sue you for the loss."

"You always have been a penny pincher Fanshaw. What insurance have you covered us for? Perhaps a couple of million? Split only between you and Stanton? I'll bet our Mr Silienko here, doesn't know about it!" Ben sniped as he looked at Silienko who was looking at Stanton in puzzlement.

"Now then, lets be sensible McGill. If you give us all the films you've taken over the last few days, then we'll forget the price of replacing your equipment. And for good measures, you both can have a nice ten day vacation to wherever you choose." Stanton said smoothly.

"Yes and I'll even chip a few dollars to spend too." Fanshaw croaked.

"Yes! A nice few weeks on the Black sea should bring back the warmth in your bones again. I'll lend you my private villa, my concubines and even my yacht for the occasion." Silienko offered generously.

Ben and Frank had known something like this would happen again, instead of a hero's return. This time they were going to play their bosses along with their own charades that they were setting up.

"Well let's see now," Ben started, as he delved into his sack and dug out the scanner. "The scanner has taken about twelve hours of scan data from the area, which as you both know goes directly via the microwave radio link into the monitor console in the lab. Both of you have already got all that material.

"Have you Silienko? If so, then why do you need the video films?"

His question to Silienko and the look he got back told Ben that something was up, as if someone was double dealing somewhere.

"You know the scanner only gives technical data but it was useless for our purposes because someone forgot to switch the transmitter on. We have had no data from it for days now." Stanton snapped

"Besides, it's only the video film that shows exactly what's what, as it's on real time happening."

"So if we give you the films you will make it into a publicity stunt, yes, and hail us as heroes?" Frank asked testing his theory.

"Yes, now you've got it. So just hand them over so that we can all go home." Fanshaw said in a pleading voice.

"Bullshit! Crap with a capital K!" Frank shouted and spat on the floor of the van.

"We've discovered a natural phenomena, witnessed it live and are the only survivors to tell what happened. Unless something special happened to make that mountain crack open like a pea pod and fall down like that? Maybe that's where you come in, is it Silienko?" Frank shouted vehemently at Stanton and Fanshaw

"If that's the case, then where are we heading for now Stanton? Making a deal with the Commies to hide their nuclear explosion that went wrong?" Ben asked with equal vehemence, but kept his eye on Silienko who started to look furtively around the cavernous van.

"We're going back to my office. Mr Silienko here needs to examine the films before any can be used." Stanton replied flatly.

"Frank I hope you've got one of your feelings right now, because I've the feeling we won't make the night out." Ben whispered.

"Yes, that's what my gut tells me too, unless we play it smart."

"The thing is Stanton, why are you doing all this? Surely you know that the government has the Special Investigation Branch on this, because you did not give us a SABRE to take with us over our last section?" Ben asked, then threatened them with: "Unless you are as stupid as you look, kidnapping us will put you into deeper water than just with the Minister for Defence. Because one phone call or contact with them is all it will take. No doubt, your own government would like to know of your dealings with us so called filthy capitalists Silienko."

Fanshaw just laughed in Ben's face and said

"You'll be too deep in financial trouble when I've finished with you punks, to be able to afford even a penny phone call."

Stanton and Silienko whispered quietly to each other as Fanshaw held a gun out to show the brothers they were not to try anything rash.

"Well here we all are gentlemen. Back safe and sound at my office. I think you'll see some changes around here since you've been away McGill." Stanton announced, as the van came to a juddering halt.

As the brothers stepped out of the van, Stanton grabbed the sack Ben was carrying and said

"I'll take the video camera McGill. It's all mine now. I'll give you a receipt when we get up to my office."

"Yeah! I bet you will. And a one way ticket out, wearing a concrete overcoat." Ben hissed as he looked angrily at Stanton.

Fanshaw relieved Frank of the sack he was carrying, and shoved him roughly towards an open lift that was to take them up the tall building.

"Now just get in there McGill." he growled.

"Welcome gentlemen! Come in." it was the voice of the hauty female TV reporter.

Before the brothers realised that they were in Stanton's office, they were grabbed from behind and frog-marched towards a metal trellis frame, to which they were brutally and unceremoniously tied. Their assailants left the room leaving the woman and the large man they met earlier.

"I hate loose ends gentlemen." she purred as she inspected the tightly bound brothers.

"Now, what where you saying about my fanny?" she asked Ben as she grabbed him roughly by his genitals..

"Hmm! You're much smaller than you speak for such a big man." she said as she belittled him.

"I'll have these pitiful excuses for genitals off you quicker than that, unless you tell me what I want to know." she said as she clicked her fingers then continued to toy purposefully with a large hunting knife.

Frank looked around and saw the big man who had rescued them from the media circus.

"Well what do you know. There's Bluto over there. And I suppose you're Olive " he snarled at the woman, as he tried to wriggle out of his bonds.

The man advanced menacingly over to the brothers, but was stopped by the woman who said soothingly to calm him down

"Now now Victor, don't damage the goods just yet. Not until I have finished with them, then you can have your fun."

The man just roared like a lion and stood where he was.

"See! All you men are just like pussy cats, when it gets down to it. Now let's see just who is the best." she stated as she karate chopped Frank across the throat, making him cough and gasp for air.

"What's your point, Fanny features! What is it you want?" Ben shouted to prevent the woman hitting Frank again.

"Me? Little Fanny features like me?" she asked demurely before she aimed a kick at Ben's crotch, but missed as he managed to dodge it.

Victor! You stupid moron, I thought I told you to tie them up tight. This one is able to walk around the room. You stupid cretin, get it fixed so that he doesn't move one muscle unless I decide which one he can." she shouted.

Victor walked over meekly and re tied Ben's bonds.

Ben looked into Victor's eyes but saw an empty glaze over them as if he was in a trance.

"Now then Ben McGill lets try that one more time." she said, as she ripped Ben's trousers open with the knife, grabbed a hold of his exposed genitals then held the knife to them.

"Now now Pussykins! You've had your fun for now, don't damage the merchandise until we examine the films!" It was Stanton's unwitting but timely interruption that stopped her.

"Thanks for the surprise Stanton. Apart from about to make me into a eunuch like Lurch over there, what has she got to do with everything? I thought she was just a snooty TV reporter." Ben gasped as the woman finally let go of him.

"On the contrary McGill. She is my little pussycat from across the border. It's her government that wants the films you took. All I want is the money those films will cost them."

"So Lurch here is one of her men is he? What about Silienko? Where does he fit into all this?"

"Mr Silienko is none of your business. Let's say, he's just a business associate with mutual interests."

Ben looked at Silienko and saw that it was patently obvious that he was not part of this little set up.

"What's your cut out of all this Silienko? How about you Lurch?" Ben shouted.

"I'll bet Fanshaw's done you a deal on the scanner but not the films. I reckon that when you've seen the films may not be of use to you, you'll be wanting compensation for your trouble. In fact, I'd also bet that having killed me and my brother afterwards, even with a nice little two million dollar pay out on our insurance, you'll get nothing, and the deal we did with a journalist will only go to Fanny features here!"

Ben's outburst started to unsettle Silienko who just shrugged his shoulders and turned round to speak to Lurch.

An awkward silence fell onto the room, that was suddenly broken by Fanshaw as he burst out of the private lift.

"What's up Fanshaw?" Stanton asked anxiously as he stared at the red-faced man who was literally foaming at the mouth.

"I'll tell you what's up. We've been double-crossed that's what!" Fanshaw screamed.

"Calm down and tell us exactly what you mean by double-crossed?" Stanton commanded sternly, as he looked at Silienko and then at the brothers.

Fanshaw walked over to a large desk, and threw the terrain scanner and videocam roughly onto it, making several dents in the highly polished veneer.

"Exhibit One." he commenced. "The scanner transmitter must have got damaged, as we've no data for the last few days, right? So it means that any data not transmitted would be contained in its memory chip, and transmitted on the next occasion, right? So where is the micro chip? If it's not in the scanner, who took it?"

Before Fanshaw could say anything else, Silienko rushed over to the scanner and examined it closely.

"You promised me the micro chip to this machine of yours. I hope you have a spare one Stanton. The films better be here too." Silienko hissed ominously.

"No, it's the only one of its kind, and besides it's the only one with the terrain memory in it." Frank said with glee, as if to rub the point in.

Ben managed to catch Frank's eye and gave him a wink. Both knew there was going to be one hell of a ding dong argument here.

The woman walked swiftly over to the scanner then over to Frank again.

"One or both of you must have taken it out and hidden it somewhere. Strip search them and let's find out." she said with rising anger in her voice.

"We're wasting our time and its no good searching them. They don't have the key to open this box, and anyway, where could they have done that when we were with them all the time." Stanton said swiftly.

"Before you go any further, that's not all." Fanshaw said, which stopped any further move towards the brothers.

"The films for the video camera are missing too. Which means –"

"Which means you've got diddley squat! And fancy letting Fanshaw look after the merchandise." Frank laughed, which brought swift retribution in the form of another karate chop from the woman.

"Yes! Even Fanny features here, she was one of the reporters we did a swift deal with too." Ben added with a convincing nod.

Silienko signalled to Lurch who produced a large automatic machine pistol from his waist-belt and waved it at Stanton and Fanshaw.

"It appears Stanton, and you Fanshaw, that my trust in you is misplaced. It seems you both like to play roulette." Silienko said as he pulled out a revolver and placed it at the head of Fanshaw.

"Now then Stanton. Tell me how you planned to get away with all this? Maybe, if when I get to three and you don't tell me, your friend Fanshaw will suffer from instant lead poisoning." he threatened and counted as far as two.

"It's no good shooting him Silienko, he's just the bookkeeper. You can catch up with him later. It's Stanton who has the secret keys." Ben said as he egged Silienko on.

"Miss TV, search them all and lets see what we can find." Silienko demanded, and she started to do his bidding without ceremony.

"So you're in with Silienko, Fanny features? I got you down for a pet lap dancer that Stanton uses on a daily basis." Frank rasped as his throat was still sore.

"Nothing from the mountain men." she stated as she went over to Stanton and Fanshaw.

Lurch had, by now, stood close to Ben and was watching the proceedings.

"What about you Lurch? You've been stuffed just like my brother and me. Maybe it's Silienko you should be searching. He's the only one that was tampering with our rucksacks when we got into the van." Ben insinuated.

"Yeah! Come to think of it, it was pretty dark in the back where he was." Frank said as he joined in the baiting with his brother.

The woman finished searching Stanton and Fanshaw and stated that there was nothing on them either.

"Ring a ring a rosies a pocket full of camfilms" Ben started to chant, which brought an instant response from Silienko, who fired a shot at Ben but missed.

Lurch, who was momentarily surprised by this, thinking the shot was meant for him, shot back, but hit Fanshaw instead. Before Silienko could fire again, Stanton snatched a gun from the dead Fanshaw's jacket pocket, then grabbed the woman and held it to her head.

"Okay you double crossing Soviet son of a prostitute, drop your guns or she gets it. You too Quasimodo, drop it!" he said menacingly.

Silienko threw his gun down, but Lurch hesitated and was shot through the chest.

"Now get out of my way!" Stanton hissed as he moved slowly over to the open lift dragging the woman backwards with him.

"Where will you go Stanton? The minute you get out of this place, you're a dead man. Besides, we know where the films are kept. Sorry for spoiling your little bit of fun Fanny, but you know how it is." Ben stated.

"Oh you do, do you! Then I'm obviously taking the wrong patsy here." Stanton said as he clubbed the woman savagely over the head with his gun, knocking her out.

Stanton came over to Ben, waving the gun in his face.

"If you tell me where they are I'll let you live. If not then your brother is next to die."

"Stanton. You don't want to do that otherwise you'll never find them."

"Why's that McGill?" Stanton snarled as he held his gun at Franks head.

"Because I know only half of what you want. He knows only the other. So you'll need us both. But won't that be risky handling two men instead of a piece of fanny? After all, she was the one that offered us a good deal!" Ben said convincingly, as he glanced over to Silienko, to see that he was moving very slowly over towards the gun he threw down.

"Yes. Untie us and we'll help you. All we want is to go home and have a nice holiday. You can have all the glory, but you must kill Silienko first." Frank chipped in to goad Stanton, who was beginning to look nervously around to see what his next move would be?

Silienko managed to grab hold of his gun again just as Stanton spun round and shot him, and Silienko fell dead under the table next to Lurch.

He untied Frank from his rack but re-tied his hands up behind him, and did the same to Ben.

"Then there was three." Ben said sarcastically.

"Right you two, move." Stanton said as he kept shoving the brothers towards the lift.

Ben was a bit taller than Frank, and shielded him when he saw that Frank had managed to untie his wrists and was pretending that he was still tied up.

Frank flicked two fingers at Ben to indicate that he was about to do something and very soon.

Frank went into the lift followed closely by Ben and they stood there pretending to wait for Stanton.

As Stanton entered the lift, Frank leapt towards him, taking him by surprise, and shoved him away with such force that it made him stumble and fall backwards over the unconscious woman. Frank pressed the lift door button and took the lift down to the next floor, where they got out and phoned the SIB. and the Sheriff.

They didn't wait long for several well dressed men sporting SIB badges, to arrive on the scene.

"Hey, what's the score with all them upstairs?" Frank asked off handedly.

"Stanton was selling state secrets to Silienko. Fanshaw was the money man. Miss Turnbull, is one of our double agents. The other one was one of Silienko's top agents." The chief SIB agent explained.

"Some double agent. Fanny features, Miss Turnbull that is, was almost ready to make me speak with a permanently high voice, if Stanton hadn't turned up when he did." Ben quipped sardonically.

"Just doing her job, like all of us McGill." another agent stated in a high pitched voice and without emotion, then left to take charge of the heavily armed policemen strutting around the place.

Shortly after the SIB men disappeared leaving the brothers to their own devices, they heard the echo of a single gunshot coming from the lift shaft.

"Stanton's pay off, probably from Fanny features, Ben." Frank said knowingly as he patted his stomach.

The brothers recovered the vital films and records and showed them to the world, not only the result of a rogue nuclear explosion, but also the catastrophic phenomena it caused, that was never seen before.

For their services, they were promoted to become joint Head of the Ordinance Survey Department. Ben and Frank went back several years later, for just one more time before they retired.

They discovered that the lakes had refilled themselves from a brand new waterfall that cascaded from the fallen mountain.

New trees had grown in place of the ones that were washed

away, forming a so called 'Trim Line' which was their true discovery. It was called that because that's where the light green of the new trees make a nice neat line against the darker green of the much older trees higher up on the mountain side.

The remains of the mountain were called Pebble Mountain.

Lake Long was re-designated as Rocky Lake.

The village of Lucky Creek was rebuilt with all the felled trees and is now a favourite tourist attraction but re-designated, ironically, as Dead Lucky Creek.

The tall column of rocks that was the remains of their promontory camp has now got a large log chalet on it, built by some intrepid woodsman.
　　It is now a fixture on the new Ordinance Surveyor's map of the area, and designated as 'Ben Frank' as in the 'Ben Nevis' mountain in Scotland.
And so dear reader, the next time you look at an ordinance survey map or even a road map, try and imagine how and why all the places you see got those names.
　　I did!

Moreland & Other Stories

The Crow's Nest

Wally Green slung his bag over his shoulder, picked up his life jacket, and shut the door of his house as he left to walk down the steep cobbled streets towards the harbour.

"Mornin' Wally Green. Off fishing again? Give me a kiss before you go then." Sarah asked as she stood in the doorway of her house.

On seeing her, he walked over and pecked her lightly on her cheeks. He was a shy young man in front of female company, even though the two of them were childhood sweethearts.

"Is that all I get. Is that all I'm worth Wally Green?" she asked angrily.

He looked at her, shrugged his shoulders, hugged her quickly then started back down the steep hill again.

"A girl can't wait forever you know, Wally Green. It's always your ship and the sea. I always come last with you. There's other boys who fancy me, just you wait and see Wally Green. " she sobbed as she watched him go.

"Mornin Wally!". It was his Father, who was the skipper and owner of the fishing trawler Wally sailed on.

"Mornin skipper."

"Seen Sarah before you came down?" he asked but never waited for an answer.

"Never mind. Once we bring home a good catch, you'll be able to court her decent." his father said softly as he looked at his tall, slim built 18 year old son.

"I need the money to wed her Father. But we can't seem to catch enough fish to earn it. I'm always at sea and that Jimmy Logan who's been seen hanging around her, will get her for sure." Wally stated with sadness.

"Never mind him. That Logan and his ilk are a bad lot, end up in jail before long. She'll see sense in keeping faith with you, my Maggie Morton is proof of that, you just wait and see what I mean." his father said cheerfully and slapped Wally gently on the back as he walked over the gangway.

Sarah wanted them to get married and earn enough money to own a whole fleet of fishing vessels, like her father used to own, but now only operates just the one.

But Wally wanted to go to sea in the ocean going liners, and maybe one day be the captain of a big ship, or even own one himself instead of staying as a crewman on his Fathers' vessel.

"Get your gear stowed below Wally we're sailing on this next tide and we have the nets still to be winched and feathered aboard yet."

Wally did as he was told and appeared on deck some minutes later.

"How long this time skipper?" it was old Sid Beer, the only survivor of the last vessel he was on, that sank during a severe storm earlier in the year.

"We've got to go up north and join up with the Scottish Fishermen at some place called Stromness which is way up in the Orkney Islands off Scotland." Green started.

"That'll take us nearly a week. Why so far?" Beer butted in.

"The official line is that we have to go up to get the

Icelandic cod instead of fishing in the Channel. According to my orders we'll up there for about three months before coming home again." Green stated.

By now the twenty man crew were crowded around the skipper listening and asking questions that bothered them, and generally getting very anxious about their families ashore.

"To put you all at rest." he said.

"There are other vessels from other places along the way, who will be coming with us. It's the King's Order." he announced, which seemed to allay the fears of the crew.

The vessels cast their ropes from the jetty and puffed their way out of their sheltered harbour, through the narrow entrance and out into the open waters of the Channel. Wally stood in the bridge of the ship and looked at the sight that always made him feel as if he belonged to the sea, as he saw the others steaming away in a line behind him. His fathers' ship was named after him and was the fastest in the whole southern fishing fleet, and lived up to its name as the GREEN ARROW. It was a new ship with lots of new fangled equipment on board to use. As it was much bigger and more powerful than all the others, and able to race through the waters at a handsome 18 knots. The smaller and less equipped fishing vessels used it as a kind of mother ship to them when in any difficulty or bother.

For three days the little flotilla of fishing boats steamed their way up through the choppy waters of the Irish sea, gathering in large numbers as they went until there was an armada of them snaking their way ever northwards, playing follow the leader.

"Gather round men!" Green announced, as he unrolled a large sea map out onto the crew's living quarters table.

"We'll be arriving into Campbeltown shortly to get our nets changed, pick up coal and other provisions, before we can make our way through the islands and up to the Orkneys. This means we can enjoy a few extra hours in port, as we wait for the others to catch up with us."

This announcement brought a hearty cheer from the crew.

"We will be in port for about a day or so, which means that each of you will have time get whatever extra clothing you need and also to write off home."

"Beggin' yer pardon skipper." It was Beardmore the Engineer.

"We need to get proper steam coal for this next run, else we'll coke up the boilers too quickly with the rubbish we're burning now."

"Good point! I've been promised Welsh steam, and even an extra twenty tons of it per vessel."

"I can manage that skipper, but what about the SPINTAIL, she'd be too low in the water with that and her full cargo of fish?"

"That's for their skipper to worry about. Just you keep this ship moving and us warm inside it. Besides, we can carry some of her coal for her for when she needs it" Green said with a smile, which brought a nod of approval from the men.

"Will we get special Sou'westers and special clothing skipper?" It was Pardoe one of the winch operators.

"Only if we're going fishing up in the Arctic we'd need better protection against the freezing waters." he asked with concern.

Green met each question posed with the genuine responses that his crew had always received from him. They knew that he was a plain-speaker, nor has ever lied to his men, and he was always ready to help any of his crew who was in difficulty, which was the very reason why he was much liked and respected.

The GREEN ARROW tied up alongside the Campbeltown's long wooden jetty that had large pyramids of coal next to it.

"Good Mornin' Captain! I'm John Petrie the yard manager here." he shouted cheerfully as he introduced himself to Green who had just walked over the narrow gangway and stepped on shore.

"Good morning Mr Petrie. I'm Captain Ted Green. You've

got some handsome piles of coal over there. Is some of that mine?" he asked as he shook hands with Petrie.

"All that pile in the corner over there is just for you, if you can handle it. There's over a hundred tons of it, but you're to take as much as you can as there isn't much coal left where you're going. It's brown coal, but it's steam grade. The WELSH CORGI and the PEMBROKE QUEEN are not due up there until next week with the Welsh steam, so that's all I can give you." Petrie explained civilly.

Green looked at the coal heap, which was much bigger than he was used to ordering, and felt for his wallet.

"Don't even think about that Captain. All the piles you see, are special loads for each of your vessels as paid by the King's Navy."

"The King's Navy? What do they want with me? It's a good measure of coal I grant you, which should keep me seagoing for about 10 weeks. I'm sure my Engineer will be pleased with it, and we thank you for it anyway Mr Petrie." Green replied then went on to ask about his other supplies which drew various answers and explanations from Petrie.

"Before we speak any further, there's a couple of people who would like to see you back in the office over yonder. Once we've spoken with them, then we'll get you fitted out. Where's the rest of your vessels Captain?"

"There's another five vessels from my lot coming in behind us, they should be here in about an hour or so. There's a further ten vessels coming, according to my reckoning about two hours behind them again."

"Och nae bother! Ann dinny fash yerself! I'll have your vessel coaled before that. When your vessel is finished you'll have to move over to the other jetty so the other vessels can come alongside here and get theirs. Your stokers will enjoy themselves as we've got a special machine with belts on it that will pick up the coal from its pile and carry it directly down into your bunkers. Saves all that shovelling and the rest of it.

You must see it working to appreciate it." Petrie bragged.
"Sounds interesting Mr Petrie, I'd like that. Maybe I'll be able to get one for my yard too." Green admitted, then turned round to look for his son.
"Wally! Come with me!" Green shouted over to Wally, who was working on deck. Wally put his brush down and followed his father and Petrie along to a brick building that had wooden steps going up one side of it.

They climbed up them and entered a large room with windows all around it to look out of. Over the doorway was the name Harbour Master.
"Captain Green off the GREEN ARROW meet Captain Rose the Harbourmaster." Petrie announced, as he introduced Green.
"Good morning Harbourmaster. This is my son Wally, but he's also my First Mate."
"Ah good morning Captain Green, I have Mr Joliffe here from the Lords of the Admiralty and a Mr Brown, from Marconi who will be your temporary Radio Officer." Rose stated as he introduced the other men waiting patiently beside him.
"You and the two others over a hundred feet will be fitted out with items not normally used on your type of vessel. A Naval gun with gunners to operate it. A special ramp over the back where your nets are hauled in, and the necessary wireless equipment for Mr Brown's usage. These will be done at no cost to your good self, as they have been financed by the Lords of the Admiralty." Rose commenced, then went into details of what lay ahead of Green and the other captains in the flotilla of fishing vessels.
Green took it all in what was said before he made his own conclusions.
"So, we're going to fish in a new sea area, drop off a few lobster pots, and report any ships we see. Huns did you call them?"

"Yes, Captain! Since you put to sea to come up here, and since you've not equipped your ship with a wireless, you missed out on the news that we'd declared a punch up with an upstart in Germany. It should all be over by Hogmanay." Rose said smugly.

"The wireless is fair comment, but we're only fishermen. Why can't you send the Kings'' Navy to do what is asked?"

"The simple reason is, that for the moment and until Scapa Flow is rigged out and equipped to take the battleships of our Home fleet, we of the Merchant Navy must plug the gap." Mr Brown offered.

"If we're going north to stooge around and fish at the same time, then the poor person in the crows' nest will be in for a stiff time." Wally observed.

"What do you mean exactly?" Petrie asked

"Well, you see sir! Our crows nest is very open, and is only used for just an hour or so, before we cast our nets out to fish. If you need someone as lookouts to stay up there longer than that, unless there's some sort of cover or heat to keep warm, he'll freeze and die. The masts would need to be re-inforced to take the extra weight, or with one big whip from the mast would snap it off like a matchstick.

Besides the fact that the poor person keeping a long watch up there would be subjected to a much wider arc of motion, giving that it would be further out from the ship's centre of gravity" Wally stated respectfully.

"Hmm! He's raised some valid points there." Rose conceded, and stood for a moment, thinking of a solution to the problems.

"Maybe if we strengthen the main mast, put a good shelter with a roof over it, and put in one of those new electric heaters that Mr Brown will be using to keep his wireless equipment warm. The rest would be down to the stamina of the crewman that will man this raised observation post. He would have to be a volunteer, as it's no fun being stuck up a 60foot mast in the middle of a gale, and I speak from long experience of such matters." Rose stated, after several minutes.

The subject was thrashed through at length before they went onto other matters.

"Then what about the extra men? We'd need extra rations and other supplies. We have just enough space for all that, but what about the other smaller vessels like the SPINTAIL or the KINGFISHER, that came with me? As you say, there's about three of us over a hundred foot long, the others average of about forty foot less than me." Green asked, which started another round of discussions.

No sooner than the meeting was satisfactorily concluded, there was the sound of the other vessels tooting their horns, as they came into the harbour.

"Well Mr Green! You are now a Captain of a Naval Volunteer Force, and it is for you now to organise your ships according to our instructions. You will be given all the recognition and accord of a Captain of the Royal Navy for the duration of your command." Rose said magnanimously.

"He means that you'll get more pay in one month than what you'd probably make in six months fishing." Joliffe said with a smile.

"If my ship is to be used as an armed merchantman, then will you pay the crew the going rate too, and recompense me if my ship is damaged or lost, Mr Joliffe?"

"You can be sure of one thing Captain Green, if you've been given an unlimited supply of coal for your ship and supplies for your crew then we would not baulk at paying your men whatever is their due."

"Very well Mr Joliffe, I accept your charge." Green stated.

"But what about the other Captains and their crews, Harbourmaster?" Wally asked politely

"They will act under Captain Green's orders, and will be

paid according to the duties they will perform." was the reply.

"Well gentlemen! Its time to get ourselves organised and get this flotilla back out to sea." Joliffe said swiftly to prevent any further delays and discussions.

Wally and his Father walked back down the yard with Petrie, who was pointing out the different features that his new yard was given, and arrived back at the wooden jetty where all the other Captains stood waiting for Greens' return.

Green was not the most senior captain in terms of years at sea, but he was mutually accepted as the spokesperson for them all, including the Captains of the other fishing villages that joined them.

"Greetings to you all. Glad you all made it then, even if some of you were down to your last shovel of coal." Green started, which created a swell of banter from the waiting fishermen.

Green waited for a moment then introduced Petrie, then he went on to give them a brief run down on what he was told, and what was to be expected from them. All of which brought jeers and catcalls, which Green let die down before he spoke again.

"We will have the rest of today in port, so get yourselves and your crews organised. Mr Petrie here has very kindly donated a case of the finest whiskey, which will be sampled later on in, and with the Harbourmaster at nineteen hundred hours." he managed to finish, as the men cheered loudly when they heard about the free whiskey.

That day saw frantic preparations and innovative additions to the vessels, with the last possible nook or cranny used up with the extra stores and equipment that was to be taken with them. Even the fish cargo holds were loaded up with supplies and materials.

It was dusk when everything stopped, time for the men to have a good bath and a meal, with Green and his Captains enjoying a bottle of home comforts in the warmth of the

Harbourmasters office.

It took the flotilla a further three days to reach their destination, as the seas were getting bigger and much colder the further north they went. They sailed into the large natural harbour of Scapa Flow and made a raft of themselves as they tied up alongside one another, with the GREEN ARROW next to the small stone jetty that represented the docks of Stromness.

"Ahoy Mr Green. Glad to see that you all arrived together." it was Joliffe.

"How did you get here Mr Joliffe, Angel wings?" Green asked in astonishment.

"Came up on the train and then by that destroyer you see anchored in the bay."

"Come aboard and see me in the bridge." Green invited, which Joliffe did as soon as the gangway ladder was put safely into position.

"Remember Captain Rose from Campbeltown? Well he's been brought out of semi-retirement and promoted to Rear Admiral, and will be arriving soon on one of the fast destroyers. He's to set up a yard suitable for your little ships. He will have all your requirements and support facilities as and when you need them." Joliffe said as he shook hands with Green.

"Captain Rose? Hope he brings Mr Petrie and another case of that fine whiskey with him for good measure."

"I feel sure that Admiral Rose will furnish all your captains with a case each, if all goes well. In the meantime, you are to prepare your flotilla for an initial patrol of the islands north and east of here. But first, you are to take your supplies and land them over on the other side of the harbour at St Margaret's Hope.

There's a small inlet marked on the chart there, and earmarked just for you." Petrie informed Green as he handed out a large chart of the harbour. Then added

"Tomorrow, once you have discharged your loads over there, you will pick six vessels for your first patrol; the others will be suitably employed during your absence."

"Very well Mr Joliffe. But first you must meet some of the skippers and their crews off the other vessels. Maybe take some notes on the different sizes and types of vessels I have to look after."

The crewmen went ashore to stretch their legs and get to know the local people of Stromness, whilst Green and Joliffe stayed on board talking the evening away with the other skippers who came over to join them.

The morning was a bright and breezy one, as the flotilla sailed out of Scapa Bay.

They had deposited all their cargo and stores on a small slipway near a little village on the opposite end of the big harbour and finally made their way out to sea for their first fishing trip and sea patrol.

The extra men and stores on board made it very cramped, which meant that Green had to live on the bridge. The Naval Telegraphist was given a small area at the back of the bridge, where he also worked and lived.

Whilst the gun was not in use, the gunners and the 'lobster potters' were very popular with the rest of the crew, as they took great delight in helping out in any way they could. Wally volunteered to become the permanent lookout and had the crows nest re-designed so that he could even sleep there in relative comfort, if necessary.

It looked like an eggcup with a little hood over the top and skewered by a cocktail stick. In fact it had a proper wooden roof, and fitted with glass portholes to look out of when the weather was too bad. Brown's new fangled electric heater kept him warm, and he even found it was useful to make himself a brew up when he needed it. Any sightings he made with the high powered binoculars he had, he would tug on a length of wire that would ring a bell in the bridge warning them.

Each tug of the wire meant a different message on both ends, thus solving the problem of having to climb up and down the mast just to say something.

Their first patrol that lasted five days was uneventful apart from the good haul of fish they caught. The weather was getting worse as the men returned back to the safety of their new harbour now set up in a bay that had a large village on its shore line.

"How did it go Mr Green?" Petrie asked, as Green had his vessel tied up to the new jetty built for them.

"Hello Mr Petrie. I was told you'd be coming up here to keep us company. We've all got a good catch that we haven't seen for ages down south." Green replied cheerfully from his bridge.

"That's good, it will be well received ashore. No doubt your crew will be celebrating in the nearby alehouse, but you are requested to see the Admiral as soon as you're ready. I'll take you there."

"Be with you in a moment." Green said swiftly, as he went to get his hat and coat.

Petrie opened the car door for Green then drove off up the little hill towards the village.

"This is a pretty little place, much on the same lines as a village near us, except with a Scottish air to it." Green said pleasantly as he looked around him.

Petrie just chuckled and said patriotically.

"Well you're in the isles of Bonny Scotland after all."

The car took only a few minutes to arrive at a drab stone building that had a naval White Ensign fluttering on a flagpole over the door entrance. There was a large sign that said Naval Patrol and Boom Defence Flotilla.

"My, that's a handsome sign our Admiral has got, Mr Petrie." Green observed.

"Yes, he will be separate from the entire Home Fleet which is going to be based here. That's why we have been given a little bay and village to ourselves. We had a few sheds for supplies and the like, built whilst you were away. No doubt the Admiral will fill you in on the details." Petrie explained.

"Good morning Captain. I'm pleased you had a successful voyage up here, and had a chance to look around the islands" Rose greeted heartily.

"Congratulations on your promotion Admiral. Yes, we've managed." he said amiably as he shook hands with Rose.

Green was briefly introduced to two more officers from the Royal Navy, then settled down at a large table full of maps and charts.

"Gentlemen," Rose commenced. "We have to set up a series of mine fields and a patrol for the sea defence around the islands. Captain Green here will be in charge of the northern area. In his guise as a fishing fleet, he will be laying 'lobster pot' mines, and keeping watch for enemy ship movements north from here to the Faroe Islands. He will co-ordinate his squadron accordingly and will be under my direct control. Our job this end is to support them and to provide a boom defence for the whole Scapa Flow area." Rose explained, then went through various charts and detailed instructions, which lasted nearly four hours. The meeting went well, bringing up various points and observations that were dealt with efficiently and purposefully, punctuated by several cups of tea and biscuits.

Green and his flotilla were to be kept up in those waters until relieved, but he made the point that his crews were only meant to be out for about two to three months. The consideration was that they were only a scratch Naval Volunteer force, compared with the dreadnoughts and other mighty battleships already arriving in the harbour in great numbers.

This was now their temporary home and here Wally would try and earn enough 'catch money' to be able to get home and marry his childhood sweetheart.

"Ahoy ELLY MAY! Cap'n Weeks!" Green shouted into his loudhailer over to the next vessel.

"Speaking. What's up Ted?' Weeks shouted back, as he emerged from his wheelhouse.

"Follow me out and keep about 1 cable astern until we reach point Charlie. Pass it down the line." Green ordered as he tooted his fog horn

Weeks agreed as he waved and started to hail the next vessel behind him. Each vessel tooted their foghorn, to let Green know that they had their message

The small line of assorted fishing vessels puffed their way out of the bay, leaving the sleeping leviathans of battleships far behind them.

As they got further north the rain- squalls got more severe, the water started to create liquid mountains in front of the little ships. They bobbed up and down the watery troughs, but still making their way to their fishing grounds even further north to where the water turns to solid ice.

Wally was in his nest at the top of the foremast, which was way above the rest of the ship and was able to see the other vessels that stationed themselves either side of him.

His father chose him to be the eyes of the little fleet. His new job was that he stayed aloft all the time but was given the time off when he needed a toilet, or to get some hot food inside him.

For Wally, this little cocoon was his Kingdom. That, as far as he was concerned, only lacked the one thing that he longed for, his beloved Sarah Weeks. She was in his mind all the time and he felt angry with himself on times when he thought of how he shied away from her advances. He had resolved in himself that as soon as he had saved enough money, he'd marry Sarah and move away to somewhere, where his arch-rival in the village, Jimmy Logan, would not get to them. Logan was a son of a wealthy merchant and had always managed to outshine Wally at almost everything, except when it came to fishing, the vessels and the sea.

Wally may have lacked the scholastic achievement of Logan, but he was innovative and practically minded, enough to be able to understudy his father for when he became a skipper in his own vessel. None of the young men in his village had his mental ability to appreciate the handling and workings' of ships, or how to be able to handle the crew as his father did. This made him stand out from all the rest of his erstwhile school friends, which served as the constant and main source of annoyance to Logan. Even Sarah's father, Skipper Weeks, had taught him a thing or two. His favourite past time was to think of various situations or problems that he had seen or encountered, and try to solve them in a manner that he would have done.

It was during one of these moments as he looked out through his powerful binoculars, that he saw a small flickering light shining in the darkness ahead of him.

His eyes were accustomed to the dark, but he had to make another search around to see if there was any more to be found.

"Now where did I see you. Ah yes. Looks like a single mast head light of a fishing vessel. Must report it anyway." He muttered as he looked up the signal to use. Two pulls three times.

He pulled the lanyard that was tied to the wire as directed, which was repeated back to him to indicate that the bridge heard his instruction.

'I didn't know we had vessels up in front of us, unless one of our lot went ahead too far from the line we are trawling'. Wally thought as he used his glasses to count the rest of the vessels alongside him.

"Yes, all correct and accounted for, then who's in front of us?" He muttered, and made his signal again. His reply was to keep searching in that direction but make sure there's nothing else around. Wally looked all around and saw nothing but when he looked back again to the strange light, it had disappeared never to be seen again. His signal to the bridge told them so.

The dawn broke over the grey and white marbled sea, as Wally finally climbed down from his nest to stretch his legs and get some hot breakfast. He passed the other members of the crew who were singing their shanty songs, happy and joking as their nets were being hauled in, loaded with a bumper catch.

"Wally look at all this lovely fish! We should get a handsome price for this load when we get back" Sid said merrily.

"Aye and pay it all back if you don't watch the nets coming aboard." Jan Murch shouted angrily, as some of the fish cascaded all over him instead of down the fish hold. Wally laughed and scampered his way down into the crew's quarters.

He met the telegraphist who had come from his own little hideout on the bridge, and sat down next to him.

"Do you get the weather forecast on your machines? I'd like to see you work them, maybe have a go with them as well." Wally asked enthusiastically, as was his inquisitive nature.

"Yes. I get them every so often." the telegraphist started.

"But it's a pity you lost that light. We would love to know what it was and who it was. But glad it never came our way as it might have been a Hun U-boat." he concluded.

"What's the difference between a Hun ship and ours? Wally asked.

"One that shoots at you and the other waves to you." was the sarcastic reply from Johnson, one of the naval gunners who was acting as the helmsman.

"Take no notice of him Wally. You're doing a good job up there. Here's your breakfast." said Bill Harper the cook.

Wally ate his meal with gusto and declined a smoke from

one of the other gunners as he stood up and went up to the bridge to see his father.

"Morning skipper! Good catch last night?" he greeted his father.

"Morning Wally! Yes, very good! We've got room for one more load before we turn onto our next course." His father greeted, then showed him the chart where their position was marked and where they were heading for, and the return leg of their patrol.

"If we go up that far won't we hit one of those icebergs Skipper?"

"We can manoeuvre around them easily enough but we've got to stay up there for a couple of days. The Admiral sent us a signal this morning, which in effect says that the light you had seen was an enemy Battlecruiser, possibly from their Baltic fleet. According to some survivors that were picked up, it sank five out of the eight cargo ships out of Newfoundland and bound for Glasgow. If it's still around then we'll try to sight her and report her position, and with luck shadow her for a while."

"But those are very fast and dangerous ships. One shot from them and we'll all get blown out of the water. "Wally replied anxiously.

"No! We're too small a target for them to waste a shot at us. Anyway, although we can't out run them, the trick is to get under their guns so they can't hit us." Johnson advised.

Wally looked at the gunner's smiling face, which seemed to re-assure him.

"Before you go aloft again Wally." his father said quietly.

"The area we are in now, is subject to rapid forming and dense fog banks, much worse than back home. Sometimes it could last for days. There is also the added danger of rogue icebergs, which are so large they give off their own glow in the dark. You keep a sharp lookout for all our sakes, and report absolutely anything you see from up there. Remember there are five other vessels around us who will be relying on you."

"If that's the case skipper. My ladder is all iced up and very dangerous to use. I'd better grab some clean gear and extra warm clothing. I will have to eat my meals up there, so if you get the chef to put my meals into a bucket that has a lid on it, we can use it as a carrier for my things.

I shall be able to pull it up to me on a line and lower it back down on the next one. I'll also need a slop bucket with a lid, for use as a toilet."

"Fair enough. I shall see that you get anything you need sent up to you. One final and important item that our lives might be dependent on, Wally. As of tonight and every night, we will be switching off all lights and cause a black out on all the ships. Look closely at each vessel and report any lights that may be seen. We must hide ourselves as best we can if the Hun Navy decides to show up."

"In that case Skipper, I think you had better give me some more signal commands to cope with the information. Either that or rig up a small messenger line between me, and the bridge. Maybe a leather pouch or something." Wally suggested, as always the practical man.

"A messenger line sounds fine by me. I'll get the rest done for you. Good luck Son."

Wally took his time gathering up his needs and comforts before climbing back up to his own little nest. He settled himself down feeling quite secure and warm, with nothing better to do but look around the vast empty wastes of the ocean, and marvelling at the way the fishing vessels just seem to bob up and down in it, like children on a see-saw.

The day turned quickly into night, when yet another storm cloud burst itself above the fishermen, and churned the water into even bigger waves than before.

Wally looked down and around and reported to his father, all the lights he saw coming from the vessels. Slowly, one by one each was put out, leaving a total seemingly impenetrable blackness around him. As the blackness engulfed him so did an eerie silence, which seemed to put Wally onto a knife-edge of awareness.

The moon was piercing its light between the dark clouds, shining on patches of the foam topped faces of the waves when Wally saw some very large white shimmering apparitions way out in front of his ship. He carefully scrutinised these shapes that seemed quite near him due to the powerful lens of his binoculars, they were in fact some distance away.

Time 0400 hours. 2 possibly 3 icebergs spread out ahead, approx. ten miles Wally wrote in his logbook, then onto a piece of paper and sent it down the messenger line in its little string drawn pouch.

He laughed at the reply. "Draw them as accurate as you can."

But Wally obeyed, which took him a good hour to do so, and sent it back down the line.

He saw that the fishermen were moving closer to him and saw that they were moving slowly towards those bergs. Our speed's about three knots, distance to bergs about ten miles. Be there about breakfast time. Wally calculated, and was proved right.

He ate his bowl of hot porridge, bacon sandwiches and drunk his tea, all the while watching through his little porthole, watching the mountains of ice, creeping nearer to him.

This is probably what happened to that unsinkable ship. Don't fancy going swimming near those things. I hope Sarah is waiting for me. Hope the others are okay. The different thoughts raced through Wally's mind as he examined these monsters closely with his binoculars.

He saw that there were in fact five bergs in a loose cluster, with clear water in the middle. He drew another picture which took yet another hour and sent it down the line again.

No sooner had he sent the message down, he spotted several

columns of smoke coming from behind the furthest berg. Coal driven bergs? Whatever next! Funny things always happen at sea so Father says. Wally mused as he turned his attention to this new attraction.

Count 7 different columns of smoke all coming from behind and to the right of the bergs, was his next message and entry into his log.

He saw that the other trawlers were coming over to meet with his vessel, as they formed a raft around him. Then saw his father shout over to them and pointed towards the bergs. Soon his vessel was moving quite swiftly through the water followed by the others as they raced into the safety of the clear waters between the bergs.

He received a message saying that they were hiding in among the bergs, but he was to look at the pictures they sent up, to try and recognise any of the ships as they pass any gap he can see through.

Wally managed to identify three of them, which turned out to be giant battleships of the Hun navy. He could have sworn that they must have seen him as he managed to catch the eye of some officer standing on deck. He even drew the face as he sent back the information.

He held his breath waiting for the thunder of guns being fired at them, but the dark grey slabs of iron and steel warships slipped past their little hideaway, without a second glance.

It was almost midday before the little fishermen came out of hiding and started to make their way home again.

'*With luck we'll be in harbour for the weekend*' Wally thought cheerfully as he hauled up his supper in a bucket. Fish for supper! Well fancy that! Could do with a lovely bowl of broth he muttered sardonically and commenced to satisfy his hunger.

The passage back to harbour was uneventful and Wally managed to grab several hours of well-earned sleep before he finally climbed down and back onto the main deck again.

The little ships discovered that the whole bay was littered in massive warships, with all types of little boats darting in and around them.

"Phew! Just look at all that. There must be at least a million tons of iron and steel anchored out there." Downly remarked as he came up on deck from the stoke hold.

"A lot of men wanting some lovely fish for supper too." Jan Murch enthused as the rest of the crew stood gawping at all the fine, powerful looking men-o-war.

"I've got a brother on the Iron Duke over there, and a cousin on the Valiant next to it. I wish I was on one of them instead of this pokey thing." one of the gunners said with envy.

"What, and miss all that lovely fish we catch, that I cook for you every day?" Bill Harper teased, which started a round of banter between them.

Green listened quietly from his vantage point on the bridge, as his crew were getting shore happy and the sight of the entire navy waiting for them made it more worth while.

The little ships tied up to their jetty and started to unload their catches into some barges to be taken away for selling.

"We have a Kings' ransom in those catches, Ted! Wished it was like that in our areas." Weeks said softly as he watched the proceedings.

"Aye you're right there." Green echoed as he turned and stepped ashore to be greeted by Mr Petrie.

"Well done Captain! Your signal saved an awful lot of red faces with the brass hats here.

"What has the Admiral got to say then?" Green commenced but was cut short by Petrie, who said pleasantly

"Actually the Admiral would like to see you. Bring your son with you." Petrie stated as he drove Green and his son to the HQ.

Rose, who was looking out of his window at the view of the whole harbour saw that Green had arrived and greeted him.

"Ah good morning Captain. Some good job you did. I shall read your logs and reports later. Have a cup of tea won't you. You too, young man!" Rose invited.

After a while of discussing the past week's trip out to sea, Rose turned to Wally and said

"It seems young man, because of your vigilance and sharp eyes, not only did you save your little squadron of fishing boats from being sunk by icebergs or even by a whole squadron of Hun battleships, you managed to save half of the King's Navy.

We were given just enough time from the warning signal your Telegraphist sent and managed to get our big battleship squadrons out. The Hun are running flat out, all the way back to Germany."

"Well Admiral. My father did it all. I was only the lookout." Wally started modestly.

"Nonsense my boy! You're being too modest. The Royal Navy could do with your sort. I'll speak to the Home Fleet about you. You'll get a handsome reward for this young man, mark my words." Rose professed as he tapped his breast pocket.

'I know I wanted to sail on big ships, but this is not the answer,' Wally thought as he looked to his father for support.

"I'd just as soon as stay with Captain Green and the rest of the squadron, if you don't mind Admiral. I would make a better fisherman than a battleship captain." Wally said swiftly to try and get out of this sudden crises.

"Yes Admiral, besides, if anything should happen to me then who would take over my ship." Green said convincingly in defence of his son.

Mr Joliffe also spoke in Wally's defence which made Rose finally concede to the points made, but re-stated that the King would reward Wally and his Father for their services.

When the meeting was over, Petrie took the Greens' down to the local hotel where all the skippers where billeted, with the men put in the specially made huts.

"This is your home ashore. All your needs and that of your crews, within reason, will be met by the Admiralty." Petrie announced, as the car arrived outside a whitewashed building with the name 'The HOPE Hotel' emblazoned over its entrance.

The weekends in port seemed to fly past as Wally strolled lazily down the road towards his other, more familiar little home that was sleeping peacefully alongside the jetty.

His mind was filled with thoughts of Sarah and the conflicting feelings he discovered he had for Moira, the young waitress at the hotel, whom he had met and spoken several times to. Maybe it was her company that he enjoyed that spirited the weekends away.

For over the next few weeks when he stayed at the hotel, he would seek her out and go for long walks around the island. He even got to meet, to know, and to like Moira's parents and younger brothers and sisters.

But it was Weeks and his father who advised him to be very careful not to upset the pretty lass when he told her about Sarah. Or of the fact that he was fishing in these waters for a short time only before having to leave for the south coast of England

"Skipper Weeks, Father! Sarah and I have been childhood sweethearts, and we have promised to wed when we have saved enough money and the time is right for us. But we share little except life in the fishing fleet. She wants to rebuild your lost fishing fleet, Skipper Weeks. But I want to own an even bigger ship than the Green Arrow. A ship that will ply its trade across the world." Wally explained, as he sat next to them in the saloon of the hotel.

"Aye Wally! 'Tis plain you and Sarah belong, but you really must stop building up the hopes of that lass, or you will end up hurting her badly. What's her name? How are you managing with her tongue, do you understand what she says?" Weeks asked in a barrage of questions.

"Does the lass know of Sarah?" Green asked

"I have told her about what I would like to do, and." Wally started to answer this unexpected questioning.

"But have you told the lass about you and Sarah?" his Father persisted.

"Yes skipper Weeks! I can understand her tongue very well. Her name is Moira. No Father, I have not told her I have a girl back in harbour, and that I will be going back soon."

"That's very foolish of you Wally, you really should not have started playing with the affections of that girl. She might have set her sights on you, and you are a good catch especially in the fishing fraternity, but how will you end it? What would Sarah say if she found you fouling your nets?" Weeks demanded.

Before he could answer, Moira arrived with her coat and asked if Wally would walk her home. Wally accepted, and nodded to his Father and Weeks as he left them.

"Who is the man with your Father, Wally? He looks fairly angry at something, is it something you've done?" Moira asked.

"That's skipper Weeks off the Elly May" Wally said but declined to answer the second question.

The two walked hand in hand along the dirt track towards a spot they liked to sit and look over the bay at the ships coming and going. Finally as they were leaving to return back to the hotel, he embraced her and kissed her tenderly as she nestled in his strong arms.

It was seemingly a new life that had just entered his heart, as he looked deep into Moira's eyes. Somehow he had grown up, and realised that the girl in his arms had awakened something inside him that his life long girlfriend had never done.

Maybe the years of being together had made Sarah and

Wally grow so used to each others demands and rebukes, that everything seemed second nature, and as if marriage would cast its magic spell on them.

"Moira, there's something I must tell you!" he started, but Moira just kissed his lips as if to stop him from speaking.

"I know Wally, I feel the same."

Wally tried again to speak but she kissed every word from his lips as she held him tight.

"You're going to be my man. You are going to be famous one day, and I'm going to be the mother of all your bairns." Moira whispered in his ear.

They walked slowly back to the hotel savouring every moment in each other's company, then with a last kiss, Moira skipped away from him and out of sight, as he walked into the gloomy hotel lounge.

He saw his father and another skipper talking about the next fishing trip and decided to join them, sitting down quietly next to them whilst they talked.

"Ah! There you are Wally, I thought you got turned in. Have a beer?" his father said cheerfully

"Only it will be your last one before we sail tomorrow for our final patrol and then store up before returning home."

"Last one skipper? But we can't go just yet!" Wally said with alarm.

"Yes, we've got a five day patrol then call back for supplies before pulling out."

Wally didn't hear any more of what his father had said, as he rushed out of the hotel to seek Moira.

He went to her home and asked her father if he could speak with her, and apologised for the lateness of the evening for doing so.

"Wally, what's the matter?" Moira asked gently as she kissed him.

"Moira, I have to tell you!" Wally started, as he drew her

into a corner of the porch.

"Tell me that you love me and that you've got to sail again in the morning?"

Wally thought of Sarah, and then of this wonderful girl in front of him, that had woken some kind of magic within him. What am I going to say? How can I tell her?

Wally decided that he was not going to hurt Moira by telling her of Sarah, instead he decided on stating something that could explain his future absence.

"Moira, we are going on our final patrol tomorrow. We were lucky to survive the last one. The thing is, when we come back we shall be returning to our home fishing grounds immediately. It might be a while before we return." Wally blurted out, and felt the tears in his eyes that seem to burn his cheeks. He was not a deceiver, nor did he intend to hurt Moira.

Moira just looked at him, and started to weep.

"But Wally, you'll come back won't you? You have to, I won't let anything happen to you. Please say you'll come back." she sobbed.

"What's the fuss? Why are you making Moira cry?" her father asked roughly as he re-appeared on the porch.

"Mr Farr. I'm going back on patrol, when we return to collect supplies; we will sail out homeward again. I don't know when I can return as both voyages are of equal danger." Wally explained.

"Shush Moira darlin'! Wally has a war to fight these days. If he doesn't make it by the end of say Hogmanay, then you'll just have to find someone else." Farr stated gently to Moira who sobbed as she buried her face her hands.

"Moira, I cannot say what will become of me, but you are a beautiful girl, and there's bound to be some other young man somewhere out there in all those mighty ships who will love you as I do." Wally whispered in her ear, which brought more sobs from her.

Moira looked at Wally and saw that his eyes were sparkling with tears.

"Wally, It's not fair that I should love you and for you to leave me. Can't you do something so that you can return and be my man forever?"

"Moira, I cannot say what I don't know, except that I have never had such peace and happiness as when I am with you. Please believe me that I will never love anyone as much as I have grown to love you." Wally whispered, then gathered her up in his arms and kissed her long and passionately.

"You'd better go now Wally. Moira will be all right in a few days." Farr said as he took Wally gently by the arm and led him down the path towards the village.

"Mr Farr, I –" Wally started to speak.

"Wally, just don't say anything. This happened to me some twenty years ago. If it's meant to be then you'll be back." Farr said sympathetically as he patted Wally's arm then turned to comfort Moira.

Wally ran back to the hotel with a heavy heart, thinking what he had done to Moira. He thought of his betrayal of Sarah and of the possible damage he may have caused that would ruin his standing in the village. Maybe he was just as bad as Logan after all. Maybe Sarah deserved somebody better than him.

The following morning saw the familiar sight of the small line of ships sail out of the harbour and out to sea for another encounter with the elements and whatever the Hun threw their way.

Wally's self recriminations and self disgust filled his mind constantly, and was getting to be a factor in his performance on board, as it became more obvious to the rest of the crew that his mind was elsewhere instead of the here and now.

He performed all his duties almost robotically throughout

the extended patrol, but kept himself in his little nest, and only came down when they sailed back into Scapa Flow again.

"Cap'n Green!" it was Rose standing on the wooden jetty calling, as the GREEN ARROW was finally secured to it.

"Welcome back! Come ashore and accompany me back to the office. Bring your son with you."

'Mornin' Admiral. Will do!" Green acknowledged and stepped ashore with Wally following closely behind. Not a word was said during the brief ride to the HQ, until they all arrived into the Admiral's office, where there were two senior naval men waiting for them.

"This is Admiral Woods off the VENGEANCE, and Captain Hollinghead off the DAEDALUS, meet Captain Green off the GREEN ARROW, and his First Mate, Wally Green." Rose announced the brief introductions.

"Captain Green. You have done a magnificent job with your squadron of small ships, and we place the immense value upon the vigilance of your lookout. All of which, I believe is all the work of your son in particular." Woods started.

He went on to ask if Green could stay and take command of the ever increasing role required of the small ships, and that if Wally would consider an officers commission with his very own vessel.

Green thanked the visitors for their kindness but stated that he must return his vessels back to their own home port to complete his discharge of duty, but it was for his son to answer for his own ends.

Wally listened to the flow of conversation and realised that he had a future other than fishing, but that loyalty to his family needed to become foremost in the whole picture of things.

This was one of Wally's visualised pretend situations, and he decided to ask them to give him time to go home before committing himself to a life in the King's Navy.

It was finally decided that both Green and his son had made

the right choices and the Admiral agreed to wait for their final decision, although not too long considering that the war might be over very soon.

The meeting ended pleasantly, with the knowledge that both Green and his son were to be suitably rewarded for their gallant services to the King's Navy.

The GREEN ARROW had refuelled, stored and sailed homeward. It was a joyous occasion for the crewmen who had become unusually prosperous, they had earned themselves fat wages and bonuses, and were eager to return home to their loved ones. It also meant that Wally had enough to get wed, and the promise of a bounty to come from the Admirals, that would help their future plans.

It was a foggy, drizzly morning when the little fleet arrived back into their little fishing harbour. But it seemed like a summers day, as they were met by a throng of family and friends who were shouting and cheering as the vessels tied up to the jetty.

The return from a four month fishing trip was such a joyous occasion, everybody danced and sang their way along the cobbled streets, some for home, but for most, straight into the nearest ale house.

Wally and his father finished the last little chores to make the ship secure, before they stepped off the ship onto the now empty jetty.

They were always the first men on board and the last to leave, with no sign of anybody there to greet them when they came back. The two men walked slowly and silently, side by side up the hill towards their cottage that overlooked the little harbour. Wally stopped briefly at the door of Sarah's house but saw that it was in darkness and silent.

"She always stands next to the bow bollard when I come back, but she wasn't there skipper. The house is in darkness, so where could she be?" Wally asked with disappointment showing on his face.

"I expect she's with Maggie down at the 'Lobster Pot'. Come home and have some tea. Sarah should be back any time." Green said softly to his son.

For he too knew the feeling of loneliness and anticlimax of returning from a prosperous trip, with nobody to greet him and share his joy, since his wife was lost to the dreaded T.B. plague some years previous, and if it wasn't for the new love in his life, in the shape of Maggie Morton, perhaps he too would join in the commiserations. For his son to be spurned by Sarah meant that something was not right, but he would not interfere between them, save to advise his son on the pitfalls of certain relationships.

Wally finished his meal and told his father that he was going to find Sarah.

He walked into the noisy, smoky atmosphere of the Lobster Pot Inn that still had some of the fishermen swilling ale and generally enjoying themselves.

"It's Wally Green the eyes of the fleet, and the man what helped us get our big wages." Sid Beer greeted as he lifted his flagon up to toast the young arrival.

"Aye! Come and have a beer young Wally, we owe you one." someone invited, which started another round of shanty songs that were sung with gusto.

Wally saw Weeks sitting at a large wooden table with all his family around him, all except for Sarah.

"Skipper Weeks! Mrs Weeks, where is Sarah? Doesn't she know I've come home to wed her?"

"Wally Green! You poor boy. You had better sit down, I have something to tell you dear." Mrs Weeks said with consternation on her face, and a silence that befell the occupants at the table told Wally to expect the worst.

"Why Mrs Weeks what's happened to her? Skipper Weeks what's going on?"

"I think you'd better sit down Wally! My missus here has something to tell you that you should have known about long before now. None of my doing mind you." Weeks said softly and pulled a chair up for Wally to sit on.

"No, I'll stand thank you. What's wrong? Where is my Sarah? It's the TB again is it? Wally asked with the thoughts of how his dear mother had died with TB when he and his father went out for an extra trip. They had gone out to earn the money to pay for his mother's treatment, but came back and found that she had died.

"You have been away for four months and a war has started. The army have been coming round taking all young men away to fight in the trenches." Mrs Green started

"But what has that got to do with my Sarah?" Wally asked impatiently.

"Some young men were given commissions as Officers in the Army, and some of your friends have been offered places with the King's Navy. You know how Sarah loves the sight of the uniform of an Officer don't you? Well Sarah went and married one such officer of the army, and has gone away to live in the barracks over in the big city."

"Oh no! Don't tell me it's Jimmy Logan who became that officer, and took Sarah away from me?" Wally groaned and looked in despair at Mrs Green.

"It appears Wally, that when we sailed, Jimmy Logan started to court Sarah in earnest and they wed about nine weeks ago. He's now off to war in France, and hopes to be home again for Christmas. At least that's what Mr Logan has told us." Weeks volunteered.

That was such a blow to Wally. His arch rival always ruined everything he touched, then tossed it away when he had destroyed it. He ran out of the inn and made for the Logan's shop just along the street.

"Mr Logan! Mr Logan!" Wally shouted at the top of his voice.

"What, who's shouting at me?" Logan shouted roughly as he came swiftly out of his shop.

"Tell me it's not true Mr Logan! Tell me that my Sarah did not marry your Jimmy!" Wally shouted angrily, as he grabbed Logan by the lapels and lifted him off his feet.

"Unhand me you lout. I'll have the law on you."

"Never mind the law, I'll crucify the bastard starting with you." Wally snarled.

Mrs Logan came out of the shop wielding a brush and started to hit Wally with it, which made him drop Mr Logan.

"You always was a no good oaf! Now unhand my husband!" she squealed and hit Wally again. Wally grabbed the brush, snapped it in half on his knee and threw it into her face.

"It appears Wally Green, that Sarah Weeks chose the better man. He's an officer in a cavalry regiment that's just gone off to war. He'll be back wearing a chest full of medals. What about you? A fist full of smelly fish that's all you ever bring back! He was always better than you." Logan sneered.

A policeman came marching up and barged his way through the ring of onlookers,

"What is all this fuss? Why are you fighting in the Kings' highway Green?" he demanded.

"I came home today to find that my fiancee Sarah Weeks had been abducted by the Logans here, and their son had his wicked way with her, without her consent." Wally started to explain.

"Now then Wally Green, that's not true. Sarah Weeks got married good and proper, had a white wedding and all that. Lieutenant Jimmy Logan had a guard of honour too. Now that she's wed in the eyes of the law, you had better move along and stop pestering these good people." the constable barked.

Wally looked at the Logans and saw the sneering look they gave him.

"You see Wally Green, she has taste, that's why she married

our Jimmy. Now unless you unhand me I'll have this policeman arrest you for detaining me unlawfully." Mr Logan hissed.

Wally told the policeman that Sarah was to marry him when he came back. That she was betrothed to him and that he would sue the Logans for every penny as compensation.

"You'll do no such thing Wally Green. If I were you, I'd go back to your home and forget her. She is already married, and that's that." the policeman snarled as he pushed Wally away from the Logans.

Wally saw the look of triumph the Logans had, as they turned and thanked the policeman for stopping a madman. Wally walked slowly up the hill to his home, with his mind in a turmoil, and sat down heavily on a wooden stool by the fire. He was feeling empty, lonely and totally miserable, and started to weep openly in front of his father.

'What's the trouble Wally?" his father asked with great concern, as he had never seen his son cry ever since he was eight years old, on the day his mother was buried.

"Jimmy Logan got Sarah to marry him, and now he's off to the war in France. What am I going to do now Father?" Wally said slowly.

"We'll try and get you back on your feet again son. Besides, if what you feel now is anything like that lovely lass in Scotland has gone through, then perhaps its best you learn from it and get on with your life and best as you can." Green commiserated, then added.

"But in the meantime we've had a letter from the Lords of the Admiralty, saying that we have to go to London and get a nice medal each and a bounty of some several thousand pounds."

Wally didn't speak for several minutes, but looked out the window at the scenic harbour below him.

Almost as if in a trance, he asked,

"What does that mean to us Father. How will that get my Sarah back?"

"That means that we are now the richest people in the whole of the coastal villages. Sarah is lost forever to you now. So you will just have to find another who will help you spend your half of this fortune."

"What about our vessel and our home Father? What about your own affairs with the widow Morton?"

"Maggie Morton and me will wed and stay here. There's no more fishing for me. I will set up a coaling yard just like Mr Petrie has. You can have the ship, maybe use it for trade and start up what you've always wanted to do. You could use your bounty to help. Then someday you will meet the right lass for you. Unless of course you go back to Scotland and make an honest woman of Moira." Green said with gentle encouragement to his forlorn son.

It took several days for Wally to get near his normal self, but people knew the look in his eyes were of real hurt and betrayal, preventing him being the Wally Green they knew.

During that time, the word was out that the Greens were summoned to the King's court, much to the delight to most of the village folk. Also the fact that because of Wally's service to the Navy, he was to be come a very rich man. There was only one family who did not share the villagers' enthusiasm and delight for the Greens, in fact much to their disgust and bitter distaste.

Green and his son arrived back from London to a triumphant welcome given by the villagers and other fishermen who had sailed with them on that epic Scottish voyage.

It took Wally and his father a couple of weeks to sort out their lives and for Wally to take over the GREEN ARROW as its new captain.

"Well Skipper! You and Maggie are now wed, and you have a good life ahead of you. I am going to get a crew together and sail north. I have written to Moira to tell her that I am coming back for her." Wally said, as he gave a toast to his father and his new Step Mother.

"Aye young man! You will do much better up there with all that cod. We hope your nets are always full." his father replied as he lifted his mug of ale, and wrapped an arm around his new bride.

"Wally, I hope you find your happiness, and good hunting." Maggie said as she hugged Wally gently, then fell into his fathers lap and said laughingly

"Your nets are well and truly fouled now Mr Green. You've got an octopussy in your lap." which was greeted with cheers and bawdy suggestions from the rest of the customers at the inn.

For the next couple of weeks, Wally had recruited a new crew, and prepared his ship for its voyage to the Orkneys. He had warned the men that whilst he wouldn't be coming back for some time, should any of them wish to come home again, they would have to find their own way back. If they wished not to sail with him, then they were free to leave. There were no takers, as each believed they would earn the fabulous wages and bonuses from the cod fishing, and set themselves up as skippers too.

He was getting better in himself and started to dream of a new life with Moira and her family on the islands.

He received a letter from Admiral Rose stating that he was happy that Wally had decided to come back. There was also talk that he could be made a full Captain of his King's Navy, just like his father had been, and possibly earn a few more high decorations to accompany his Military Order, let alone another big bounty from his Naval pay.

One morning, just a few days before he was to sail, he was in the Ships Chandler's office attending to some business, when he looked out of the office window to see a familiar figure step out of the omnibus and walk towards the shops.

He knew the figure, the walk and now could hear the voice. He felt a coldness creep down his back as he stared at the very person who had devastated his life. The feeling slowly went, as he concentrated on his business.

"Captain Green. You look as if you've seen a ghost." The chandler stated.

"It's nothing. Must have caught a draft" Wally replied, as the solid spar he was holding snapped in his hands like matchsticks.

The chandler looked out of the window to where Wally was staring, and saw the expensively dressed woman step into a shop doorway.

"Hmm! I wonder why she is back?" he whispered almost to himself.

"What do you mean Chandler?" Wally asked

"She comes back and fore?"

"Yes. That's Mrs Logan. Her husband is a womaniser and is known for his woman beating antics back at the barracks. I don't know what she saw in him. Pity mind you." he said as his voice trailed off when he realised what he was saying and to whom.

Wally felt quite calm and composed when he told the chandler, that the woman meant absolutely nothing to him now.

Wally finally finished his business and walked out of the store towards the inn to see his men, but had to pass the Logan's shop to do so.

"Good morning Captain Green. Nice day for a walk!" Mr Logan fawned as he pretended to sweep the pavement outside his shop.

"We have a visitor who would like to see you, if that's all right with you Captain Green. You are more than welcome to come inside." Mrs Logan added invitingly, as she almost curtsied to him.

For the past few weeks, the shoe had now been on the other foot for Wally.

"Get out of my way before I break your back with your own broom" Wally hissed as he kicked the brush away from his feet.

"But Captain Green, you must speak to this person." Mrs Logan wailed, as Wally saw that Sarah was standing inside the shop.

"I don't have to speak to anyone. Besides, aren't I supposed to be the scum who only catches fish. I'm the one you treated like dogs dirt, remember?" Wally said vehemently to the Logan's.

"But now I'm a decorated man seen by the King. I'm the one with most of the money in this village now. I'm the one who didn't stab people in the back like the traitor you raised, Mr and Mrs Logan." he said raspingly, as if to rub the salt into their wounds. They had fallen from grace and became social pariahs when they denigrated Wally that day, seemingly a lifetime away. For the villagers didn't take kindly to what they and their son had done to Wally, and none had ever shopped there since. The Logan's stood with their heads hung down in shame, with Mrs Logan crying into her pinny.

Sarah stepped out through the doorway and out into the light. Wally saw that she was gaunt looking, with several bruise marks on her erstwhile pretty face, and heavily pregnant.

"Hello Sailor boy! Don't I get a kiss?" she asked softly, and puckered her lips up expectantly.

Wally just stood and looked at her, shook his head in pity and started to walk off.

"How dare you walk away from me Wally Green. You owe me Wally Green. Come back I want to speak to you." she demanded angrily.

Wally turned round slowly, looked her up and down.

"I owe you nothing. It also appears from your disposition that you are incapable to demand anything. Where's the clever husband? Bashing up yet another poor woman or hiding in some ditch afraid to come out and play with the big boys?" he asked sarcastically.

"Now don't be like that Wally! You and I were sweethearts weren't we? Besides, I need a strong man to keep me warm." she smarmed as she came up close to him.

"Then go back to Jimmy Logan. He's supposed to be your husband after all isn't he? You chose him rather than wait for me, like you promised. But it seems your promises count for nothing Sarah." Wally said with increasing anger and disdain.

"Oh don't be like that. Jimmy is just a boy compared to you. Besides you have lots of money now, and we can buy that ship you've always wanted." Sarah continued in her coyish way, trying to win his affections.

"Sarah Weeks. You had no hold over me from the very day you chose to wed Logan. You go back to him, not me." Wally said angrily as he shoved her towards her mother-in-law.

"Here! You look after her. She is your new Daughter in law and by the look of it a pregnant one, at that."

"And as for you Mr Logan." Wally stated as he turned to Logan.

"If your son ever interferes with my affairs again I will personally shoot him dead. Officer in the army or not." He whispered menacingly.

Mr Logan just hung his head and muttered that the telegram they had yesterday told them that Jimmy was killed last week and hoped that he would help them out if only for Sarahs' sake.

"Then it appears that somebody has spared me the trouble. Probably shot in the back trying to run away no doubt as he always was a coward when the going got tough. You and your money may have bought his Lieutenants commission, I am a Naval Captain, and of a much higher standing than his rank. But at least I earned mine fair and square." Wally continued icily and spoke to all three of them

"Sarah knew that Jimmy was a bad lot and always spoiled

other people's things. Now he's met his death, you were hoping that I would take her back so that your grandchild would have a good up bringing with all my money. Well Sarah Weeks, that was your choice not mine, so suffer your own consequences. If any of you ever bother me again I will have you all arrested. What you sent round Mr Logan, has now come back round to you sooner than you thought." Wally said without mercy, as he sneered then spat in Mr Logan's face and walked away leaving Sarah sobbing and pleading for Wally to forgive and come back to her.

When Wally got home and spoke to Maggie, she told him that he was too hard on Sarah, even though she did marry somebody else when his back was turned.

His father told him that he knew what happened was always a possibility, especially when he created the same misery up in Scotland, and he too had suffered in just the same way as Wally by using the expression. What goes round comes round again.

It was the following morning when Wally felt a strange sensation he tried to understand.

He felt like a new and cleansed man, with no baggage or regrets to hold him back.

He was free to chase his own fortunes and ambitions, and the spring in his step told the world that he was now his own man, beholden to no-one.

The black clouds turned day into night, the winds howled and the seas sprayed the windows of the bridge as the Green Arrow arrived into the safety of the now familiar port of Campbeltown.

"Afternoon Captain! A wee bit of a gale out there." Came a voice Wally knew.

"Is that you Mr Petrie? This is Wally Green here."

"Hello Wally. Captain Green not on board? Never mind.

Come to the harbourmasters office ashore as soon as you can." Petrie shouted as he ran back through the yard to the office.

"Greetings and welcome Wally Green." It was Admiral Rose standing in front of a roaring fire.

"Come over here and have a warm. Mr Petrie, two glasses if you please," Rose's booming voice ordered. Wally walked over to the fire and held his hands out to feel the warmth radiate throughout his body.

"My father sends his regards Admiral. I am now the owner of the GREEN ARROW, and have a young and fresh crew with me to do whatever is needed up here. I hope to emulate my father so that I can get a squadron of ships like mine." Wally said as he shook Rose's hand.

"Well said that man! Yes Wally, congratulations on your Military Order. You will make a fine Captain no doubt." Rose agreed as he offered Wally a large glass of rum

"To the King. God bless him!" all three said as they downed their drink in one go.

"Now then young Wally. We have still got our HQ in the Orkneys that I want you to take over, as I have bigger things to attend back here. You have a special mission and task to perform there." Rose opened, then went on to brief Wally on what was required.

The briefing was over when Wally left the office with Mr Petrie carrying an armful of charts and orders. He was feeling elated as he was to spend most of his time ashore whilst his ship was used for military purposes.

The Orkney coastline and jetty of their own little shore base was a marvel for the new men, but a familiar one with lots of memories for the few who came back with Wally. The hotel was the same, and even his room was the same, just as if nothing had happened in his absence.

Wally felt his heart pounding as he walked swiftly towards Moira' croft, to be met at the door by Mr and Mrs Farr with great elation and jubilation. He was a welcome visitor and was ushered inside to enjoy a welcome back drink.

His heart leapt with joy when he saw Moira come through into the room.

He moved swiftly over and took her into his arms, whispered her name and kissed her with fervour and passion.

"Wally! Oh Wally love! You've come back to me. You must be my man now!" she sighed, as she returned his kisses.

The whole world seemed to have melted as he felt the fire and passion between them, and for what seemed an eternity as they looked into each other' eyes. He kissed her once more before there was a delicate coughing noise that brought them back to reality.

"You two will have plenty to talk about. Your hearts will manage a while, but first you must eat some food for the body and soul." Mrs Farr said with a knowing smile, as Mr Farr drew on a large pipe that seemed to give off more smoke than Wally's ship.

He married Moira within weeks of returning to her, and had a house built on the very spot where they spent their time together.

Their life together was a happy one, with Moira giving him four children. All of them now enjoying a happy life as fisherfolk of the now deserted Scapa Flow. Deserted that is, except for the ghosts of the Hun Navy that drowned itself in the bay.

Wally never did return to see his father or his own fisherfolk, but kept in touch by letter now and then.

One day when Moira was reading the local paper that Wally's father had sent with the recent letter, she mentioned about the tragic death of somebody he might remember from his native village.

"It was reported that a woman called Sarah Logan, gassed

herself when she found out that her husband was branded as a coward and was in fact executed for desertion and not killed in action as reported earlier. That the army had stopped her husbands pension and she leaves a daughter behind."

"I don't know them, Moira love. Probably arrived after I left to come here." Wally lied protectively keeping the skeletons from her doorstep and shrugged his shoulders. He felt a pang of guilt at the way he remembered of how he cheated on Sarah by romancing Moira, of how he treated Sarah after he met up with her again and of the words that came flooding back what Maggie had said to him all those years ago.

He went over to Moira, caught hold of her gently and kissed her just like he did the day they were re-united.

"Wally Green!" Moira gasped breathlessly.

"What are you thinking of, as if I didn't know, you naughty boy?" she teased.

When he replied, it was with another lingering kiss.

As he held her close, looking out the window and far out to sea, he felt an icy coldness slip slowly through his body. He knew it was the memory and the ghost of Sarah, and her passing, that she was now leaving him.

But Moira' love had cured his hurt, warmed his heart, and rescued his soul for him, yet it was only now did he feel at peace with himself.

Moreland

Tom looked out from under his shady spot and saw what a lovely day it was to go swimming, but if he did it here, it would scare the fish that he had spent all morning trying to catch.

He knew that if there was nobody for a mile around his favourite fishing place, under the big sycamore tree, it would be safe for him to leave his clothes and went swimming into the inviting coolness of the slow moving river.

He splashed about in the deeper parts of the river, although for a thirteen year-old, and because it was an early June time when the river was slow and benign, it was only up to his waist.

As he came up to the surface again, he heard high pitched voices that shouted to him from the opposite side of the river, and recognised them as his village school class mates, the twins Lily and Iris Moreland.

"Tommy Wilson! You know you're not allowed to swim in Daddy's river, and if he catches you he'll have you flogged. So get out of there at once before I call one of the farmhands." Lily bossed. She was always the spokesperson and the dominant twin.

Moreland & Other Stories

"And be sides, we want to swim there, not you." Iris pouted.

"I was here first, and besides your dad only owns the land the river is on, not the water that runs down it."

"You silly boy!" retorted Iris,

"No wonder you're the class dunce. Fancy not knowing that the river *is* the water."

Tom just sighed, and went to get out of the water to move back down to his fishing tackle and his clothes. He did not want to get into any trouble, especially from the Moreland twins.

'Oh look, He's got nothing on, quite naked in fact." Lily gasped.

"What's the matter Tommy Wilson, can't afford a costume?" Iris mocked.

"You know I can't. And besides, it's much nicer and cooler without one."

"Well, we've got silk ones with our names on them, so there." Iris boasted.

"Well, put them on and we'll all have a swim, the river is big enough for all three of us."

"You know we don' t have them and thanks to you we wont be able to swim now because you're a boy and boys aren't supposed to look." Lily said petulantly.

"I will turn my back until you're in the water. Just leave all your clothes on the bank and come in, if you dare." Tom challenged

"Right Tommy Wilson, we'll do just that if only to show you we're not afraid." Iris stated emphatically.

Within minutes, Tom heard the splashes of the twins entering the water, laughing and joking to themselves, as they came up to him, just as naked as he was. All three were pubescents, with the girls showing signs of womanhood, he a skinny youth, and all three innocents abroad.

The three school chums splashed and raced each other through the water, and generally enjoying themselves.

"I have a fishing line down stream from here, so I must go and check it is okay. Stay until I come back won't you?"

"Fishing in Daddy's river as well. That's poaching, and he shoots poachers didn't you know!" Lily said ominously.

"It's the only way we can get fish to eat, and you know how poor we are." Tom defended himself.

"Oh never mind, just this once Tommy Wilson. But it will cost you a forfeit." Iris said wickedly.

"Forfeit? What's that? Wait until I get back and tell me." Tom muttered and left the girls to themselves.

Tom came back shortly, to find the girls whispering to each other and pointing to Tom, as he came slowly back up the river towards them, sensing trouble.

"Now then Tommy Wilson. What's it worth for us not telling Daddy that you've been fishing in his river and playing with us with no clothes on?" Iris asked slowly.

"What do you mean? I have nothing except the fish I've caught today."

"Come over here to us and we'll tell you. That's if you're not a scaredy cat." Lily urged.

Tom moved slowly through the water towards the twins and noticed that they were pointing to his genitals, which made him blush even in the cool water.

"We've noticed those things between your legs. We have seen those on statues, but we have not seen them for real, and we want to have a good look at them and see them properly." Lily said slowly as she watched his penis sway gently in the water.

"My sisters have told me that girls aren't supposed to touch them until they get wed." Tom replied bashfully.

"C'mon Tommy Wilson. So who's the fraidy cat now! Who's the fraidy cat! Scared that we'd laugh at you?" Iris taunted with a chanting voice.

Tom stood there whilst they kneeled down in the water to get a better look, touching, fondling, and rubbing his genitals very gently in case they hurt him.

"Ohh look! It's grown very large and strong! Look Iris, see what I mean." Lily said with amazement.

"Ohh yes! What makes it do that? I wonder what its for" Iris asked, as she took her turn to feel and fondle Tom.

When they had finished, they stood up slowly, and looked at each other.

"We are different from you, now you will look at ours as fair exchange." Lily ordered.

Tom meekly did as he was told, for he knew the squires' daughters had to be obeyed.

"Yours is called a pense, and ours are called virgins." Lily nodded her head knowingly.

"Yes, and these are called boosems, aren't they Lily." Iris said as she rubbed her hands over her budding breasts

"Wouldn't you like to feel how soft they are and rub them like I have just done." she teased, and grabbed Toms hands and placed them upon her.

The three school friends were fascinated in what they had seen and spent a long while exploring each other's bodies, trying to discover something called the birds and bees.

Finally, Lily announced that they had to go home for tea, and that Tommy should go home in case he is caught by the water bailiffs.

"We'll be here again tomorrow to have another swim. We have not finished with you yet, so you will be here too just like today." Lily ordered softly.

"But tomorrow is Sunday, and I always go fishing after dinner on a Sunday." Tom protested.

"Not if you don't want us to tell our Daddy that you were seen poaching, and playing with our bodies too." Iris said quietly.

Tom knew he had to give in to their demands and told them that he'd be there, then made his way back to his fishing rod and clothes, leaving the girls to themselves.

He got himself dried and dressed and started fishing again. Shortly afterwards as he was collecting his fish net from the river and was preparing to leave, he heard shouting and the thunder of horse hooves coming his way.

"There he is!" a loud voice shouted, as three men with some dogs came splashing across the river, coming swiftly upon Tom and surrounding him, with the squire Moreland arriving minutes afterwards walking along the river bank with a limping horse.

"You! Stand up and be recognized!" Moreland demanded sharply.

Tom stood up slowly and wondered why he had all these people around him.

"Who are you? What are you doing on my land? C'mon speak up I haven't got all day." Moreland shouted impatiently.

"He's the one what must have did it my Lord. I saw him taking liberties with your daughters. He must have drowned them after he had his evil way with them." A burly unkempt man said, pointing to Tom.

"And by the look of it, he's been poaching your fish, me lord!" said another

"What? I did what? Whatever, it's untrue." Tom shouted over the barking of the dogs.

"You were seen messing about with my daughters in the river down yonder."

Moreland pointed to the place where he had played with the girls.

"You were swimming in the river with them weren't you?" he demanded.

"Yes sir"

"You were seen to play and act very rudely towards my twin daughters Lillian and Iris. Is that right?"

Despite his fresh impromptu sex education with the twins, he was still a very confused naïve thirteen year old.

"What do you mean sir?"

"You admit playing around with my daughters and swimming without any clothes on to be decent?" Moreland snapped.

"Er yes. I suppose so. I didn't. They are my school friends, why should I hurt them?

"How dare you ask the Squire questions. Know your place and own up to it. It'll be much easier for you if you do." another man snarled at him.

"But sir, I left them to go and get dressed over by those bull rushes just opposite that oxbow, when I came down here to see to my things." Tom protested desperately, trying to save himself from this danger.

"That's just where these men found them you little scum!" Moreland snarled and raised his riding crop up to strike Tom, but missed as Tom dodged the blow.

"Judging by your fish net, you've taken some of my fish. That's stealing. I don't take kindly to thieves, let alone poachers." Moreland said, moving quickly over to him brandishing a silver handled whip.

"Hold him still whilst I give him a good whipping before you take him to the constables' house.

The men held Tom down, whilst the squire whipped him several times not caring where it landed on him.

"Now take him to the Constable in Fordham" Moreland gasped breathlessly.

Tom's badly cut body was dragged into the village and dumped at the door of the local police station

"What's all this? What 'ave we here then? What's this person doing bleeding all over my newly polished floor then?" the village constable asked with a frown on his very fat face.

"We had apprehended this person what killed the squires twins, after he'd had his way with them. And was caught poaching. The squire will be along shortly for you to do what you do with all this." the burly one said.

"I need you to identify yourselves. You! The one with the rope! Yes you, the big one. What's your name and where do you live?

"My name is Jimmy Mitchell. I'm the squire's foreman of the estate. I live down by the miller's house."

"And you, with the dogs?" the constable prompted.

"My name is Les Walker. I'm the squire's saddler. I live over the manor stables."

"And you. The third one?"

"I'm Anthony Beckett. The squire's rent collector. I live in the Manor, constable."

"Very well you lot. Come in, make your statement in my big book, sign it with your names and be off home with you. When the Squire comes, we'll have this dealt with in a good orderly fashion, I can assure you." The constable commanded.

After the men left, Tom was dragged and unceremoniously dumped into the one and only cell that represented the local village jail.

"You can stay there until Lord Moreland arrives. He's the local Magistrate who will give out your official punishment, apart from the thrashing he's already given you." the constable announced and went out through the jail door.

"Why did you have to kill those lovely girls. Wasn't you satisfied enough with having your wicked way with them, you little bastard?" he added and spat a large globule of phlegm towards the luckless Tom.

Lord Moreland arrived with two attendants and started up the proceedings.

"The charge is murder, rape, and other despicable acts of misbehaviour, and poaching, by this person standing in front of you squire, your honour." the constable stated out loud as he nodded his head towards Moreland.

He was always called the squire since he was a boy even after taking up his duties as the Lord of the Manor from his father's early demise.

"Your name is Tom Wilson, yes?" the constable asked Tom.

"Yes Constable." Tom replied disconsolately.

"And you live down the school lane with your mother and your sisters, yes?"

"Yes Constable."

"Is that Widow Wilson's boy? Her husband was the gallant Sergeant of the Royals?" Moreland enquired.

"Yes your honour. The very same. He was a very brave man, saved his entire company."

"Ah yes, I remember. He refused to join my Father's regiment formed from the men working on the estate you know. Was offered a commission too. Such a shame his only son has turned out to be such a disappointment." Moreland said and reminisced for a while with the constable whilst Tom stood shivering and moaning to himself.

"Stand still and shut your noise boy, whilst his Lordship decides what to do with you." the constable snarled.

"This is my decision. I find him guilty. You will take this wretch over to the head warden at the County Borstal. Tell him that he is to ensure that this boy is to serve his days doing hard labour. Also, when it's suitable, see to it that he gets transferred to the Missionary in the Australias. But you will tell his mother first, to learn of her shame.

Then she and her family are to be banished from the estate. His father's name is to be struck off the roll of honour on all the war memorials." Moreland paused for his instructions to be understood.

"Remember Constable 127. It has always been the long tradition and custom of my family to take care of its own affairs. We don't want the world to know about our dirty linen, now do we constable!" Moreland shook his head as if to emphasise his meaning.

"You could be promoted to sergeant if you do, otherwise you know what happens to those who do not do my bidding." He warned.

"Now have you got that? You understand what you are about to do?"

"Ye, yes, my lord. It's as good as done my lord." stuttered the constable, as he fawned over and tugged his forelock as a salute to Moreland.

"Very well, do your duty." Moreland replied, then walked slowly out of the building, satisfied with himself for doing a good day's work.

"There you have it Tommy Wilson. Because of your age, you're lucky you were not sent for a hanging party in the village cemetry."

"But constable. It wasn't me. Anyway, why should I, they were my school friends."

"According to Mitchell and the others, you were the last person to be seen with the girls before they were found murdered. So you must have been the one that killed them. That is why the magistrate has found you guilty as charged." the constable growled and left to speak to Tom's mother.

"But who saw the girls after I left them? Who was it constable? Please tell me the truth constable? My mother always told me to tell the truth, so why can't everybody else?" Tom wailed and started to cry bitterly.

"He is only an innocent thirteen year old boy. So why have they accused him of this crime?" Mrs Wilson sobbed as the constable told her to pack her things and get out.

The village square was full of spectators, cat calling and shouting at Tom's family as they walked out of the village pushing a rickety hand cart full of their belongings. The crowd did not see Tom being frog-marched out the back of the village jail and into a waiting police van, nor did he see his family being booed and spat upon when they had left.

Tom Wilson became yet another victim of the squire's justice, and his family paid the price for him not being hanged.

A few years later, Tom managed to escape from his cruel incarceration at the county Borstal, and decided to enlist in the Army. His quest was to try and be like his father, to try undo what had been his nightmare these past years. To seek retribution and justice against all that he and his family was condemned for.

According to his mother, when he was only five years old, his father had succumbed to his severe war wounds, and was buried as a hero within the estate, with his name enshrined in the local church and on the new war memorial in the village.

When WWII came and throughout its entirety, Tom was found to be in the thickest of fighting, and had served in many theatres of war.

The rigours of his life turned him from a skinny youth into a well-built young man. Several times he had proved himself as a brilliant soldier and a master tactician that some generals were most envious of.

His rapid rise up through the ranks, and the several bravery medals he had won, made him a very popular man with the men he served with, especially as he was so young.

When the war ended he was the Colonel of his regiment, but he was required to take some time off before being called back to duty.

His body held the scars of war, and the haunted look in his eyes that told of a man who had witnessed too many deaths, both friend and foe alike.

The snows of Norway and the heat of the Burma jungle took its toll on him. For although he looked weather beaten and well beyond his years in fact he was only twenty-seven.

Even though he was a celebrated hero returning from the carnage of a world war, just like his father had at the end of the so called 'WAR to end all WARS', except that for Tom Wilson, he had nobody to see or nowhere to rest.

For the first time in his life he was now in a perfect situation to deal with something that had been eating him up inside all these years.

Tom Wilson arrived in the village of his birth, and made his way down the now seemingly smaller lane than he remembered. He looked at the address on the buff envelope he held to confirm he had the right place.

Just as I thought, but how did this come about? He asked himself.

He had found himself at the front of, and looking at the very cottage that he was born in, where his family was evicted from, and seemingly never to be found again.

The cottage name was different. It looks much the same, but somehow much different, he argued with himself as he climbed out of his vehicle and stood looking at the cottage.

He saw smoke coming out of the chimney, with curtains half-drawn in the windows, as he walked down the path that was almost choked with weeds.

He felt himself tremble briefly which was something he had never done all during the war, as he reached the solid oak door. He paused and knocked it politely.

It was a young woman who answered the door, with a little girl clutched to her pinny.

"Yes? Can I help you sir?" the woman asked nervously.

"Sorry to bother you madam, but I'm looking for a Mrs. Williams whose husband is Sergeant Arthur Williams from the 2nd Commando Brigade. Are you she?" Tom asked civilly.

"Yes! Who wants to know? Where is he?" she asked as she looked past him to see if anybody else was with him.

"I'm his commanding officer, Colonel Wilson and I have an official letter for you concerning your husband. I can tell you now, that I have spoken with him recently and he's all right. He should be coming home just as soon as the army will let him." he said as he gave her the envelope.

She grasped it and started to cry as she ripped open the letter to read its contents.

She muttered out the message as she read it quickly, then grabbed her child up in her arms and danced around the room, crying and laughing and telling the child that Daddy's coming home very soon and it will be all right again.

Tom looked at this very joyous scene, but with a heavy heart, because there was nobody to dance and cheer his homecoming.

She looked at Tom standing in the doorway, wiped the tears from her cheeks with her pinny, and invited him inside for a cup of tea.

"I've been saving my rations up for when my husband came home." she told him.

"But you are welcome to have some now that you've brought me the best news since Lord knows when."

Tom sat down and sipped his tea, and engaged in a lengthy conversation with Mrs. Williams. Telling her how her husband is his best friend. Of how the two of them met up and how they fought in many a battle together.

The day seemed to have slipped by as it was now getting quite dark outside, and Tom still had to find somewhere to sleep.

"I am not allowed to take in lodgers, but there's a coaching inn at the village that you can lodge Colonel Tom. But you are welcome to call by at any time."

"Thank you, I will do just that. I would like to call by tomorrow morning to look around if I may."

"Yes that will be fine. But make it after the rent collector has been, say about ten o'clock."

Tom bade good night, parked his car in an outhouse next to the cottage and walked slowly down into the village to take in the view as if to refresh his memory of his boyhood days.

He arrived at the inn and walked silently across the foyer to speak to a woman he took to be the receptionist, but to him she looked a common floosie.

"Can I have a room for a couple of days please?'

"'Ere Charlie! There's a man 'ere that wants a room? Says can he have one?" the floosie shouted though a hatchway to the bar, as she chewed noisily on some gum.

A stout middle aged man sauntered through a doorway, rebuked the woman for being uncouth, then spoke to Tom in a slurred manner and reeking of beer.

"Sorry about that! Our Ethel hasn't had an offer now since VJ day. Did you say a room for a few days, Mr, er Mr?"

"I'm Colonel Williams. I wish to stay a while. How much is it?" Tom replied with his own question.

"Let's see now! If you just want a room its five shillings a night. Everything is extra. Hot water, or any meals, whatever."

"Make that five days then, but I'll only pay you twelve shillings in advance, as I may have to leave before the end of my stay. And landlord, I do not want to be disturbed by unwanted guests, no matter how they are dressed. Understand?" he stated as he pointed to the woman.

"Yes, I understand. Welcome to the Duke of Moreland Arms, Colonel Williams. If you have got a vehicle out the front, then you'd better take it through to the courtyard. Only our squire, Lord Moreland, does not like motor vehicles cluttering up his streets."

"Lord Moreland did you say? His streets? His village?" Tom asked innocently.

"Yes. He owns everything by ancestral right. The buildings, all land and all things living here, and even the rivers around his manor for the best part of ten miles or so. He's a judge too, so don't go crossing him or you'll end up with all your goods confiscated and thrown out of the village as always happens to unwanted guests." the landlord volunteered.

"Hmm! I'll bear that in mind. Don't worry, my vehicle is parked way out of sight. Here's your advance, and I think I will partake in some of your finest scotch and soda, landlord."

"Scotch! I haven't had that since Christmas. Don't you know about the rationing and all? There was a war on, you know! I'd recommend a good drink of the millers home made wine, or the local potato mash that tastes like whiskey, but a pint of ale is all I can offer for the moment."

Tom chuckled quietly at the revelation, and followed the innkeeper into the smoke filled semi darkness of the bar.

The hubbub of the bar fell silent as he felt several pairs of eyes staring at him as if to assess what sort of character would dare to wander into their cosy little pub.

"Make way for an *hofficer* and a gentleman. Let him sit by the fire, whilst I get his drink." the landlord announced and wiped a beer spilled table over with a filthy cloth.

Tom sat in the inglenook by the fire, drinking his ale slowly, staring at the burning logs waiting for someone to speak to him. The noise came back slowly into the room as the men turned their back on him as if to dismiss him as somebody of no account.

He did hear some mutterings from behind him about somebody going to tell the squire, there was a stranger in their midst. The Sergeant should also be told in case he was a trouble-maker of some sort.

Tom left the bar and on entering his room he found Ethel sitting on his bed.

"What are you doing here. Get out of here at once!"

"Aw come on now big boy. Lets' you and me have a party. You could do with a bit of comforting by the look of you." Ethel insisted.

Tom grabbed her roughly by the shoulders, and shoved her out through the door and locked it behind her.

"Pig! Wassamatter! The Jap's must've cut your balls off too?" she shouted at him.

The following morning after Tom had his breakfast, he took a leisurely stroll back along the village towards the war memorial in the centre of the village green. Some people stopped and looked at this stranger who had dared to come amongst them.

My father should be mentioned here, and so far nobody has recognised me yet. He thought, as he looked down the neat columns of names, carved in alphabetic sequence. To his horror he saw that his fathers name, Sergeant T.T. Wilson. DSC. Royal County Fusiliers, had been crudely scratched off the list.

Tom had fourteen long years piecing together as to who did what, to whom, and remembered faces and names as if it was only yesterday. He was accused and punished for double murder he did not commit, and his family banished from the family home and village.

What is the matter with this place. What is everybody trying to hide, as if I didn't know.

That surly man standing at the bar looked like Mitchell, and it looked like it was Walker who sat with his back to me. They haven't changed much except seemingly cocksure of themselves. There is one more for me to locate.

He walked back down the cottage path and stood at the doorway and paused, but heard furniture being dragged around, a child crying and a woman screaming in terror, all coming from inside the house.

He opened the door quietly, stepped inside the room and saw a burly man in the process of ripping the clothing from Mrs. Williams, and telling her just what he was going to do to her. All the while, another younger person who was swigging from a large stone flagon and egging the attacker on. Both men had their backs to him when he acted.

Tom went swiftly and silently behind the younger person, grabbed him by his head and wrung it like the neck of a chicken. Then with one stride he aimed one swift and almighty kick at the exposed genitals of the big man.

The force was such that it lifted him right up into the air, which made him crash back down onto the floor in a slobbering gasping heap. Tom then grabbed the man by the neck and broke it in the same manner as the other one. It was Anthony Beckett.

Mrs. Williams sobbed uncontrollably, calling her assailants filthy beasts as she tried to make herself decent in front of him.

He helped her to get dressed and managed to calm her down by giving her a cup of tea, and for her to tell him exactly what was going on. She told him that the estate farm hands were going round, raping the women and girls when the rent could not be paid.

Their husbands were beaten up, in some cases very badly, then made to work all hours without pay, and were forced to offer their womenfolk as barter. Of how some people just seem to disappear.

The squire had taken the death of his twelve year old twin girls very badly, especially as it was one of the village men-folk that had killed them. Some man by the name of Tom Wilson. He's supposed to be dead now, but we're all still suffering from it.

"Wait until my Arthur comes home. He'll sort them all out with his gun, just you wait and see." she avowed tearfully.

Tom looked into the woman's face and told her that there was nothing to worry about now. To remember that her husband is his best friend, so she was to take the five pounds he pressed into her hand. She just looked at it as if in a trance, with more tears welling into her eyes and started to cry afresh.

Tom searched and found another flagon in the bag the younger dead attacker had, and poured it all over the dead men. Then he dragged them down the lane and threw them over the little bridge that spanned the railway. He made it look as if they had sat on the bridge wall, fell off it in a drunken stupor and down onto the track below.

That evening whilst Tom was preparing himself for a another stroll, he heard a loud insistent knock at the door of his room.

"Colonel Williams. Are you in there? This is Police Sergeant 127. Open the door, I want a word with you." a deep voice commanded.

Tom slipped over quietly and opened the door to see a very large, fat policeman standing there.

"Good evening Police Sergeant 127, do come in. What can I do for you?" Tom asked abruptly. *Obviously the local bush telegraph had worked well*, he thought.

"I am here to enquire as to what business you have in this village, and how long you are planning to stay here for?'

"Well Sergeant. That is really none of your business on both accounts. I am a man who fought for King and Country, therefore am at liberty to go anywhere at any time I please. That is unless, there is some County by law that prohibits me from doing so. Do you know of any such a law?"

"The squire is the law around these parts, he's the local Magistrate." The sergeant boasted.

"What is he called?"

"It's Lord Moreland. And you'd better mind your manners when he comes into the village."

"Why is that? Has he a special license to practice his own law in the King's realm that even the King doesn't know about? So what's the purpose of your visit? Checking up on me and see if I resemble somebody you know?"

"You said your name is Williams. Have you ever lived around these parts before?"

"Where I come from, Williams is a very common name. I had sixteen Williams' in my regiment, and even twenty-five Jones' all in the one company. As for me living around these parts. I'm here, there, everywhere during the last six years, but that's enough about me. What about you? By the look of it, you must have spent your war years, with your fat belly up to the bar in the local pub no doubt. Did the squire Lord Moreland serve King and Country?"

"Yes, he was at Dunkirk. But his mother, who looked after the estate for him when he was away, had died suddenly, so he decided that he was needed here to look after the estate. Besides he is a Lord, and they're not supposed to go to war you know." the sergeant explained loftily.

"Is that so. Who told you that? The King would be very pleased to find that one of his Lords deemed himself excused for duty at the front line, especially when his two daughters were in the blitzes of London." Tom said angrily, then added.

"In fact I wonder what the War Office would say about that?'

"Now don't you start any trouble Williams, or I'll be forced to throw you in jail and await his lordships pleasure."

"It's Colonel Williams G.C. to you Police Sergeant 127. Now if you don't mind, I have things to do. Shut the door on your way out, there's a good fellow." Tom said icily, as he dismissed the scowling policeman with a clap of his hands.

"I'll tell his lordships about you." he stated as he went out slamming the door behind him.

The cool air of the summer evening gently fanned Tom's face as he walked down the lane that he knew would take him down past the orchard and on to the stone bridge that spanned the river, some half mile away from the village. He strolled along the pathway that followed the river, very soon he reached his old favourite fishing spot, under the same old tree.

Tom stood very still with his back to the tree and looked around to where his boyhood and innocence was stolen from him, and wondered what really happened here all those years ago. The slight breeze whispering over the growing grain crops and from the bushes, which made him think he heard the girls whisper his name to say "Tommee, we're over here Tommee!"

He looked around to see but saw nothing. He was not one for fancy notions, nor was he one for self-pity as the Borstal years and the carnage of war saw to that, but his eyes started to mist over at the thought of the deeds that were perpetrated against his family and of the twins.

He remembered that he lost his prize fishing rod that his father gave him, and his home made animal snares that had disappeared in all the commotion, and decided to look around to see if anything could be found after all these years.

He came to the oxbow on his side of the river and opposite the river-bank to where the twins were supposed to have been murdered. Yet again he thought he heard the girls giggling and saying.

"Here we are Tommee! You've found us Tommee!"

He looked around again but dismissed it from his mind. After a little while, he found the remains of a leather belt that still had a brass buckle with the initials J.M embossed on it. Then he found an ornate silver bauble, and recognised that it must have belonged to the squire, Moreland.

He also found a bronze horseshoe that was caught up in a snare, which was behind a row of evergreens that lined the whole length of the oxbow. *That will do for a start.* Tom said quietly to himself, and left the area to go back to his lodgings again, but stopped when he heard some rustling close by, and crouched down to conceal himself among the tall corn stalks, so that he can see what it was.

"Bleedin 'ell! He was there a minute ago, maybe he's gone further up the stream.

We'll try to cut him off, but make certain your rope is ready to string him up. We don't put up with strangers coming here uninvited." whispered a voice.

"No Mitchell! I'll just tie him up, you can do what you like. We don't know who this man is and it's certainly not Wilson 'cause he's supposed to be dead."

"Shut up you fool, Walker. It's a mystery what happened to Beckett and Thompson. But you can bet your last farthing, this stranger had something to do with it, whether he is Wilson or not. Now stop your snivelling and get on with it, or his lordship will do for us both." came the louder whisper.

Tom's army field craft and knowledge of unarmed combat had kept him alive over the battlefields of the world. Handling two beer bellied men even much larger and taller than him, would not be a problem for him.

The two men rushed past him, so he let them go until they were much further away up stream, before he moved off back the way he had come and back to his lodgings.

Yet another fine morning greeted Tom as he sought out the innkeeper.

"Mornin' Colonel!" he said with surprise on seeing Tom.

"What can I get you?"

"I'm leaving in about half an hour, but will be back in about two or three days time." Tom said curtly.

"Right ho Colonel! Going somewhere nice? Maybe a lady friend or something?"

"Let's put it this way landlord. I'll be back, so try and keep this room free for me." Tom knew that there were no other guests in residence except him, and knew that his room would be exactly the same one.

"I'll try and do just that." the innkeeper replied.

Tom carried his packed suitcase, but he made it look empty as he walked down the lane towards his old home. Everybody was forced to walk unless they had a horse and cart, as horsepower was still King throughout the whole estate and especially in the two villages.

Apart from the country bus service or the trains coming through the estate, there was no mechanical vehicle to be seen all day. But Tom's horsepower was an open-topped sports car that was hidden away in an outhouse.

The outhouse used to be his Father's carpentry shed and he knew where the key was always hidden. Having taken the car out then re-locked the shed and put the key back, he roared off down the country lanes, splashing through the shallow ford that gave its name to the village of FORDHAM and of MORELAND. But purely as of the whim by the Lord, thus giving its name of Fordham in Moreland.

The twin village on the other side of the estate was called Woodham (because of the woods) in Moreland.

The Manor in Moreland, was the original Moreland's castle built in the 12th century, but was much renovated and adapted over the centuries to suit the image of the Aristocracy of that era. It was situated on top of a hill, which helped to form a triangle with the two villages in the estate.

The whole estate had a high stone wall surrounding it, with thick barbed wire fence running along the railway branch line and right down even to the rivers' edge. All designed as a giant 'Trespassers and strangers keep out or else' sign.

Moreland & Other Stories

But Tom knew that he would be safe, once he passed out through the twin towers of a portcullis type of gate that marked one of the two the entrances to the estate.

This was a place where time seemed to have stood still, and where everybody was under the total dominance of Lord Moreland and his cronies.

It took him several hours to reach his Brigade HQ. He wanted to seek out his friend Brigadier Sir Geoffrey Collins then afterwards, his best mate Sergeant 'Thumper' Williams MC. Williams' nickname of 'Thumper' was given to him because he was always fighting, and lucky he was still a sergeant, thanks to Tom's interventions.

The Brigadier was an old war-horse with plenty of the right connections, which suited Tom's myriad of questions into the background and other records of Lord Moreland. Having renewed his acquaintances and briefed the Brigadier on what he needed, he then left to see Williams who was in the nearby military hospital.

"Sergeant Williams. Get on your feet! Tom commanded sternly.

Williams, through military conditioning started to obey, but sneaked a glance as to who gave the order.

"Colonel Tom! You rascal, you nearly 'ad me going there for a minute! How's me missus? When can I get out of here?" Williams greeted him with a series of questions.

"How dare you come into this ward unannounced. Who are you and what do you want with this patient?" the ward sister demanded angrily as she intercepted Tom.

Tom looked at the irate female Captain.

"Hello Matron. I'm Colonel Wilson of the 2nd Commando Brigade. I need this man on duty today if he can be discharged, that is." he explained politely.

"I don't know Colonel. I'll have to see the M.O. first." The matron said starchily as she gave him a salute and left the ward.

"As for you Sergeant Williams. We're getting you out of here. This is only for the sick men. You know my feelings about lead swingers and skivers." Tom chided mockingly.

Before Williams could reply, the Medical officer quickly appeared, surrounded by a bevy of nurses and ward matrons.

"Colonel Wilson? I know that name, but is that you, Tom?" he asked.

Tom looked round to see a man dressed in a Colonel's uniform.

"Colonel! Why it's old Captain Taffy Jones, from Torbruk. Last time I saw you, you were knee deep in blood and guts. Belated congratulations on your promotions Taffy. How the devil are you?" Tom said elatedly as he recognised and shook the hand of this old friend of his, much to the dismay of the ward matron.

"I understand that you're wanting to take this nuisance of a sergeant off my hands?"

"He is needed for special duties, but I need your clearance providing he's fit."

"He'll do. Some fresh air and exercise is what he needs. He's to report back in about 1 month." Jones said, then turned to his staff.

"Matron. See that this patient is given sufficient medicine and discharge him if you please."

"Very well sir!" the matron said promptly, then turned to Williams.

"Now then sergeant! Come along now, get yourself dressed. The M.O. wants your bed for a really sick soldier. Your transport is about to leave." the matron ordered.

Williams finally got dressed, then went slowly around the ward, bidding farewell to his fellow ward mates. He kissed each nurse in turn, even the ward matron, who went red faced as it was all done in front of, and much to the amusement of the two Colonels.

"Well Taffy, many thanks for this. We really must be getting along now. I shall bring our old sergeant friend back for you again soon." Tom said quietly as they shook hands goodbye, bringing the jubilant Williams with him, who was still waving to the nursing staff as they went out of the building.

"We are billeted in a local hotel for the night Thumper, all expenses paid by the War Office. We need to discuss certain items that up to now, was neither the time nor the place to do so."

"What's up Colonel Tom? If I know you, you're up to something and you need me to bail you out again, like as not. What's the Brigadier want us for? But never mind all that. First, and I needn't really ask you this, but how did you find the village, my missus and my little lass Sarah?"

"No problem. But that is just what we need to talk about. Where you are living, is only just the start. We can discuss this over lunch and a few beers tonight, as I'm due to see the Brigadier tomorrow."

"Well then let's get started by parking this little beauty up somewhere." Williams chuckled and happy to be with his comrade in arms again!

They checked into the hotel, then after their evening meal, settled down into two very large and cavernous leather armchairs. Armed with a couple of drinks, they started talking well into the evening.

Tom told him why and how easy it was to find where Thumper lived. Of how Moreland treated Tom and his family; of how Moreland was running the place by sheer terror and brute force, and other such unpleasantries.

Afterwards he wanted to know, by the strangest co-incidences, how Williams ended up living in his old home.

"That's easy! My mother in law was the chief cook up at the manor and my wife was a chambermaid at the time. I lived in the other village with my family and as you already know, one of the water baliffs for the whole estate. So when her mother was retired from the manor, the squire gave her a grace and favour cottage to live in. She died not long after our wedding, and shortly after that I went and joined up. That made the house a rent paying house again, costing me seven shillings a week. I made sure that Susan had my pay from the Post Office every month, but then as you know, sometimes the pay was late going out.

It was thanks to some money that Susan inherited that she managed to cope somehow. Mind you though, it's a mystery where it came from." Williams explained.

Tom paused to get another drink, then on his return went on to explain what he was planning to do when they got back to the village, but that everything was dependent on the information given him by the Brigadier.

Whereas, as far as the squire and his cronies were concerned, he needed Williams as his back up for the inevitable confrontation. He told Williams that if need be, even the Brigadier will help when the time comes.

Williams nodded his head and said.

"I knew it! I knew it all along from the moment I met you, that there was something eating away at you. You never did let on, but I could always tell. No wonder the Jerries and Japs got a load of grief from you. Everyone must have been a Mitchell, Walker and Beckett. Don't you worry, I'll watch your back and be your shadow, just like old times in the jungle. Okay Colonel Tom?"

Tom thanked his friend to conclude the business then climbed their weary way up the stairs to their respective rooms.

"You can remain here until I come back from HQ, but have everything packed and ready for moving out and the homeward march. See you in the morning." Tom said as he bade his sergeant good night.

The following morning was a cool showery day for Tom to go back to see his Brigadier and get the information he needed.

"Its all there Tom. That Lord Moreland's a scoundrel and a coward by all accounts. He should have been court martialled! If I can help out or if there's anything else you need, just say the word." Collins stated, and offered a brown package to him.

"You have a good plan, but beware of Moreland if you tangle with him, he's an excellent swordsman. He starts off with his left hand but in fact is right handed. I know, I've crossed swords with him before the war. Hence this gammy arm of mine." Collins revealed, as he tapped his shoulder gently.

"Thank you for your help Sir Geoffrey. I will certainly do that. Give my regards to Lady Sybil, won't you." Tom said, as he first shook hands then bade farewell in traditional military style.

He arrived back to find Williams waiting in the foyer and standing guard over their baggage.

"Its raining outside, but it's a lovely day, because we are both going home, sergeant."

"Amen to all that. Lets go!" Williams replied softly, picking up all the baggage and barging his way through anybody who stood in his way.

Williams drove steadily onwards for home, whilst Tom read some of the neatly typed reports.

"It says here, there was a Home Office inquiry into the irregularities of law and order in Moreland. But our squire managed to wangle his way out of it. That and the one from the War Office, concerning him not returning to duty, after Dunkirk."

"Must have pulled a few strings in the Lords then. What else has he dodged Colonel Tom?"

"There's a whole string of them. But this report from the Brigadier concerning the background of our friend and the rules governing aristocracy and so on, is just what I need. But we can talk about that later, soon after you've had a night at home with your good wife and your little girl."

"Aw is that all you're giving me Tom? I thought at least a week and I deserve that."

"No. What I told you earlier about the goings on in the village was only the half of it. Speak to your wife about what I mean, so I think we had better stick close for a while." Tom advised.

"But don't worry old friend. I'll be discreet and be out of sight as and when you feel the urge." Tom added.

"Thanks Tom. For one 'orrible moment I thought we'd have a threesome, and not just to keep warm either like we did in Norway."

Both men fell silent for a while, lost in their own thoughts and feelings that lasted until they arrived into the estate.

"Better pull up here Thumper. I'll go and see if the coast is clear." Tom advised, as they arrived outside Williams' cottage.

"We don't want snooping eyes or flapping ears. You will have to pretend that you came off the last train and that I had just given you a lift. This is where Operation Whiplash begins. This is your final briefing so remember as its important.

Tell your wife that, for the moment, the both of you don't know me. If you have anything that goes against the run of play try to contact me, in our usual manner. Understood Sergeant?"

"Yeah! Just like old times Colonel, just like old times." Williams whispered his acknowledgement with a far away look. Between the two of them and in special commando units, they had done a lot of covert activity behind enemy lines. For them, this plan would only be a walk in the park.

"Right then. Have a good homecoming Thumper, and I'll see you in the morning." Tom concluded and waved to Williams as he drove off down the lane to his lodgings.

Moreland & Other Stories

* * *

The sign above the coaching inn was dimly lit, but Tom could recognise the heraldic coat of arms and translated the Latin motto underneath it 'Hold in Honour'. *So much for the family motto for the Duke of Moreland, or should I say Duc Du Muelande and kiss your erstwhile French arse.*

You have been a disgrace to all your forefathers going right back to William I.

Yet you dare to preach to my family about disgracing the family honour. Tom muttered to himself as he drove the car slowly into the courtyard and parked it inside a converted stable.

"Welcome back Colonel. I've kept your room. How long do you plan to stay this time?" the innkeeper greeted heartily.

"Good evening Innkeeper. Say about three days this time." Tom replied civilly, all the while looking through the open hatchway to the bar to see who was there.

"Here's your room key. I'll have some supper sent up to your room if you wish."

'No thank you. I will just have a couple of beers in the lounge before retiring to bed. I've had a long drive, and my car is parked in the courtyard as you advised me last time I was here. Don't want to upset the squire, now do we."

"No, that's a fact. Mind you, he is still away on business and won't be back until Saturday. He had asked about you and gave me this letter for you. He would like you to pay him a visit before you go away again."

"Oh really! Whoever told him when I was here last time, had done me a good service, because I would like to meet a real Lord in his manor. We'll see anyway Innkeeper." Tom concluded the conversation by accepting the envelope and carrying his suitcases up the broad stairway leading to the landing of his room.

That bush telegraph was as good as its reputation. The innkeeper certainly knew what was in my letter. At least that solves one problem as I get to see the squire officially instead of creeping about his premises after him. Tom thought as he put his heavy case on the floor and locked the door behind him.

The crowing of the rooster brought Tom back to reality, as he slowly opened his room curtains to be greeted with a bright sunny morning.

He felt the warmth of the sun on his face and opened the window and took several breaths of fresh air into his lungs then prepared himself for the day.

"Good morning Colonel! Here's your breakfast, all hot and tasty!" The innkeeper said affably.

"Is there anything else you like. Maybe a paper or something Colonel?"

"Thank you my good man." *Operation WHIPLASH was now in operation. So must keep him sweet.*

"Yes there is. I noticed that there are some horses stabled in the courtyard. I would like to spend the next couple of days riding around the estate. Just like the squire does. Do you think that I could borrow one?"

"That's what they're there for, Colonel. I'll have a word with the groom whilst you enjoy your breakfast. I shan't be long."

Shortly afterwards, the man came back huffing and puffing.

"The groom said it's okay, but you'd have to pay him in advance for the horse's upkeep and the like. "

"Fair enough. But before that, I need to pay you for my lodgings. How much do I owe you?"

"Well let me see now. It's –" the innkeeper started to count out as he saw Tom opening his wallet.

"Its fifteen shillings for your board, and say eight shillings for your meals and ten shillings for your ale, that makes it thirty-five shillings, no make that extra for the ale, so that's –"

he stammered and licking his lips, as Tom flashed a wad of five pound notes.

"Let's put it this way Innkeeper. You'll have three guineas for my board and lodgings now." Tom stated, as he start putting his wallet away before putting another hand into one of his trouser pockets.

"Here's some loose change. Let's see, say about fifteen shillings should do for the horse. We are quits now, yes?" Tom asked as he put the coins into the innkeepers' grubby hands.

"Yes! Thank you Colonel. You're very generous. I'll go and tell the stable hand to saddle up a good horse for you." the innkeeper replied, as he slipped all the money into his pocket then scampered off to the stables.

It's been a while since I was in a saddle. Plenty of mules and camels yes, but a long time since riding a horse. Tom thought as he went up to his room and got prepared for a day in the saddle.

The innkeeper stood in the doorway of the bar and watched Tom ride off.

"I'll be back for lunch and a cold pint of your best ale, innkeeper." Tom shouted to him, as he rode the chestnut coloured animal down through village.

The horse trotted down the village lane as Tom guided it towards the garden gate to his old cottage. When he reached it he stopped the horse, dismounted and let it drink from the stream running down the side of the lane. He saw that Williams was already at the gate, looking as if he was fixing it.

"Good morning sir, what lane would take me down to the river." Tom asked as part of the pretence.

"If you take this lane on the right." Williams stated his instructions in a loud voice, as Tom whispered his messages.

"Oxbow. Chestnut tree and back, this way. At pub for 1200. Invite at Manor 1100hrs this Saturday."

"Have you got that sir?" Williams finally concluded his instructions.

"Yes. Down lane half mile, bridge, turn right onto bridle to ford and back. Thank you very much sir." Tom replied and nodded his head as he started to climb back onto the saddle.

"Rent men due shortly. Don't know how many. Might see you at the chestnut tree. Call in on way back, or pub 1200." Williams whispered as he reached over to pat the horse's nose.

God help those rent men if they try it again. Tom chuckled to himself and went on his way, but not as instructed.

Yes, the old hay barn was still there. The styles and gates to the fields were in the same positions. Apart from the odd tree felling or new growth, everything was just the same. He knew the terrain well even after fourteen years absence, and he felt a great joy in its re-discovery.

Before long, he found himself down by the river and near to where he used to set his rabbit snares and wild hog traps. He stopped by the evergreens he used as a den to hide when the water bailiffs were due along. The evergreens had grown very tall and much thicker, but still a good hideaway. *Fancy me not recognising Williams as one of the bailiffs. They must have sent him over to the rivers of the former estate lands to work.*

There was something flashing down stream of the river and beyond the chestnut tree, which caught Tom's attention. He quickly dismounted and led his horse into his old den, then pulled out an apple from the saddlebag and gave it to the horse to keep it quiet.

There was someone on a horse carrying a rifle, accompanied by two men on foot, coming quickly towards him. Tom reached back into his saddlebag and took out his powerful binoculars to see who it was. It was a youth on the horse, and Mitchell as one of the men, but he didn't know the other one.

Tom made the horse lie down keeping it quiet all the time by softly whispering in its' ear. He had learned of this trick in the jungles of Burma, to save himself from the inquisitive Japanese patrols.

It took several minutes for the boy and the two men to pass, who talked about the stranger in the pub and that the water bailiff, Williams was now back from the war to take over again. Tom waited until the trio disappeared around the tree-lined bend before Tom coming out from his den. After mounting his horse, he galloped the other way towards the chestnut tree and stopped for Williams to show up.

Thumper must have had a good time with those rent men otherwise he'd be hiding up this tree. Better go back and see he's all right. He spun the horse round and galloped up through the meadow, jumped over gates and ditches and clattered down the lane towards the house, slowing down as he rounded the bend to come into view of the house.

He saw that Mrs Williams was humming to herself as she swept the front door step. The little girl playing with her doll under the apple tree, and Thumper throwing the bodies of three men over a wall on the other side of the road as if putting out the rubbish.

Those men had the misfortune not to know that Sergeant Williams was a martial arts expert, and a thoroughly nasty piece of work. Thank God he's my best friend.

"Good morning again sir, did you enjoy your ride?" Williams greeted.

"Why yes thank you. I see you've had a spot of bother here. Everything all right?"

"Just a few uninvited guests that's all, no problem." Williams replied with a large grin on his face.

"Well if you're sure. I'll be in the pub if you care to join me. That is of course if your lady wife can spare you."

"Well I don't know." Williams said uncertainly as his wife took her cue to speak.

"Yes husband. You have done a good job today, go and join him. He will see you shortly sir, and thank you for your concern." Mrs Williams concluded as she finished brushing the garden path, as Tom rode back to the stables.

"Here you are groom! He's a good horse, no trouble. I wish to use him again later on if I may." Tom stated as he dismounted from his horse handing the reins to him.

"That's okay sir, but I need money for to look after the horse. The Innkeeper only gave me three shillings." was the disgruntled reply.

"Three shillings you say! Well, I'll just have to see the innkeeper about that. I had given him a good fifteen shillings like you asked. "

"Oh no sir! I said it was twelve shillings for three days including feed, the mucking out and the like."

"Let me sort this out for you. I'll see you are paid fairly, and the horse fed properly." Tom stated and strode out of the stables towards the inn.

"Innkeeper, a word in your ear if you please!" Tom shouted out to the innkeeper, who walked over to him slowly.

When he reached the bar opposite Tom, Tom grabbed him by the collars and almost dragged him right over the counter.

"Now look here Innkeeper! Don't take advantage of strangers staying at your inn, especially me! I gave you good money to pay the groom to feed the horse I had been riding. Now cough up or I'll be forced to re arrange some features around here, starting with your face! Have you got that innkeeper?" Tom snarled at him

'Y, Y, Yes! Anything Colonel! Just let me breathe, you're choking me!" the innkeeper pleaded and started to cough as Tom let go of him.

"I thought you were an honest Innkeeper! Now be off with you and pay the man what I gave you. When you come back

I'll have a flagon of your coldest ale, which will be on the house seeing as you made me loose my temper."

The innkeeper waddled out through the back of the bar and came back shortly with Tom's flagon of ale.

"All paid now Colonel. I was going to pay him, but forgot all about it. There was no need to get cross with me. Here's your flagon, it's on the house." he said and slammed the wooden tankard down in front of Tom, spilling some of its contents.

The bar was starting to fill up with the farmhands eager to sup some cool ale to slake their thirst, but taking no notice of Tom as he sat in his chair by the unlit log fire. It was not until he noticed Williams had made an appearance which caused a deathly hush from the rest of the customers standing in the bar.

"Pint of ale Charlie! Make it a cold one!" Williams demanded loudly as he entered the bar.

"Who are you calling me Charlie? Do I know you mister?" the innkeeper asked annoyingly as he peered into William's face.

Williams looked around at some of the staring faces and started to name some of them.

"Seth Booker, you're the village shepherd. Freddy Lowe, you look after the piggery down by the black stream. Frank Swanson, you're the miller down by the ford." Williams explained and rattled them off in quick succession.

"We know who we are, but who are you? "asked one.

"Wait a minute. Why, it must be the water bailiff. It's Arthur Williams from Woodham in Moreland. " the innkeeper said with surprise.

"What! The bailiff Arthur Williams that went off to war?" the miller asked aloud.

"Yes, that's him. Welcome back bailiff. Innkeeper, give that man some of the finest ale that hasn't got watered down." stated another as he ran over to shake Williams' hand.

"Tell us about the war, bailiff. I'll bet you've got lots of medals to wear." shouted another.

Tom sat in his chair pretending not to notice, sipping his ale. *Welcome the conquering hero Thumper. Wait until they find the bodies of the rent men.*

Two of the farmers came over to Tom and demanded quite belligerently, that he stood up and pay respects to their village war hero. Tom obliged so as not to spoil Operation Whiplash.

"It seems that I am required to buy you a pint sergeant! Seeing as I had already given you a lift from the station, maybe we could swap war experiences some time." Tom stated quietly to Williams, while the others looked on with approval.

"Yes! maybe another time" Williams replied and dismissed him to drink the toasts with his fellow villagers.

"What did you do. Where you a high ranking officer with the commandos or something?" one man asked.

"Yes, what medals 'ave you got bailiff?" the men started to ask and warmed to Williams, and taking a dislike to the seemingly disrespectful Tom who did not seem to share their enthusiasm for him.

Tom slipped out the door quietly without anybody noticing him, and went out the back to retrieve his horse. He had a few items to check on, whilst Williams kept the farmhands busy at the bar, which was getting a little more noisy as he finally left the stables.

The notice on the cemetery gate stated that all animals must be tied up to the rails provided, and silence must be observed when paying respects to the dead. Not by the request of the parish Minister, but by order of Lord Moreland.

So who was to argue this fine tradition, except those who desecrate the tombs and monuments to the Glorious Dead.

Moreland & Other Stories

Tom mused as he walked slowly up the gravel path towards the headstone that marked his Father's grave.

Before he got there, he recognised the golden haired youth he saw earlier with the gun, and walked slowly towards him. The boy stood in front of two identical white marble grave stones, with his head bowed and a large bunch of flowers in his arms and was speaking softly to himself as Tom drew along side him.

"Here's a bunch of your favourite flowers my dearest sisters. It is to mark the day of your demise." the boy whispered sadly.

Tom looked at the gravestones and saw that it was the graves of Lily and Iris that this boy was whispering to, and felt the sadness of the loss of these lovely girls that he had whiled away a summer afternoon with. His anger to whoever killed them was welling up inside him which only served to re-enforce his resolve to find the killers of these girls.

"It is good to remember loved ones young man. They will always be alive and free for as long as they are remembered by those who are left behind." Tom said quietly as he stooped down beside the boy. Yet again he thought he heard their voices calling him as he looked at their neat graves.

"Yes, I have always felt them as if they were sitting on their headstones and waving to me, every time I come here." the boy started.

"Who are you sir? Why have you disturbed me? You have no business in the cemetery until after I have left." the boy said with annoyance as he stood up to confront this stranger.

"Then who might you be to command the dead to remain unvisited until you leave?" Tom challenged him with his own question.

"You are either an imbecile or an ignorant person not to know that I am the Squire of Moreland. I hold that title as Heir to the Moreland estate after my father who is the current Lord of Moreland." the boy said haughtily.

"But who are you? State your business!" He challenged boldly.

Tom stood up and looked over to his father's gravestone some yards away.

"I am a visitor seeking the last resting place of my last known relatives that were reported to be interred within this place." he stated flatly.

"You are but an adolescent. Do you hold power of attorney over such visitors, guests to your estate, preventing the succour you get with your lost ones?"

"No sir I do not! I hold command until my Father returns." the boy retorted swiftly, but with a more conciliatory tone in his voice added

"You are welcome to continue your quest. Never let it be said that the future Lord of Moreland would be so crass as to deny such a basic right that you seek."

"Thank you squire. I hope we meet again soon." Tom said civilly and looked at this boy standing by at the two graves. The twins were twelve, 'Murdered by Tom Wilson'.

"Now be off with you and leave me with my sisters, or I'll call the foreman to escort you away." He ordered.

The Brigadiers' records were right and just as I thought. Two lovely girls dead on the very week their brother was born. Just one more coincidence on this estate, or was it?

His afternoon ride took him across the estate to the other village, and to the home farm of the manor where most villagers were not allowed to venture. This was for the privileged few and the favoured cronies of the squire.

He was amazed at the lushness of the place, of its open grasslands, of the magnificent building standing on the top of the hill, that was almost obscured by tall well established trees brought from distant lands. Of the neat but well spaced lodges dotted around, instead of the cramped run down hovels that formed the villages. *A totally different world for the rich,* Tom shouted out his disgust to the world, as he galloped away back to his own village.

"Here you are again groom. He needs a good rub down, and see that he gets a nice feed of oats. I would like him again tomorrow, if that's all right? You had your money?"

"Yes thank you very much sir. I'll see the horse is well looked after and ready for you after breakfast time." The groom replied, leading the horse back into its stable.

'Good evening Innkeeper! Be a good man and fetch me a light supper with a cup of sweet tea. I need to make a phone call, so if it's all right with you, I'll make it from here in the foyer." Tom stated.

"Yes, you go right ahead. I'll have your tea ready in the lounge." The innkeeper replied sullenly.

The dust on the phone spoke of disuse, as Tom dialled the operator and requested he put through to his Brigade HQ. He knew there were people listening to him speak. *The phone tap at the switchboard was part of the bush telegraph after all.* He thought.

He spoke in a foreign language and in code to keep his conversation private, as the switchboard operator interrupted him and told him to speak the King's language. Tom laughed at the barefaced cheek and told her to get off the line as he concluded his business.

The deed was set for the following day after the return of the Lord Moreland, and at the allotted time. But first, he needed to muster his forces.

"Morning groom! I need a favour of you but I'll pay you handsomely." Tom spoke quietly so as not to be overheard.

"Good morning Colonel! Your horse is ready. Am at your service, what is it that I can do for you?" was the genial reply.

"I need you to saddle up another horse of equal nature to mine. Please make it quick as I have to attend Lord Moreland very soon. Here's two florins for your trouble."

"Lord Moreland? If you're going there then you'd better be careful 'cause there's a mob going around hunting for the killers of the three rent men that were found yesterday down the school lane next to the water bailiff's cottage."

"Three men killed you say? Now who'd do a thing like that?"

"There's a rumour that Williams the water bailiff did it, 'cause his house was the last one to have been visited by the rent collectors. But he's suffering from his war wounds, so he couldn't have done it. Mind you Colonel, you were seen there at the time so you might get the fault." the groom volunteered.

"Thank you for your concern. No doubt the squire will see that I have safe passage throughout the estate."

"Maybe so. But the police sergeant is looking to bring you to account, before the Lord arrives this morning. Nobody does anything without the sergeant's knowledge in case you didn't know."

"Thanks for telling me. I shall take that into account during my ride today."

"Well if there's anything else Colonel, I'll get that horse for you."

Tom waited patiently until the other horse was brought out to him.

"Groom, I would ask you to do me one more favour." Tom paused to see the grooms' reaction.

"Yes Colonel. At your service."

"I need to speak to you somewhere private for what I am about to say to you."

"I think you'd better come into the stables here." the groom said as he ushered Tom to a secluded place.

Tom explained carefully what was needed and entrusted the groom to do it. He gave the groom some maps and a piece of paper that would be used for the groom to understand.

When he had finished telling the groom he demanded absolute obedience from him in order to comply with what Tom had given him.

"Will you do this for me?" Tom asked.

"You are asking me to risk my job, home, wife and family just to help you! What if I fail, what guarantee have I got against all this?" the groom asked suspiciously.

"If you do what I have entrusted you with, you will live to celebrate your own liberation day. I am prepared to bargain within reason with you. So what do you say?"

"So that's all I have to do. Is it? Mind you I have to watch with whom I speak to, which is not very many, certainly within this village, but maybe my friends in the other village would help."

"I have someone who will help you in those matters, all I need to know is if you'll do it.

"I too am taking a terrible risk talking to you, if you decide not to take this task on mind you."

The groom sat on a bale of hay for a moment weighing up his proposition.

"I will agree to this Colonel, but what's in it for me and my family?" he asked

"For a start. I will give you straw and oats for all your horses and a five gallon barrel of ale for yourself." Tom said for openers.

"A barrel of ale you say?"

"Yes. That and maybe something for your lady wife?" Tom said as he upped the stakes.

"I have to watch my step around here." the groom pondered and thought for a moment.

"But if you make that several yards of fine cloth for my wife and a leather hide as well, we have a deal."
"You drive a hard bargain, Groom! Very well then! Let's agree on that!" Tom said, spitting on his hand and offering it to the groom to shake it. The groom did the same that sealed their bargain by that handshake.

Tom took the other horse and tied its reins to his saddle and steered his own horse out through the courtyard and down the lane towards Williams' cottage.
"Good morning Colonel! Planning another ride?" Williams called from his open front door.
"See you've got a second horse. Maybe a long ride this time?"
"Good morning Sergeant Williams!" Tom said politely.
"I brought him along in case you care to join me."
"Sounds inviting. Yes I'll join you." he replied. Williams then turned to his wife, spoke to her quietly then kissed her and walked swiftly towards the waiting horse.
The two men walked their horses down the lanes. Through woods, and streams until they had skirted the village, to come out by the lower orchard lane below the policeman's house.
All the while they talked about the deed ahead, kept a sharp lookout for followers or potential ambushes from the other villagers that the groom spoke about.
'Two men on horseback with dogs tracking us on my left moving along the river bank." Tom warned his friend.
"Yes I see them way back. There's five men on horseback up in the woods in front of us to my right. Unless I'm mistaken, it looks like a welcoming party coming to greet us Tom."
"We'll duck out of sight along this gully that comes up behind them on the hill."
Both men dismounted and went along the gully before remounting their horses and riding full gallop right through the

waiting men, taking them by total surprise.

Tom dropped a red smoke flare and a thunderflash that boomed its echo all over the estate.

"That's my signal." the groom said quietly to himself as he heard the echoing bang.

The two friends galloped their horse up the long grassy hill towards the side of the manor, jumping their horses over fences and gates with ease, until they finally arrived into the cobbled courtyard of the old castle. There they slowed down and trotted calmly up the drive-way leading to the grand entrance of the manor.

They led their horses to a drinking trough and after the horses were watered, the two friends tied their horses to a hitching rail next to some grass where the horses could eat whilst they were inside.

As they walked into the dark hallway of the manor, they were grabbed roughly by several men. Tom saw that Mitchell and Walker were standing, watching, from some distance away guarding an open doorway with what he made out to be Lord Moreland standing inside it.

"So this is how you treat your invited guests is it Moreland. A coward who has others to fight for him?" Tom challenged, but getting a blow to his stomach for his troubles.

"Shut your filthy mouth. It's Lord Moreland to you, you decrepid old man" growled one of his attackers.

"Code Viper!" Tom whispered to Williams.

As both men broke free, Williams started laying into the group of men whilst Tom leapt towards Moreland's henchmen.

Tom's fight with the two men took him into a large hall where Moreland was, which had a lot of old weapons adorning the walls. He guessed that this was the Moreland's inner sanctum, and that all the suits of armour and battle flags around came from Moreland's famous forefathers.

"I'll deal with you in a minute Moreland," Tom shouted, as he slammed the door behind him and karate chopped the two henchmen to unconsciousness.

As he stood over them he felt a steel object pressing against him, and saw it was Moreland holding a duelling sword to his throat, forcing him to stand up.

"You fight well Colonel! But you forgot about me. All I have to do is flick my wrist and your windpipe will spew forth your life's blood." Moreland said softly as he gave a menacing prick to Tom's throat.

"Why have you come to my estate? Who are you, and I don't mean a Colonel. I demand to know exactly what you're up to and I intend finding out. Do I make myself clear, Colonel?" Moreland stated as he flicked the point over Tom's face making one of his cheeks bleed.

Tom looked at the still unconscious men quickly, then at Moreland.

"So this is how the Moreland's greet their guests. It appears that when the Lords of Moreland fight, they make certain of superior numbers, and their opponents unarmed before they lift a sword in anger?" Tom goaded Moreland.

"If you wish to emulate your forefathers then you would at least fight fair."

"Fight fair!" Moreland scoffed.

"Who told the Jerries and the Japs to fight fair. Fighting fair is only for the doomed and the dead."

"You are supposed to be an Officer and a soldier like me. Why not at least give me the chance. Officer to Officer. I'll fight you with any weapon you choose. What do you say Moreland?" Tom challenged.

Moreland forced Tom backwards with the point of his sword, towards an array of swords fixed to a wall and stood back.

"Take your pick Colonel, and face me in the middle of the room. In fact you can take two if you can handle them. I'll show you how to fight." Moreland hissed.

Tom looked at the array of weapons and chose one, then followed Moreland into the middle of the room.

"Hmm! The tenth Duke of Moreland's favourite sword I believe. A good choice! Prepare to answer my questions when I've finished with you. En Guard!" Moreland said swiftly as he lunged at Tom.

Remember. He starts off left handed just so that his opponents get used to it then changes over for the final flourish Tom, was the advice his Brigadier had given him.

The two men lunged and parried and moved all over the room as their fencing got more intense. Tom managed to work his way back to kick the head of one of the henchmen that started to come round, knocking him out again.

"Kicking men when they're down is all you appear to do Colonel." Moreland rasped as he managed to slice into Tom's upper arm.

Tom was beginning to appreciate the magnificence of sword fighting as he'd been told several times in the officer's mess. But for him, he'd rather a hand to hand scrap any day and was getting tired of this charade.

"That cut will cost you Moreland." Tom fought off another parry and sliced the thigh of Moreland.

"See what I mean? You should have stuck to the proper appointment time."

"It's your fault that you arrived early. You are fighting like an old woman Colonel, and I'm tired of all this. Now let's fight properly." Moreland snarled, as he swiftly changed his sword over to his other hand and lashed out to catch Tom's exposed chest.

But Tom saw the switch and was ready for him. He grabbed Moreland's sword hand and arm then with a judo throw, threw Moreland across the room scattering suits of armour all over the place. Moreland looked at Tom with total surprise, cursed him for his ungentlemanly behaviour and came back at him flaying his sword quickly trying to force Tom against a wall.

Tom merely dodged the flashing blade and with a karate kick to Moreland's crotch and a blow to Moreland's temple with the hilt of his sword, Moreland dropped like a stone, unconscious.

Tom had time to tie Mitchell and Walker up against some stair bannisters, before Moreland came round. He too was tied up but facing the two henchmen.

Williams entered the room, looking dishevelled and breathing hard, but with a large grin on his face.

"Didn't think I'd take this long. Must be getting soft or something Colonel Tom. Just as I was warming up, and looked around, they had all fell down on me!"

"Yes, I was beginning to give up on you. Maybe you're getting too greedy taking on those five men. Or maybe they didn't know they were supposed to fall down." Tom mused and shook his sergeants hand, delighted that he too had survived.

"I need you to bring them all in here and tie them up. Then stand guard by the door, I have some unfinished business with the Lord here." Tom said quietly.

Williams had all the men trussed up and sitting in a line in front of Tom and was standing behind the door when Tom saw the youth who walked into the room with a rifle aimed directly at him.

"It's you again. What have you done to my father. Untie him before I shoot you like a dog." the youth ordered and raised his rifle to take aim. He did not see Williams, who crept up behind the boy, knocked the rifle from his grasp and delivered a punch that knocked him out.

"Careful not to damage the boy. He's a star witness. Just put him to sit over on that chair by the table." Tom ordered.

"Make certain that the next person that comes through that door is somebody we know, Sergeant."

Williams nodded and carried out his orders.

Tom put his hand into one of his trouser pockets and fished out the three items he'd found the other day, and laid them on the table beside Moreland's silver handled riding whip.

Moreland came to, and realised that his wrists were tied to the stair bannisters.

"Just who really are you? Why have you come to pester us? I am a magistrate and I will see you hang for all this, who ever you are. Now untie me before the police sergeant comes."

Tom sighed loudly, strode over to Moreland, slapping his face.

"Just shut up and listen. You will be told exactly what is what, all in good time."

The scene was set for the truth, but there was yet an audience to ensure what was about, that would be deemed fair and proper. Also, to protect Tom and his sergeant against the Lords of the realm.

"Ah there you are Colonel! I've brought a few friends with me. We've gathered up some of the locals we met on our way here, and also have brought the local constabulary along with us as you requested." It was Brigadier Collins.

Tom was introduced to Berkdale. Pollard and Smythe, three lords of the realm, a host of local villagers, and a platoon of soldiers marching into the hall with the police sergeant 127 and four constables that were tied up and stringed together.

"Lord Moreland you're the magistrate tell them to untie us and place them under arrest." the fat sergeant whined.

"Shut up you fool!" hissed Moreland.

"Colonel. I hope all this is to a purpose?" Berkdale asked.

"Yes indeed your lordships. I needed three lords to bear witness against another lord. That was why I had asked the Brigadier to request your indulgence to attend. All will become clear." Tom stated, and asked them to sit down at the large table next to the youth.

The clock in the tower rang loud as it struck the eleventh hour silencing all around it.

Tom walked slowly over to Moreland, brandishing the silver riding whip, and struck him across the chest.

"It is now eleven o'clock, the time you had requested my presence. So pay attention the 40th Lord of Moreland! Any question that you do not answer from now on, will get the same treatment. Do you understand?"

Moreland nodded his reluctant agreement, but still tried to struggle against his bonds.

"I say! Easy on Colonel," gasped Smythe.

Undeterred, Tom started his speech: "We have been assembled here today in order for me to prove a double murder that was committed some fourteen years ago. According to the King's laws of the land, I need three things: A motive, a body and the murder weapon." Tom paused.

"We already have the bodies, but now for the other two items." then continued in a loud voice.

"Far be it for me to tell you, your family history Moreland. The original was the Duke du Mue Leande, who was William the conqueror's Knights champion. For his service he was given a large piece of land that would represent most of the Mid-shires of today. The area was to be known as MORES LAND, but over the centuries it was shortened to MORELAND. The title and land had one big proviso for it to be hereditary and in perpetuity, as was common with such ancient titles. In order for it to be inherited it must go to the legitimate first-born, and to be a male, otherwise all titles and or all lands would be forfeit. Due to infant mortality among the aristocracy, that first born had to be registered as the next heir on or near its fourteenth birthday. Also, that the rulings of hereditary titles, and so on was up for review every century, by the current monarch, who at that time was our late King George."

"So what! Don't tell me you've come into my house, creating mayhem, tying me up just to give me a history lesson, Williams? If that's your real name." Moreland said angrily.

"Yes he's got a point there Colonel." Pollard and Smythe agreed.

"If you please bear with me gentlemen." Tom recommenced after that outburst from Moreland.

"The motive for the murder, Moreland, was that you had to get rid of your twin girls, for your son to be the first born, when the time came for registering him for hereditary considerations. You seized the opportunity to kill your girls the week your son was born, then blamed it all on a thirteen year-old youth.

"But what you failed to check out, and the tragedy of it all is, that a couple of years before the late King died, he had made a decree which stated 'All hereditary land and titles to ancient titles' such as yours, Moreland, 'could now be passed on to any first born child'.

This decree was held up due to various reasons and then because of the war. You had killed your own daughters for nothing Moreland." Tom stated vehemently.

Tom paused and turned to the Brigadier and the three lords.

"That my lords, is the opening gambit and the motive for the said murders. Now my first evidence of proof." Tom stated in the now completely silent hall.

Tom looked over at Moreland who was now muttering to himself, then walked over to the table to retrieve the brass buckle.

He walked over to Mitchell and Walker, but as he passed Moreland who was angrily protesting his plight, struck him another blow with the riding crop telling him to be quiet.

"Now then Mitchell. This is a brass buckle taken from a leather belt, that has the initials of J.M. embossed on it" Tom announced and showed it to Mitchell.

"You can see the initials clearly can't you?"

"Yes! So what?" Mitchell growled.
"Your name is Jimmy Mitchell, yes?" Tom asked sharply.
"Yes! But how do you know me? We haven't met before." Mitchell stated.
"The initials of this buckle has yours on it hasn't it Mitchell?"
"That might be so, but I've never seen it before." was the reply.
"Yes you're right Mitchell! Because in between the letters there is a small mark that I had to examine more closely, and found that the mark formed the letters, D and U." Tom stated as he held up the buckle for Mitchell to see.
"Can you see the mark Mitchell?"
"Yes I can! But what does all this mean!"
"It means, Mitchell, that you are too fat to fit the leather belt this belonged to, and that you are not now the person I am seeking." Tom said quietly and menacingly.
Tom walked over to Moreland, struck him again, and showed him the buckle.
"You can see the mark in between the initials, can't you Moreland?"
"Yes. So what? That's got nothing to do with me. Anyway prove it!"
Tom replied with another strike of the whip that drew objections from the seated lords.
"That's exactly what I intend doing." Tom stated and walked over to the boy and gave him the buckle. Then picked up the silver object and walked over to the lords.
"I have here an object that bears a coat of arms." he said and showed it to them and to his Brigadier.
"I think that I can safely say that it belongs to none other than Jaques Du Moreland. Those are the same initials on the buckle, and the very same 40th Lord of Moreland. Yes gentlemen?"

All four nodded their heads and edged closer to the table as they had began to realise what was unfolding.

Tom came over to Moreland, striking him again.

"Do you recognise this object Moreland? You should do because it's got your coat of arms on it"

"If you say so, then yes. So what? I don't know what your game is but you'd better untie me. Anyway just who the devil are you?" Moreland protested loudly.

Tom struck him again making Moreland cry in pain.

"Render unto Caesar! Moreland"

Tom went back to the table and gave that object to the youth to examine. Then came back to Mitchell holding the bronze horseshoe.

"Mitchell! No you Walker, you're the farrier. Do either of you recognise this shoe? Do your horses have such a fine set? Who in the estate would have a horse shod with such a fine shoe with a number on them?"

"The only person who had their horse shod in that metal was the squire, and he puts numbers on to keep count of them." Walker confirmed.

"I thought as much. That means that you are not the murderer either Walker. That leaves only Beckett, but he's since been found dead, there can only be one other." Tom concluded then threw the horseshoe at Moreland.

"Pah! So what! First its buckles, then baubles now lousy horseshoes." Moreland shouted angrily but gained another heavy blow for his troubles.

"I'll trouble you to keep quiet Moreland." Tom silenced his outburst.

"Gentlemen this is the very reason why we are all gathered to witness." Tom announced.

"Lord Moreland, I am accusing you of a double murder that took place with its fourteenth anniversary today. I am stating that you killed your two daughters known as Lily and Iris, in the very week that your wife gave birth to your son who is sitting at that table over there."

"What? What is he saying?" the boy asked out loud. "I did have two sisters called Lily and Iris, but what's that got to with this man?"

The boy's outcry prompted a few questions from the lords, but Tom took no notice.

"Isn't that right Lord Moreland!" Tom prompted with yet another blow of the whip.

"NO! No you're wrong" snapped Moreland

"Mitchell and the other two saw the boy Tom Wilson fooling around with the girls, that's who did it."

"Yes! Mitchell and his pals did see a boy with them. But they were too far away. The only way they could tell was by looking through a telescope that Mitchell used to carry around. That's because he was spying on them." Tom said aloud as he walked over to Mitchell.

"You were known to have a small brass telescope. Where is it now Mitchell?"

"I, I don't know. I lost it years ago." Mitchell stammered.

Tom pulled out that very object from one of his trouser pockets and thrust it into Mitchell's face.

"Is this yours Mitchell? It should be because it's got your name on it, right here." Tom stated as he showed the telescope to Mitchell.

"But! But I've got another one now. Where did you find that one?" Mitchell gasped.

"You must have dropped it down into the bushes by the stone bridge, where I found it last week. Beckett, you and your pals like to spy on people and when you saw the two girls messing around with that boy you decided you wanted a piece of the action."

"No! That's not right!" Mitchell protested. "It is right, because you and your pals had a taste for young girls and it's you lot that have been going around raping them if the rent is not paid on time! Isn't it Walker!" Tom shouted.

"Isn't it Mitchell." Then gave both of them a heavy blow with the whip.

This revelation drew an angry response from some of the soldiers, guarding the prisoners.

"Murder, arson, sabotage, terrorism, spying and rape is a hanging offence in this country. So the men found dead by the village constabulary met their just rewards, as they were part of your gang of cronies raping the womenfolk of the estate. But then you should know that Moreland." Tom shouted at Moreland, before landing yet cutting blow to his body.

"The thing is Mitchell, you failed to spot that our Lord Moreland had been hiding behind the evergreens alongside the oxbow." he said slowly then turned to Moreland "And that's where you murdered the girls, because that's where I found your horseshoe, and the silver ornament. Isn't that right Moreland?"

"No! That's not true." Moreland said nervously.

"How could I, was riding my horse when Mitchell told me what happened."

"Ah yes! Indeed you were riding your horse. You rode through the oxbow and hid it behind the evergreens as I had said. It was there that your horse had cast its shoe, and exactly where I said. It takes about ten minutes to get from the bridge to the oxbow even on horseback. That gave you the time to drag the girls from over the other side of the river, murder them in the oxbow before Mitchell and friends arrived. You also had time to retrieve your horse and leave, to be found elsewhere " Tom stated loudly.

"How do you know all this! You're only guessing! It was the boy Tom Wilson, who killed them. He's been reported dead from the bomb that blew up the county Borstal." Moreland bluffed.

'Oh! How do you know that"? Tom asked, sensing that the time was near.

"Because in my capacity as the county Magistrate, I'd sent him there. He was too young to hang so that's what happened to him."

"You a magistrate? Since when 'Lord' Moreland?" Tom asked sarcastically.

"It's a hereditary title given me by my Father the 39th Lord of Moreland, and I merely exercise that right as bestowed upon me. Now if you've finished your charade, just untie me and let me do my duty. I promise I'll be lenient with you." Moreland said loftily.

"Lord Berkdale. This is your domain. Am I right to state that the title of Magistrate does not become a hereditary title, only attained by personal endeavour?"

'Correct! No Magistrate is allowed to practice unless he had been suitably qualified and acknowledged by the Lord Chancellor. As I am his deputy, I do not recognise this person as one." Was the reply.

"So you see Moreland, that is just one more explanation you will have to make to the King." Tom stated as if to reinforce Berkdale's revelation.

"I put it to you again Moreland. It was you who murdered your own girls. You killed them and used your leather belt to drag them over from the oxbow. Because when your cronies surrounded the boy, they came from over the other side of the river, yet you were walking a limping horse along the oxbow track. The very horse that lost its shoe in a game snare in among the evergreens. That's why it was limping and the reason why you had arrived on the scene later than the rest, because you had to walk the animal instead of riding it."

That explanation drew a gasp from everybody and a surprised look on Mitchell's face.

Moreland gasped and fidgeted in his confined ropes.

"You're only guessing. Prove it. Where is the weapon. How the hell do you know all this. Just tell us just who you are." Moreland pleaded.

"I have provided the motive, and where the murder took place. Now for the murder weapon and how, my lords." Tom said calmly, that seemed to chill the atmosphere of the chamber.

Tom took off his shirt to expose the whiplashes than had embossed themselves on his body then turned to Moreland.

"Now do you recognise me! Mitchell, Beckett and Walker held me down whilst you gave me a good whipping. These are the scars to prove it." he said vehemently and walked around the chamber to show the rest of the onlookers.

"That shiny bauble as you called it came from your whip, because it got broken off when you hit the girls with it. That was why the metal dug into my flesh leaving these strange 'star' marks." Tom said with menace, as he turned his back to Mitchell then to Moreland then held up the whip to show it was the very same one.

"You see the damage on this whip? Sergeant Williams, bring me the bauble over here and see if it matches the hole on the whip." Tom stated as he walked around showing everybody the whip. The sergeant was able to match the silver object to the whip and went around showing everybody how it fitted, then gave it back to Tom.

"You see Moreland. That whip, the very same one in my hand? If you care to look at the marks of the whip that I have just given you, they will match the exact same scars as mine. The beating I have given you today was for a reason Moreland, and should prove it beyond doubt." Tom stated triumphantly as he ripped Moreland's shirt off him to expose the whip marks Tom gave him.

"Why it's true!" Walker declared.

"We did hold Wilson down. Those marks are what he said." Mitchell declared.

"But, but, you can't be. You're not Tom Wilson, you just can't be!" Moreland stammered.

"I can state quite categorically that I am Tommy Wilson, the boy you sent away by this policeman now Sergeant 127, to the county Borstal. Further to that you had my family banished from the village. On top of that you had my father's name scratched off the village war memorials. He was Sergeant TT Wilson DSC. Need I go on?"

"That's all rubbish! All you have proved is that the whipping I gave you matches the marks on the whip. You still haven't proved that it was the murder weapon used on the victims. Therefore you have no case. I know the law." Moreland stated defiantly.

"Lord Smythe! Have you brought the Scotland Yard's forensic reports and photographs of the victims' wounds? If so can you give them to Sergeant Williams for me." Tom asked.

Everybody was talking quietly among themselves discussing what they had witnessed, but still not believing what they saw or heard until a hush settled over the room.

An elegant woman, dressed in a long blue dress seemed to float silently down the large stairway that Moreland was tied to. She came over to the table and comforted the youth for a moment, then took the photographs off Williams and went over to Tom.

"I have heard every word of what has gone on here this morning, but did not believe it until you mentioned the whip. You seem to have a dispute over the murder weapon. Colonel, I need to see this whip." she said and grabbed the whip from him.

She took several minutes examining the photographs, Tom's wounds, and the whip.

"That explains it Colonel." she stated. "You see Colonel. My daughters were virgins up to that day, and no matter the size of the man, there's no way he could damage my daughters privates with it the way that they had suffered." she said as she gave the pictures to Tom.

"Do you see the marks on their privates? Now don't be shy colonel. Can you see that they match up to the marks of your body? The only thing that would do that was from this whip, as it penetrated them. They had been viciously defiled as well, am I right Colonel?" she demanded.

"Then there's the dent made on one head matches that of the bauble. The mark on the other head shows the same star marks because the bauble was missing. The strangle marks around their necks was made from the belt and buckle you found. Am I right in all accounts Colonel?"

Tom nodded his head and said.

"It's a perfect match in every detail."

"Indeed Colonel Wilson. This whip is definitely the weapon that killed them." she declared as she brandished the heavy silver whip over her head.

She shouted an obscenity towards her husband and gave him a vicious kick into his groin that made him gasp and scream with agony.

As she was about to take another kick, Tom managed to embrace her from behind and stopped her in her tracks.

"Lady Moreland. This is not one of your husband's kangaroo courts. So if you don't mind I would ask you to desist your struggle against me." he said sternly, as he held her until she stopped struggling.

"Sergeant Williams, please escort Lady Moreland to the table next to her son." Tom commanded as he left her to his sergeant.

Before the two men could do anything else, she broke free and gave her husband another hefty kick in the groin, which made him gasp before going momentarily unconscious.

"And that's for Iris. That's what it feels like. I hope it hurts, you bastard." she snarled and spat into her husband's face.

The sergeant grabbed hold of her and moved her forcibly over to the table. Warning her to sit down.

The boy got off his seat and moved swiftly over to his father.

"Did you kill my sisters? How could you do this to all of us?" the boy sobbed as he started to question his father, who finally came round from his assault.

"Aaah shut your snivelling mouth! Why you ungrateful pup. I did all this for you." Moreland gasped in pain as he shouted over his son's questions.

Tom took hold of the boy and escorted him back to his seat before returning back to Moreland.

"So you see Moreland, not only are you a murderer and a thief of peoples lives, but you are also a coward who leaves his men to die on the battlefields. You are not fit to remain in this castle or bear your title."

"That's enough Colonel." Collins said loudly but without conviction.

Tom shouted for and waited for the silence in the hall. Then after a deep breath and a voice, that carried up into the rafters, he declared

"As a citizen of the realm, I Colonel Tom Wilson, erstwhile of this village, arrest you, the 40th Lord of Moreland for the murders of your daughters Lily and Iris Moreland. This is done in the witness of your peers, the Lords Berkdale, Pollard and Smyth and of Brigadier Sir Geoffrey Collins.

I have vindicated myself as innocent of the said crime alleged against me and of my family.

My investigation is at an end, and for you Lord Moreland, to be taken away to await the King's pleasure." That was his 'coup de gras'.

His announcement created a spellbound hush for several moments, before the sharp commands from Collins shattered it.

"Sergeant Williams. Take all these men and hand them over to the Platoon commander. Captain Green, place them all under close arrest, including Lord Moreland, and take them to barracks for further questioning."

The offenders were marched out of the large hall leaving it sounding hollow and empty, with Lady Moreland comforting the boy, tears streaming down her cheeks.

"Now then Lady Moreland, this is no time to let go of yourself. Must keep tradition and show the world that aristocracy are above all that sort of thing." Lord Pollard whispered in her ear.

She walked over to Tom, wiping her tears away with a handkerchief, took hold of his hand and said quietly

"You must really hate the Moreland family for all this. I cannot undo what my husband did to you and your kinfolk Colonel Wilson. My daughters and you have suffered greatly from his hands. What can we do to try and put things right?"

Before Tom could answer, Collins interrupted him.

"Lady Moreland! I too am a knight of the realm. As Colonel Wilson's commanding officer, I would suggest that he takes up residence here and become your boys' guide and mentor in regard to the finer points of rearing up the future 41st Lord Moreland."

"Yes that's a fine suggestion Lady Moreland." Lord Berkdale enthused as he bowed slightly towards her.

The other Lords added their voice to the idea as the group started to discuss the next Lord Moreland's future.

"Brigadier, my men are waiting to move off. Request you and your party leave now." Captain Green interrupted the group.

"Very well Captain. Well must dash now Lady Moreland. Tom send me an invite soon and tell me about your duel." Collins said as he patted his gammy shoulder like last time.

The three lords encouraged Tom and Lady Moreland to think over what they had said very carefully, as they bade everybody goodbye.

Lady Moreland and her son stood between Tom and his sergeant in the manor gateway. They watched and waved goodbye as the motorcade left slowly down the driveway and out of the manor grounds.

The boy looked over the estate with a faraway look in his eyes, while his mother wept softly to into her handkerchief.

"Colonel Wilson. In view of our strange but tragic meeting today I would like you to call on us soon. I understand that you are due back to your regiment, but would like to discuss some arrangements before you leave." Lady Moreland said abruptly as she turned to him.

"That would be most helpful. Lady Moreland." Tom started but was interrupted once more.

"Er! Excuse me Colonel but we best be getting back." Williams said as he butted into the conversation.

"My sergeant is anxious to get back home to his wife and his little five year-old daughter." Tom said gently as he explained away the intrusion.

"So Lady Moreland I must take my leave of you. I shall be staying at the inn should you wish to see me." Tom said as he dismissed himself from her.

The two soldiers mounted their horses and rode slowly down the grassy slopes and out of the manor gates for home.

When they arrived at the cottage, Mrs. Williams met them at the doorway and kissed the both of them, with Sarah demanding hugs and kisses too.

"I thought of all sorts of things that might have happened to you when I heard loud bangs, shots and all sorts of fireworks going off. What happened at the manor Arthur?" She asked

"It's a long story Susan dear. We need to have time to discuss things for the future and with Colonel Tom, which can wait until tomorrow. But for now, we are going to the inn for a large jug of ale. We'll be home again for supper dearest." he said and kissed her tenderly again.

"And me Colly Tom!" Sarah said, as she couldn't pronounce the word Colonel.

"I want a kiss too." she insisted, which Tom duly obliged, as he gathered her gently into his arms.

"Ooh Colly Tom! You have such prickly cheeks. Not like mine all nice and soft, because I'm a girl." she said as she ran her hands over Tom's unshaven face, then her own. Tom placed her gently back onto the floor as her parents laughed at the comparison.

They waved to the girls, mounted their horses and galloped off down the lane to the inn, for what they always did, drink a toast to the end of another successful operation.

The entire estate was in an uproar of celebrations, which lasted well into the following week, thanks to the ever-efficient bush telegraph that spread the news about the Moreland investigation at the manor and the outcome.

In total contrast, Tom spent the next few days in peace and quiet, staying at the home in the company of his friend and family. The two friends talked long hours about many things except the Moreland operation, as both knew that it was still unresolved.

Tom's leave was at an end and he was preparing himself to return to his regiment, when a letter arrived from Lady Moreland with the request that both he and his sergeant attend the manor that day.

"I wonder what Lady Moreland wants. Have you any clue Susan?"

"According to the gossip, she's had word about Lord Moreland, and I expect you have not gone back to the manor to see to her private comfort and welfare." Susan replied with womanly intuition.

Thumper drove the sports car up into the manor courtyard and was met by a footman who escorted them into the large hallway.

"Now this is more like it Colonel. No stupid asses trying to knobble us this time."

"Indeed Thumper, but more likely it will come from the wiles of a Lady Moreland, if Susan is correct."

"Good morning Colonel! Good morning Sergeant!" Lady Moreland greeted civilly, but looked very pale.

"I have just received a telegram sent by Lord Smythe. It appears that my husband took his own life by gun, late last night as 'Honour' rather than 'Dishonour' by hanging."

"Lady Moreland. I do not grieve for your husband. It is in the memory of your daughters that you will always have my sorrow and pain, but my anger has gone now. Maybe your son will regain the former glory of the Moreland' name. Just give him time and the guidance he needs." Tom replied gently.

"Is this goodbye then Colonel Wilson? What will you do now? Will I see you again?" she asked slowly and nervously.

Tom looked at the distressed woman and felt guilty at seeing what she was going through.

He thought of all the things he wanted to say to her, but realised that what was done could not be undone and there was therefore only one outcome to this visit, brutal as it may appear.

"I do have one or two more things to do before I leave to serve King and country once more. I'll only come back to visit my sergeant as the estate holds nothing for me now except sad memories."

"Wish it was as simple as that for me Colonel! I too would like to move on." she said disappointedly as she started to weep into her handkerchief.

Tom looked at Williams with unease. *Susan was right on the button this time,* he thought

"Lady Moreland! I am to resume my water bailiff duties now. I will see that you will come to no harm. I am certain that Colonel Tom will see to that." Williams volunteered.

"You are kind Sergeant Williams, I will remember these words of yours. As for you Colonel, go and do your duty." she sniffed, wiping the tears from her cheeks.

Tom took his leave from Lady Moreland, and with his sergeant at his side, drove back to the village to collect his things before leaving.

"There you are Colonel Williams, or should I say Wilson." the innkeeper greeted jovially.

"Not now innkeeper. I have things to do. First I need to settle my bill. How much?" Tom asked gruffly.

"On the house Colonel!" the innkeeper beamed.

"How much for the stables?"

"On the house." was the same reply.

Tom thanked him and walking out of the building made his way to the cemetery.

He stopped at the little florist shop and picked two big bunches of flowers.

"How much madam?" he enquired.

"For you Tommy Wilson, and the memory of your poor mother. On the house." the old lady whispered as she gave him a toothless smile.

He walked into the cemetery and laid the flowers on the girls' graves, stood for a moment talking to them in a whisper, then turned to leave.

"Colonel Tom Wilson! I knew you would return to visit my sisters. That's why I've been waiting for you." It was the youth who was now the new Lord of Moreland.

"What do you want?" Tom said, cross at the intrusion into his privacy.

"My sister' thank you for what you have done for them. They are at peace now, I just know it, because they do not waken me up in the nights anymore. I also thank you for myself for letting me have a fresh start with the estate. I will show the villagers that I am no tyrant like my father was, that many things will change for the better. Should you decide to return one day, please let us know at the manor. My mother and I bid you goodbye Colonel Tom Wilson." the youth concluded and held out his hand.

"Yes young man. My sergeant will help you in your endeavours. Bid your mother goodbye for me, as I am needed elsewhere for my King and country." Tom replied as he shook the strong hand of the youth, and left the cemetery without looking back.

The walk to the war memorial was a slow one for Tom, as he held a large poppy wreath in his hands. He stopped and placed his wreath on the white marble stone then stood to attention and saluted 'THE GLORIOUS DEAD'.

He hesitated for a moment but it was the sad echoes of a bugle that he heard nearby, sounding the LAST POST, made him remain at the salute.

He looked at all the names of those warriors, and felt tears trickle down his cheeks when he saw that his fathers name was re-enscribed into the stone in large bold black letters. Sgt. T.T. Wilson. DSC. Royal County Fusiliers. It was only as the last sad note of the bugle faded away that Tom finished his salute.

He spun on his heels and marched back to his car where, through the tears in his eyes, he saw Williams putting his bugle away and waiting by the car.

Susan and little Sarah were also there.

"Colonel Tom! We hope you feel better now." Susan said as she hugged him and kissed his damp cheeks. Then tenderly gave them a wipe with her handkerchief.

"Colly Tom! Pick me up and kiss me too." Sarah insisted as she tugged at his hands.

Tom picked her up and hugged her gently.

"Colly Tom your cheeks are all wet now. Can I dry them for you?" she whispered loudly into his ear, as she rubbed the hem of her dress on him and dried his cheeks with a flourish.

"There Colly Tom! All nice and clean again." she said proudly as she hugged him again, before Tom putting her gently back onto the ground again.

"Well Thumper, I'd best be off now. Any problem just let the Brigadier know. I'll try and come back some day. Mind how you go my old friend, and take care of the girls." Tom said softly, as they embraced each other goodbye, before he climbed into his car and drove out of the village.

The wind in the trees still seemed to call to him, but they fell silent as he left the estate behind.

He left with the knowledge that one record had been put straight. The anger in him that had spurred him on all these years had now gone. But his heart still ached as he still had no family to return to, nor a home to rest.

Would Tom ever find his lost family? Would he return to his native village again?

Moreland & Other Stories

Moreland & Other Stories

About the Author

Frederick A Read was born in Norwich, but grew up in Northern Ireland. He is a retired sub-mariner and ex-lecturer and is married with two grown-up children. He has been living in South Wales for over thirty years.

This is his first book.

Coming Soon from
www.guaranteedbooks.com

A Fatal Encounter
Book One of the Adventure Series

The opening chapter in the life of John Grey and his journey through the ranks of the Merchant Navy.

Written in the style of C S Forrester's Hornblower series, but set post-World War II.

LB	7/07
DU	04/10
SA	10/11
FL	6/12